The Scyra Society

k.r. sawyer

Copyright © 2020 by k.r. sawyer

All rights reserved. No part of this publication may be reproduced, distributed, or transmitted in any form or by any means, including photocopying, recording, or other electronic or mechanical methods, without the prior written permission of the publisher, except in the case of brief quotations embodied in critical reviews and certain other noncommercial uses permitted by copyright law.

ISBN: 9798647767431

First edition, 2020

DEDICATION

Mom, Dad, Sophia, Kamille

For the greatest gift anybody could bestow, unconditional love.

CONTENTS

Part I   1

Part II   54

Part III   129

Part IV   158

Part V   196

PART I

Chicago, Illinois – 2018 – Trip

Every time I make love, it feels like it's for the first time ever. I mean really make love, like glance into the depths of their being. That shift from when you're just fucking someone to touching souls. On the second date I'm on all fours, with his hands on my waist, while he slams into me with abandon. For the third, I go to his place and – high as hell – spin a wild sociology theory around him. How it relates to the anecdote that started me on this thread is revealed in the last sentence. The theory is personal, grounded in science, and relatable all at once. He kisses me on the forehead after my last word finishes ringing in my mouth, enthralled now that he's seen me in a more vulnerable and brilliant light, then gets up to refill our wine glasses.

    Hours later, after moving to the couch, after I move close but innocently enough to make him think he initiated sex, we're finally both completely naked. This time though, when it goes in, I look up and we lock eyes. He watches my face through each stroke and I can feel hormones bursting in my brain. It's slow, intimate, sensual. Afterwards, we just pet each other and chat in the darkness, making small confessions.

    It feels special with him, even more so than the other hundreds of times men and women have made love to me. This time, he's different. This guy is kind, like, mad kind. He actually listens to me and remembers small details I slip into conversation. On the third date, I notice that there are tulips in the vase on his kitchen counter, after I told him that on the second I love tulips but fail at growing them every spring. He bought red wine, even though he told me white is his favorite on our first date.

I stay the night and wait for him to fall into a deep sleep. You can tell by the way someone's eyeballs twitch under their eyelids how far into REM they are. Regular sleep is peaceful, gentle movements and sighs. REM is erratic, the entire length of your body paralyzed by deep sleep, except for the tender meat under your eyelids. I slip out of his bed and quietly into the living room. From my backpack, I pull out black leggings and a black sweater, then take off my wig and nose. Within thirty seconds, I'm dressed and everything else is secured in my bag. I softly turn the handle of the front door to let in the person I know is waiting outside.

Her order said she wanted to torture and threaten him. It was a date rape, so she felt that it wasn't worth the effort of getting him to turn himself in to the cops. She's dressed head to toe in black so that no DNA escapes. She hands me a black ski mask that's identical to hers and I put it on after gesturing towards the knife rack. She's well prepped, drilled by my favorite handler, an old hand at dealing with men from her former job on Wall Street.

My client knows he's lightly drugged, just enough for us to bind him quickly before he wakes up. I handle tying his wrists, blindfolding him, taping his mouth, and shackling his legs. Now it's her show. My partner takes the glass of water from his night stand and pours it fluidly over his head. He thrashes, his startled yelps muffled by the duct tape.

"Sit the fuck up," she growls. He's obedient, clearly trying to gather information on how to get out of this situation. I shudder a little from the pleasure his confusion brings me, the pleasure of being a master of your craft. There's no getting out. I move to stand behind him, armed with more ropes in the rare case of an escape attempt.

Once he's properly tied up, my partner chooses to take off his blindfold. Her head tips softly to the side, savoring the fear and adrenaline in his eyes. I hand her the first knife from my arsenal laid out on his bedroom floor. Sobs rack his body even before she begins to cut his inner thighs. I maintain a keen watch on her face, looking for signs of losing control, as well as the wounds she's inflicting. The client decided to go with just knives as her weapons of choice. His place was somewhat limited in weapons since he's a minimalist, so all I could offer her were lighters, knives, and scissors.

She does a fine job, lovely even, keeping her cuts in the same direction, evenly dispersed throughout all the sensitive parts of his body. The handler should have prepped her on areas to avoid — there's no point of all this work to torture him if he's just going to die anyway

— but the creativity is all borne of her own mind and will.

After about an hour of careful, meticulous work, he's nearly passed out. The client's own adrenaline and blood thirst are also wearing off. She sits back on her heels and I mime, ready? She nods and stands, stretching lightly before walking the knives to his kitchen sink. I escort her to the door and return to him. Someone posing as a neighbor will be in the hallway to make sure she exits the building and leaves the premises.

I load a syringe with a clear liquid and inject him in the thigh, then go into my speech, "Jacob, now you know that we know where you live. We are watching you. You're a rapist." He gathers up the strength to shake his head defiantly. I reach up and grab his chin, forcing him to look into my eyes. "Yes, you are. You raped someone. This is only a taste of what's to come if it happens again. I will know. Scyra will know."

I take out my Scyra brand iron. The emblem is the size and shape of a quarter. It only takes the power of a corner store lighter to make it scaldingly hot. I heat it thoroughly and press it into his crotch, right above his dick. Once he's passed out from the pain, stress, and drugs, I untie his hands and leave the rest for him to deal with in the morning. I inspect each cut to my best ability. Some are already starting to scab up. I grab my backpack and head out, taking the stairs just in case there's any hidden cameras in the complex.

I feel calm and satisfied. Everything went according to plan. My favorite jobs are the ones where I get to fuck them beforehand. It makes it all the more violating.

Chicago, Illinois – 2018 – Detective Lendo

I scanned the precinct for my partner. He was hard to find in the sea of beige skinned and clothed men, most all balding and pudgy. I sighed and gave up, deciding to just text him and tell him to meet me in the interview room. I ran my hands through my hair, pulling idly at tangles, and did a few breathing techniques to calm myself into objectivity.

Jacob Boon was seated in the interview room, quite literally on the edge of his seat, waiting to tell us his story. He was pale and shaken up. Illinois Masonic sent him straight over to us after taking care of his wounds. I skimmed the hospital's report. Shallow knife wounds all over his body, Quaaludes in his blood, and a burn on his groin. The burn was the most bizarre aspect of the report. It was perfectly round; branded like a steer. The scabbing made the image hard to make out, but it kind of looked like a horse's body, bucking wildly. I didn't want to traumatize him further, but he was going to have to let me get a closer look at that.

"Len, ready to go?"

My partner, Shane Ghurt, strolled up. His belly rolled over the top of his pants. His face was beat red and from its main, gaping orifice came huffing and puffing, a result of the physical exertion of walking down the precinct hallway. I liked Len okay, but the man was a walking cliché.

"Ghurt, did you read the report the hospital sent over? You should take a look before we head in."

Ghurt shuffled through the papers I handed him. His eyebrows wiggled all over his forehead, ending as high up on his balding head as possible. He finally looked up at me blankly and I pushed upon the door to the interview room.

"Hi Jacob, my name is Detective Lendo and this is Detective Ghurt. We understand you were assaulted last night. We'd like to hear your story, ask a few questions, maybe. See what we can figure out together. I know this may be difficult to discuss, so please, take your time. There's no rush."

Jacob muttered hello and clenched and unclenched his right fist. I could tell he was reluctant to file a report. He was most likely only here because of pressure from the hospital. After a few seconds, he decided where to begin.

"I met this girl in a bar a few weeks ago. She was this gorgeous blonde with big eyes. I took her home and got her number in the morning so I could take her on a real date. Second date was great, we had dinner. I took her back to my place again. She was super normal, has a job in marketing. Yesterday, I had her over for wine at my place. Again, super normal. I tell her she's welcome to sleep over and we fall asleep. Next thing…"

Jacob paused. His eyes were starting to well. Ghurt and I looked away, anywhere but at Jacob crying, to give him space to compose himself. He launched back in after a minute or two, talking too fast for me to take good notes. I sighed internally and pushed the recorder a little closer to him.

"I woke up tied up, blindfolded and everything. They took the blindfold off and then she cut me all over. It was two people in ski masks."

"Can you describe them?" Ghurt interrupted, a little too forcefully for my taste.

"They were in all black with black masks on. Same height? Both kind of skinny. I think they were both women."

"Was the girl you brought home one of them?" I asked.

"She had to have been. Had to. Nothing else makes sense," Jacob said, shaking his head woefully and the tile floor.

Ghurt asked, "Are you absolutely sure one of them was the girl you were dating? It's okay to not be sure."

Jacob cleared his throat and stuttered, "It...I... no. I guess I'm not."

"That's okay, Jacob. Go on," I said encouragingly.

"She cut me all over my body and then I think injected me with roofies or something. Then she threatened me, telling me she knew who I was, and she had it out for me. I think she said her name was

Kira or Kiara. I woke up covered in blood and went to the hospital immediately." Jacob hung his head.

I have him a moment, hoping an awkward silence would bring forth more detail. Witnesses, victims, they always lied. Intentionally or not, my real job was to whittle down to the truth. He didn't take the bait, so I furnished my concluding statement. "Thank you for sharing your story with us Jacob. I have one last question before you head out. Can you show me the burn mark on your groin? And email me a picture when it heals a little?"

"I... I don't know—"

I held up my hands, palms out in submission. "Say no more. You don't have to undress for me. Just email me a picture when it's healed. Here."

I passed him my card and said goodbye. Ghurt followed suit. We went straight to my office to debrief.

I sat down behind my desk. Ghurt sat in a chair across from me, put his feet up on my desk, hands threaded behind his head, and started working through the details out loud.

"Seems like a freak incident. Guess someone wanted revenge. The guy's testimony isn't great. I mean he was pretty heavily drugged. Not that I don't believe him. I'm just not sure he has a firm grasp on what happened. Also, two skinny chicks were able to tie him up like that? Why didn't he fight?"

"Yeah, he clearly didn't want to file this report. I'm surprised he even went to the hospital. He doesn't want us to swab his apartment for DNA and didn't get a rape kit done at North Shore. I would normally file this away and call it a day. Except, there's one thing that's bothering me. You should take a better look at the burn."

I slid the picture of the burn mark to Ghurt. He stared at it, clearly confused as to why it was interesting. I was instantly annoyed that I had to explain.

"Ghurt, it's perfectly round. It's the only burn mark. Most importantly, I think it's some kind of image. It looks like an animal, maybe a horse. That's why I want a better picture."

"Len, this just further proves to me it was some one–off psycho revenge thing." He shrugged and moved to leave the office.

"It probably was, but, just in case, I'm going to get that picture from Jacob Boon. Not every day a guy walks in with a brand mark on his crotch." Ghurt shrugged again and walked out.

Chicago, Illinois – 2018 – Trip

I followed Jacob from the hospital to the police station to watch him file his complaint. The final phase was always figuring out how many people — that mattered — knew that a Scyra mission had occurred and what information they had. I went through the process of filing a report, faking like my wallet had been stolen on the subway. It seemed like Jacob was interviewed by the only woman in the entire precinct. She was tall and fit with dark hair. Her office was down a small hall, all glass. In my head, I mapped out the best entrance and path to use when I came back later that night to read the report Jacob filed.

  I asked to use the bathroom so I could get close enough to read the detective's name on her office door. Detective Diana Lendo. Diana, how ironic. I hovered, watching her lock her office door and head towards the station's front exit. Without really thinking through why, I decided to follow her.

  She walked at a clip. Despite my agility and many years of practice dodging slow city pedestrians, I had a hard time tailing her. Diana squeezed through bite-size openings in crowds, breezily sidestepping tourists and natives alike. Finally, we got to her target destination, a cafe on a quiet side street. She picked a table outside and sat in the wrought-chair facing the street. From her satchel, she pulled out a book, then deftly swept through the pages using one finger and thumb, finally coming to rest on where she had left off. I noted a wedding ring on her left hand and a faded tattoo on her ankle. Classic fucking cop.

  I'd always had a thing for big hands. It looked like hers were big enough to fully wrap around my throat. I started watching her more intently when I noticed that she was reading 'On Beauty' by Zadie Smith. Books were my one vice. They were the only way to quiet my brain. I imagined that her face was more expressive while reading the novel than it was the entire time she interviewed Jacob. Through rote articulation, that assumption would quickly become fact in my mind. Her lips moved delicately when she got to passages or sentences she seemed to like, as if she were savoring the feelings they expressed, running them over her taste buds. I could've watched her taste that novel all damn day, like I was starving for something myself.

After twenty minutes, I decided it was time to go. I had a potential client interview in a few hours and needed to shower and change, plus fix my long, blonde wig I'd been favoring lately. I'd shoved it my backpack pretty roughly last night. I left cash for the waitress for my coffee then I reached into the pouch on my chest and blipped home.

I always land in the closet, just in case the tenant was home. She was a consultant who kept her calendar projected on her living room wall at all times. The only other person that ever entered her apartment was a housekeeper who came to stock the fridge, throw out any old food, and clean the minuscule bits of dust that gathered. I cased the rooms to make sure nobody was home then showered and changed. My meeting was at a Wendy's in West Town. I'd have to take public transportation.

I arrived first, making sure my back was to the door so that the Scyra insignia on my hoodie faced everybody that walked in. A minute late, my client slid into the booth across from me. George had bags under his eyes and was wearing gray sweats and a black hoodie, pulled down like a safety blanket over his hands. The open sadness in his face made me sick.

"Hi, George Snow? Do you have the form?"

He nodded and abruptly slid a wrinkled sheet of paper across the table to me.

"Great, thank you. As long as you filled it out to the absolute best of your ability, then we're good to go. My only question is, do you want to do it yourself or would you like me to?"

"You, please," George replied politely.

"Okay, the protocol in a situation like this is up to you. I can send you a picture that confirms the job was completed or meet with you again and give you the details, as well as pictures if you would like them."

"I don't think I need anything. I trust you," he said, while shrugging.

    I nodded and George slid out of the booth to leave. Shoulders stooped, I watched him leave, noted which direction he went in, then counted to fifteen and headed his way. I tailed him to make sure he wasn't doing the same to me. He seemed to be ambling instead of heading anywhere, definitely not worried about where or who I was. After a few blocks, I ducked into an alley and blipped home to prepare.

Wyoming, Ohio – 2001 – Trip

Disguised in flared jeans and a light blue Abercrombie sweater, I rang the doorbell of a two–story suburban home, light brown brick with a small porch. A busted bottled blonde answered, her breasts spilling out of a too–tight V–neck shirt.

"Hi, I'm George's mom. I just stopped by to talk about his progress on piano and how everything's going. Is this a good time?"

Tammy smiled broadly and nodded, letting me into her home. As soon as she turned her back on me, I covertly injected her with a syringe by pretending to accidentally stumble and catch myself on her arm. She apologized, the rug sometimes got bunched up, and led me into the living room. Within minutes, she passed out mid–sentence. I worked quickly, focusing my energy on tying her arm up so it could point a gun at her head but not be used to hurt me or aid an escape. I heated up my Scyra brand and hiked her sweater up to expose her midriff. The searing woke her up. She tried to scream but her mouth was sealed shut with duct–tape.

With one foot on the ground and a knee in her chest, I braced to lean forward and loom over her. "Hi Tammy. Shut the fuck up. I know you've been grooming George. Bear with me during the last few moments of your pitiful life. I'm going to make a lot of assumptions here. I'm assuming you're going to ruin this kid's life with your perversion. I'm assuming you're going to ruin a lot of boy's lives after him. Call this speculation, call it an opinion. I, personally, feel that 17 years from now you still aren't shit and never will be shit. Whether you live or die doesn't matter in the grand scheme of the universe. So, I choose death."

I watched her eyes bulge while I took out the pistol I found while casing her house on previous trips. She squirmed even harder, but my bonds held and I was able to put the gun snuggly in her hand. I crushed her pointed finger into the loop of the trigger, pressing up, careful not to let her shoot too early, then pushed the gun up to her temple. I took a deep breath to prepare myself to move quickly once the gun fired. My fingers wrapped and pressed into hers, squeezing the trigger like a snap, and her eyes immediately rolled up into her head. I untied her so it looked self–inflicted, left a note on her chest confessing her penchant for young boys, and blipped home.

Chicago, Illinois – 2018 – Trip

It's hard to know how much someone's life is going to change when you intervene so decisively. The day after executing Tammy, I did a quick look into George to see how he'd turned out. Taking the time to follow-up was part research and part vanity. Knowing George's full name and hometown made him easy to find on social media. In this new timeline, he still lived in Chicago. I spent half an afternoon tracking down his exact address and the other half waiting outside his apartment. Around 6:30 pm, he came outside. He was wearing gray slacks and a navy blue, short–sleeved button–up, same haircut as when we met at Wendy's. There was more color in his cheeks and no bags under his eyes. I followed him to a small Italian restaurant within walking distance and watched him light up when his date walked in. It looked like love or maybe budding love. Both men leaned into the conversation and didn't notice the waiter hovering until she cleared her throat. I blipped home to finally get some sleep, before heading to the precinct to finally read Jacob's file.

  I woke up around 10 pm and swished some mouthwash around before teleporting to the station. Not fully awake yet, I didn't stick my landing quite as well as usual. My knee twisted and I slammed a hip into a desk corner. I'd probably over done it with the space–time shit that day. Immediately after recovering my balance, I noticed a light on in Diana's office and ducked down behind a desk.

  I peeked over the desk and watched her leaning over files, parsing them with her long fingers, moving her lips in silence, just as she had done earlier in the week with that novel. Heat spread out across my face. Why did I feel so drawn to her? Maybe this was how my mentor felt when she first noticed me. I mean not romantic or anything in that way, I was a kid when she took me in, but like that intangible chemistry you notice with friends, your favorite uncle. I'd always felt too young to start thinking about a successor, but maybe it was time. It kind of made sense for a cop to take over for me or at least be a party of Scyra. Mama Scyra's dad had been a cop, which is how she got her start. Most importantly, who the fuck would believe Diana if I took her into my confidence and she told other people? I didn't have much to lose, if anything.

No move seemed right or safe, so I chose unabashed confidence and strolled right up to her office. In seconds, she was on her feet, gun drawn.

"Hands where I can see them."

I slowly put my hands up. "Hi, Diana. I'm here to talk to you about Jacob Boon."

Chicago, Illinois – 2018 – Diana

After checking her for weapons and taking down her name and address, I was ready to listen. Trip sat across from me, feet up on the desk, just like Ghurt sits, but much more disrespectful somehow. Maybe it was her unearned ease in my presence and in my office. I clasped my hands, elbows on my desk, and touched the tip of my nose to the index finger of my left hand, waiting for her to begin.

"We can talk somewhere else at a later date. I just have a couple things I want you to know right now. I don't trust you not to record me. Not that it makes that much of a difference. I just would rather not have to deal with it."

"Is that a threat, Trip?"

"Definitely not, I just mean practically speaking I would go back, like in time, and stop it from happening."

I rolled my eyes. "Sure, okay."

Trip went on, unbothered by my disbelief. "Jacob Boon is a rapist. He locked himself in a bedroom with one of his female friends in college, knowing she had a boyfriend and no interest in Jacob, and pressured – theatened, really – her into having sex. She was pretty drunk and terrified he would hurt her if she didn't go along with it. So she brought me in to handle him, make sure he never does it again. I mean, let's be honest, this case would never have made it very far in court, if it even made it to a judge at all."

I kept my face carefully blank, but Trip was right about it not making it into court.

She continued, "I give my clients a menu of options. This one chose to torture and threaten Jacob so he, hopefully, is too scared to ever hurt someone again."

I sat back in my chair and unclasped my hands. "You know Jacob is the only one with a police report and evidence of assault, right? I could tell him all of this so he could identify the woman who tortured him."

Trip snickered. "Diana, first of all, there will be no hard evidence of this woman having been there. I can promise you that. Second of all, like I said, I'll just travel back in time so that this conversation never happened. It'll be a little time consuming, but I protect my clients at all cost. Let's save us both sometime and not involve Jacob. He's not even why I'm here anyway. I'm here for you. To recruit you."

At that, Trip stood up and walked towards the door. Her transitions from stillness to movement were imperceptible, the fluidity of water pouring out of a tap. I examined her shaved head, delicate from the back, and a sharp contrast to her broad facial features. She looked back at me before leaving my office and said "I'll be back soon. Think about it."

"About what? Joining your "time-traveling" fucking vigilante shtick?" I yelled, with more exasperation than menace, at my suddenly empty doorway.

Chicago, Illinois – 2018 – Trip

I was light on clients for the week and took to trailing Diana. She lived in a snazzy condo in Lincoln Park, came home late most nights, and didn't seem to do shit else outside of work. Sometimes she visited her mom at a nursing home or picked up a pizza to eat in front of the TV with her husband. The only time she read was on her lunch break, always at the same table at the same cafe. I usually settled in across the street, obscured by bushes or dumpsters, and zoned out to the image of her parsing through a novel for the full forty minutes of her lunch break. Diana was as consistent as I was chaotic.

    I puzzled over how to bring her into the fold, or even how to make that decision and be sure about it. A week into watching her, I went over to the bank to access my safety deposit box. It was hard to safely track time-traveling, mine and my predecessors'. A tattered notebook was the best I could do. I couldn't keep all those moments in a computer or phone or anything else unsecure. At least if someone took this or read it meaningfully, it was one physical, handwritten thing and not a spawn of good data. I found a date and time that Ma was likely to be home and entered it in the journal. After thrifting a good outfit for a trip to 1971. I scarfed down a light meal back at the apartment, changed, and blipped to Oak Park.

Oak Park, Illinois – 1971 – Eloise

Four sharp knocks and one awkward cough was how Trip announced herself. In comparison, Charli's raps were always just as urgent, but with two loud pounds on the door. It's funny how three people can share so many of the same traits, like a particular brand of feminine aggression, but express them in such different ways. Trip ducked in like an alley cat and hugged me briefly, then accepted my offer of a cup of coffee.

 Her energy was restless which wasn't normal for Trip. Coiled, sure, but not usually fidgety. Meaningless movement was a waste of her energy. I estimated her to be in her late–twenties, but I could've been off. I knew she traveled back in time so often that she'd begun to look older than she technically is. Trip answered a few questions about her health and well–being without protest and I asked what year was the present. It was still 2018. I had seen Trip a handful of times in 2018 over the years and she'd aged noticeably since the last visit.

"Trip, you're traveling back in time too much."

"I know, I look fucking old. That's kind of what I'm here about, though. I might have found a Quatro."

I raised an eyebrow, surprised Trip had forged a connection beyond Scyra. "So, you can stop traveling back in time so much?"

"So, I can do it until I crumble and there's someone there to take over."

I pursed my lips slightly and blew out a jab of air.

Trip held up her hands, mea culpa. "Look, you have to trust me. I literally can see it all spread out in front of me. This woman fits perfectly into my dream. Now I'll have inside information. She's a cop, like your dad, Ma. What a great addition to my legacy, our legacy. Imagine not having that information from your dad. Scyra may never have even been borne."

"It did work to my advantage, but gossip from people in the community was just as good as tips from my father. He had his own bias and agenda, just like anyone else. His own shortcomings, too. I can't imagine cops are more competent forty years from now, are they?"

I saw Trip calculating how much energy she wanted to expend on arguing with someone who was trapped in the past. She relaxed, likely realizing this wasn't going to go anywhere.

"Her name's Diana. Detective Diana Lendo. I can tell she's very intelligent and 'keen' on justice. I have a plan. I'll ease into the relationship, just to get information from her at first. Then show her how much easier it is to change the world this way. To change Chicago for the better. I don't know, Ma. There's just something about her. She feels like one of us, like a warrior."

"Have you talked to Charli about this?" I asked, knowing full well Trip hadn't.

"No. I know she wouldn't approve of a cop. That's almost as bad as a man or a politician."

I smiled and changed the subject, asking Trip about 2018. We chatted for a while, enjoying reheated coffee and inane, juicy conversations about the present. She left around midnight and I logged her visit in my journal.

Chicago, Illinois – 2018 – Trip

Even after sleeping for six hours straight, I was still exhausted from all the recent time-traveling. In the mirror, I was wariness dripping down my face and into my shoulders. It was 3:27 pm, just enough time to shower and then head back out for an appointment. A potential client, Marcelle, was supposed to meet me at a Panera during the senior citizens dinner rush. I got there early and she was a little late. While waiting, I idly went over my conversation with Ma, like fingers worrying a zipper. This was the most alone I had felt in my entire life, even worse than when Charli died. Even work wasn't enough of a distraction. Ma and Charli were dead. I had no real rules or guidance.

Someone sat down heavily across from me, interrupting my train of thought. Marcelle was pale with stringy, straight black hair. She immediately focused all of her energy and attention on me. Her presence of mind was slightly unnerving. The stark contrast between her intensity and the cloud of numbness clients usually gave off jolted me out of my haze of exhaustion. I took in this new energy, thick as December rain, slightly dampened but focused as she started.

"Hi, thank you for taking the time to meet with me."

I nodded, letting her take charge and allowing myself to pay attention to everything about her. She hunched heavily but had a controlled stillness, always ready to react. It was a little like sitting across from myself and, at that moment, desperately in need of twelve to fourteen hours of sleep, I found it difficult to put my finger on the significant differences between us.

"Okay, I don't exactly know how this works so I'm not sure

how much you can help me because it's someone…someone who thinks they're untouchable and I'm also not here for myself. My sister Cassie, little sister, she's been through enough. I'm working on getting her into therapy and the past is ya know, the past. I just, if you can, I want you to stop this from happening to someone else."

"Did you bring the form?"

"I did, yes. I felt like it needed some context though it's a big ask. He's a cop and me and my sister are just so bottom of the totem pole, estranged from our mom, on welfare–"

"It's not a problem that he's a cop," I interrupted, trying to make sure my tone left no room for doubt. Marcelle slumped further down in her chair, leaning away from the table with what seemed like a bit of relief.

"I'm assuming it's on the form, but what precinct?" I asked.

Marcelle rustled in her bag and pulled out the form, tracing it with her finger to find "20th, 20th ward or district, whatever. His full name's on here."

Diana's. I tossed this information around my head restlessly, from side to side, up as high as I could, and against the walls of my skull. I definitely needed sleep to deal with this or use it to my advantage. I glimpsed from the form that Marcelle, seemingly very down to earth, selected to just have him stopped by me, not stop the situation from having never happened in the first place. I didn't give clients or potential clients details on how I was going to accomplish the offered methods of reparations. She probably thought the option to erase the event involved digging around in her kid sister's skull, not something as hokey as time travel. I'd have to decide if I was going to honor her wishes or do some digging into this guy and travel back. I was feeling the second option. Cop assaulting a young woman, potentially a teen based on Marcelle's apparent age, made me almost sure, despite the lack of detail, that this was a recurring offence for him.

Marcelle sat in companionable silence while all of this ran through my head. I stood up, took the form, and folded it up to tuck into my jacket pocket. She stood up and we shook hands. I was glad she was content to trust me. I followed her home without her noticing, noted the address, and promptly blipped away to sleep the rest of the day.

Chicago, Illinois – 2018 – Diana

"Jesus Christ, one of these days I'm going to accidentally shoot you". Trip had fucking popped up out of nowhere once again, this time actually in my office. "What if you accidentally arrived, appeared, arrived, and I was already sitting there? And then we were molded together?" I growled.

"Do you sit in this chair?"

"No, but still. You don't know that."

Trip smiled like actually, she did, and I frowned but dropped it. I had a good sense of who I should be afraid of at this point in my life. Trip was not currently on that list.

"Can I help you with something?"

"Yes, actually. Do you know a cop named Danny Dupree?"

"I do, we've worked together a few times. He hasn't been in this precinct for very long, or in Chicago."

"No, no he hasn't. I think I know why, too. Got in some trouble at his last job and I'm guessing they transferred him to try and avoid a scandal. He's not only a serial rapist, but also one who does it on the job."

My skin bristled.

"So, first you come in here confessing to a crime I'm working and now you're threatening one of my own? Get the fuck out of here before I arrest you."

Trip stared at me, maddeningly unfazed, getting a last sentence in before walking out. "I'd like to remind you, Diana, in all seriousness, I am untouchable."

I paced around my office angrily. It was violating to have this woman pop into my life, my cases, my office. After drilling a rut into the tile, I huffily sat down at my computer to look into Dupree, clear his name for myself. Whatever he had done, I didn't have the clearance level to view. I sat back heavily and rubbed my eyes until I saw stars. Shit, it was late. There were still a few things I wanted to add to the Boon case file, namely some research on the sigil that was burned into his groin. I wasn't afraid of Trip, sure, but I did feel like I needed to arm myself against her and definitely had to take her down. I didn't even know where to start to figure out her magic trick of disappearing into thin air. What kind of cop would I be if I just let this chick run lose around Chicago, punishing guys as she saw fit? Whatever it was that she felt strong enough to brand onto her victims would be useful in figuring out her psyche. I put in a request to have Officer Dupree stop by Boon's place tomorrow and try to get a picture of the burn mark.

  I could keep Dupree close in case Trip came for him and quietly continue building a case against her. Feeding two birds with one scone left me feeling satisfied and I called it a night. The drive home was peaceful. As long as you weren't close to any bars, the northside was quiet at night. I did the bare minimum to get ready for bed and slid in under the sheet next to my husband. He stirred slightly and I wrapped my arm around his chest, falling asleep with my nose pressed into the fuzz on his neck.

Chicago, Illinois – 2018 – Trip

I lingered across the street from Cassie and Marcelle's apartment, smoking a chain of cigarettes as cover for my loitering. Cassie came out around 7:00 am dressed in all black. I tailed her as she took two buses to a Dunkin Donuts and slipped into the back door of the building. It looked like she was a cashier there. That's one way she could've come across Dupree. I felt so sure this was a pathological thing and desperately wanted to prove that to Diana.

    My internet searches the night before brought up a couple of pictures of Dupree, but I couldn't tell which was more recent. He was a basic looking white guy. Pale, straight brown hair that could probably use some conditioner, cop haircut. The bridge of his nose was too wide for his face and nostrils. I pretended to read a book at the bus stop across the street from Dunkin, keeping my eye out for any cops. None showed during Cassie's eight–hour shift, soI followed her back home. She didn't come out again until around 9:00 pm. Two girls met her outside her apartment, and they walked to a nearby park. The way they all fell into familiar positions on the playground equipment made me think that this was pretty routine for them to hang out here. That would be another great way to come across Dupree. Maybe he was patrolling, yelled at the girls for being in the park after hours, and offered to drive Cassie home.

    I could've gotten all this from Marcelle, but I couldn't bring myself to summon her to rehash all the trauma. Besides, I'd picked up a lot from observing that Marcelle or Cassie wouldn't notice as civilians.

    Cassie went home and I went to the precinct to update myself on Diana's progress on the Boon case. I walked past the building to make sure no one was there and then blipped inside. Diana's file cabinet was easy to break into. I found Boon's file under the B's. There was a new picture of his burn. Healed, Diana has been able to correctly identify the shape as a horse. Her scrawl noted that Boon mentioned someone named "Kiera" during his interview but had no new details to share after being asked a few questions again yesterday.

I sat back in her chair, picturing Diana's reaction if I told her about the origins of Scyra. Her puppy brown eyes would hold a playful amusement as she pushed her hair out of her face while I told her about Charli's research. This woman who hadn't even made it through high school was suddenly trying to learn Greek and find old texts at the local library. Assured that Diana wasn't going to get anywhere with Boon, I went home and fell asleep within minutes.

The next morning, I sent a few messages to people in my network to try to find other potential clients that lived around Dupree's beat. My goons sent me dozens of new client forms that took me hours to read through. Only one looked promising, alluding to a tricky situation because of the abuser's job. I texted them asking to meet that day.

Chicago, Illinois – 2018 – Diana

"God–fucking–damnit!" I yelled, slamming the file down on my desk that Officer Dupree had brought me. It was Boon all over again: lite–torture, drugging, unidentifiable assailants, a burn mark, and a reluctant–fucking–witness. My record was going to have another unsolved if I didn't figure this out. The media would be all over this if they knew I was dealing with a serial perp.

Ghurt came in munching on a chocolate chip cookie, tie and comb over askew. I glanced up at the clock. Definitely too early for a cookie. He sat down heavily in a chair across from me.

"I heard we have a new case, Len."

"We do, suspects in an interview room. The bad news is that this looks like it's connected to the Boon case."

"Boon case?"

"Guy who came in with weird cuts and a round burn about a month ago? Here, I'll jog your memory."

I pulled out Boon's case file and tossed it across my desk. Ghurt wiped his hands on my chair, likely smearing chocolate on the upholstery. I rubbed my temples as I watched him goggle over the file.

"Oh yeah, yeah this guy. I remember him. What makes you think they're connected?"

"Similar M.O. Plus the same burn mark. This time on his dick."

Ghurt's eyes widened even more. He whistled and leaned back. "We're gonna have to go to the big boss about this."

"I know, but first let's interview the victim so we have some fodder to reassure the Captain. Let me take the lead. We need to wring every little detail out of this guy. His name's Michael Forte."

"You got it, Len."

I headed to the interview room with a purpose, waited briefly outside the door for Ghurt to catch up, then burst in. Michael jumped about a foot. Still deeply unnerved, I noted, ready to use it against him. I pulled my chair out, making sure it scraped against the concrete floor and noisily dropped the file on the desk. Michael winced at each unpleasant noise and shifted uneasily in his chair. I wanted him strung up, feeling like he was the criminal, ready to tell me everything I needed to take Trip down.

"Michael, I'm Detective Lendo and this is Detective Ghurt. I read through your file but need you to start from the top and tell me everything in your very own words. Don't leave out a single detail. You never know what's going to be important."

He looked at me briefly then trained his eyes on the table and started talking.

"I met this girl at a bar, took her home, woke up tied up and bleeding…that's it. Went to the hospital now I'm here."

I waited, hoping the silence would goad him.

"…she had brown hair. Long. Not sure what color eyes. Pretty short and lean except…she had a, like, a fat ass for her size."

Ghurt took down notes; I saw him carefully write down the phrase "fat ass". That didn't really fit Trip's description. I mean I guess she could fake an ass, hair could be a wig. Wouldn't help me, though, that it was different from Boon's description.

"I need you to recount for me every single thing she said to you or that you talked about, Michael."

"I mean we didn't talk that much. I saw her giving me eyes at the bar and chatted her up. It was already real late, maybe like 2:30 am, so we were both super drunk, ready to go home."

"Okay, and when you got home?"

"We hooked up and I went to sleep. When I woke up in the morning she was gone, and I was…I was…there were ropes on my ankles and my body hurt everywhere. I don't know what the fuck happened. She didn't take anything."

I let the loudest sound in the room be my fingers tapping rhythmically on the table and put on my contemplative mask, never once breaking eye contact with Michael's insipid, lying face. He looked at me briefly, slumped down in his chair, and pulled his hoodie tighter around him. I took a long, deep breath.

"Michael, I think you're lying to me and I think I know why. I think last night you did wake up and your attacker spoke to you."

His eyes flit up at me then back down again. I leaned forward to loom over his hunched body.

"Not just spoke to you, she accused you. She accused you of being a rapist." I sat back suddenly and shrugged, arms open. "Look, I have nothing on you. I'm investigating this crime and only this crime. I don't need any information other than what happened last night." I turned to Ghurt. "I'm parched. I'm going to grab a glass of water. You think hard about what I just said," the last part tossed in Michael's direction.

I walked out of the interrogation room, winking at Ghurt on my way out. The water cooler was right next to our interview room, so I listened to Ghurt work his man–magic while I filled up. He was all meaty hands and shoulder shrugs.

"Michael, I get it. No one likes to be bested by a female. This wasn't a fair fight though. That's why we gotta step in and even out the playing field. What if this woman hurts someone else? We need you, man." I couldn't see Michael's face, but I saw his posture relax. Ghurt chuckled to himself. "At least help me put her away so this scary bitch doesn't show up at my house in the middle of the night. These days, everyone's throwing the word 'rape' around. We all know what it really is, right buddy? Just women being women. Blaming men for their own problems."

Disgusting. I charged back in and sat down carefully.

"Okay, memory starting to come back to you?"

Michael cleared his throat and sat up a little straighter, empowered by Ghurt's pep talk.

"Yeah, actually. I did wake up for like a minute but it's hazy. I'm pretty sure it was at least one female, maybe two, and one of them was talking crazy. She said I made her do this and threatened to...to, uhm, hurt me worse if I ever came near another girl."

"Did she name any names? Recognize the voice at all?"

"I didn't. No, no details. Just raving about what a bad dude I am."

Internally, I had my head in my hands ready to scream and tear my hair out. This guy was absolutely useless. And now I had to go talk to the Captain.

Iowa City, Iowa – 2003 – Trip

I had to do a bang-up make-up job to look the part of a high schooler. Luckily, the foundation and eye shadow trends from the aughts hid a lot of wrinkles and age. The party was raging. I asked around for Dupree, getting knowing smirks from guys. Finally, some girl, through hormonal tears, told me she last saw him on the roof.

    I had nothing to say to this guy. No warnings, no threats, no words of vengeance. I'd followed him in 2018 for weeks, watched him spread his filth all over Chicago with his partner. Hassling black kids, using excessive force, bursting into homes without a warrant, tasting cocaine he pilfered after unwarranted searches. I didn't need to see what he did to Cassie. The scumbag had it coming when I pushed him off the roof.

Chicago, Illinois – 2018 – Trip

For weeks after taking down Dupree I rode a pleasant high and felt healthier than I had in a long time from spending more time in the present. Maybe the effects of time traveling were just temporary, like a disease your body fought off.

It was my slow season, when everyone was busy heading back to school, so I only had a couple applications to review on Monday. The second one was from someone named Marcelle. I groaned loudly. What the fuck? Was it the same person? I thought I solved this weeks ago. Dupree must have recovered from that fall. What if I made him an even worse person? I reached out to Marcelle immediately and scheduled an interview.

We met at Panera three days later. Marcelle charged in like a storm and sat down heavily.

"Marcelle." I said, with a short nod.

"Hi, thanks for taking the time to meet me."

"It's no problem, what's going on with Cassie?"

She looked at me, confused. "Did I mention Cassie in my app? I totally thought I hadn't."

I searched her face. Was Diana setting me up? This was unnerving. I told Marcelle I had to go to the bathroom and did a lap, checking for anybody who looked suspicious, then sat next to her this time, so I could see the whole restaurant. My proximity made her shift uncomfortably.

"Sorry, just need to make sure no one's tailing me. Tough business, you know?"

"Uhm, sure. Anyway, so here's the form, filled out. I feel like it needs some context, though, it's a big ask. He's a cop and me and my sister are just so bottom of the totem pole, estranged from our mom, on welfare–."

I interrupted, "So Danny Dupree again?"

Marcelle somehow got into an even more uncomfortable position, hunching over further in her seat, like a wolf guarding a haunch of meat. "Do I...do I know you? Who is Danny Dupree?"

We stared into each other's eyes, both confused and scared. I had to get on top of this situation.

"You know, I think I just got you confused with somebody else, honestly. Sorry, long week. So, what's this cops name?"

She relaxed, accepting my lie, not because it was well delivered, but probably because she was desperate to get this over with.

"Marshall Roberts."

"Precinct?"

She looked down at the sheet. "Uhm, 20th district or ward or whatever."

Jesus, what was going on.

"Okay, really quick, what happened?"

Marcelle caught him hassling her little sister, Cassie, while she was hanging out at the playground by her house. Luckily, Marcelle was coming by to grab her for dinner and was able to intervene, but she didn't want him to do it to anyone else or accost her sister again.

So, I did fuck up. I pulled up the stem but missed the roots.

"How's your sister?"

"Oh, she's fine. Not even shaken up. You know how kids are. She probably won't even realize how disgusting it was until she's way older, some forty–year–old cop hitting on a teen girl."

"Yeah, until it comes up in therapy twenty years from now."

We cracked smiles at each other, and then I wrapped things up. Three blocks away, I was shaking my head furiously. How could I have missed this?

Chicago, Illinois – 2018 – Diana

I took two bites of saccharine cake from the Jewels down the street and then tossed my Styrofoam plate, dabbing my lips lightly to get any frosting off but keep my lipstick on. Thirty-five more minutes at the Captain's retirement party, then I could make an excuse to head out. The testosterone in the room was pumping, men all vying for his spot. His last day would be next week, but he planned on going straight to Cancun from work, so we held the party today.

Ghurt was even getting in the mix, missing sneers from the younger men, colts ready to burst out of their skin. I generally tried to ignore the obvious abuse of steroids and gym equipment in the 'cint. Being a cop was tough on your body. I couldn't begrudge them some extra juice.

I headed to my office to put together files to bring home. While bent over I felt someone come up behind me, rubbing directly up against my butt. I stood slowly and turned to face Roberts.

"Whoa Diana, way to come onto me. Still got that husband?"

I sneered at him and walked to the other side of my desk.

"Yeah, Roberts, I've 'still got' my loving husband of six years. Can I help you?"

He held up his hands, like chill out bitch, and sat on my desk, right on top of the files I needed. "What's with the attitude? Just stopping by for a friendly chat. Figured I'd get to know everyone better. Word on the street is that I'm climbing the ranks fast. Need to know who I'll be overseeing, so I can...tailor...my management style," he said, licking his lips and looking around my office.

I laughed, "Congrats, Roberts. Nothing like having the Captain as your uncle, am I right?"

He stood, knocking my files off my desk. "Excuse you?"

Ignoring his sudden anger, I squatted to put my files back together, muttering "Jesus Christ."

I felt Marshall squat down over me and paused, head parallel to the ground, to assess the situation. He pressed down slowly on the top of my head with a meaty hand. I tried to resist or get out from under it, but his hand covered the expanse of my skull. He deftly pressed my head all the way to the tile. I said nothing and went still, letting him grind my ear into the bleached floor.

He leaned down towards my ear and growled. "Rich, coming from a woman. No more diversity hires when I'm the boss." Roberts lifted his hand and stormed out.

I stayed on the ground, getting my breath back and counting my bpm until it slowed down.

Chicago, Illinois – 2018 – Trip

I felt like I was starting to get wrapped up in my own web. Diana knew I was the "criminal" behind Jacob and Michael's reports. Surely someone else had noticed the connection, if she hadn't already told her boss. I considered laying off the brand, but it was important. The whole point of Scyra now, my goal, my baby, was to cause a ripple effect. Those men woke up every day and saw that. It stopped them, it stopped god knows who else.

My second issue was Marshall Roberts. I hated his fucking face from the moment I saw him with Danny. Pretty baby, big grin, ears made to be boxed in. I wanted to gut punch his organs, wrench his tongue out of his throat, crash my knees into his twenty-four ribs. I needed more info, though, insider info. Logic follows that the conversation with Diana about Danny had never happened, seeing as he was a paraplegic in Iowa now, so I could tap back into her.

I needed to be nice to her somehow, win her over. That wasn't exactly my strong suit, being charming. People liked me for my honesty, I think. I guess I'll go be honest? Maybe in a nice way, somehow.

After my meeting with Marcelle, I started watching Cassie at the park every night, making sure Roberts didn't slide by. This whole situation felt paralyzing. What if I caught him, only to find another nesting doll, mentoring him on his filth?

Before accosting Diana, I stopped by the park and journaled, brainstorming a few nice things to say to her. I decided not to sneak up on her this time. I walked into the precinct wearing a wig and normal clothes, joggers and a sweatshirt with a logo, a generous pink. She was sitting at her desk when I knocked on the door.

Diana looked at me for a long time, rubbed her eyes, and waved me in.

"Trip," she said, leaning back in her chair.

"Hey, Diana, look I'm here to call a truce. I think I've been kind of combative on my end."

"Sure, that's the word. Combative. Maybe toss a few more in there. Criminal, mocking—"

I gave her a tight smile. "Sure, yep, yep, okay. All of that. But I just want to say, I do really respect you. It must be hard here, dealing with all these men."

Nothing on her end. I cleared my throat, awkwardly.

"I think we have a lot in common. We both want to make the world a better place, yeah? We just go about it...differently."

"Yep, I'm not a criminal."

I put up my shit-eating grin as a wall and kept powering through.

"I need your help. I'm worried about some young girls and well, this isn't easy to say – I'm really putting my heart on my sleeve with this one – but the trouble's coming from someone in your precinct."

Her eyes flashed. "Who?"

"Uhm, this guy named Marshall Roberts."

She brought a hand up to cover her mouth and said nothing, but kept boring into my eyes with her own.

"He was harassing a fifteen-year-old. And I've seen him do some other not so great stuff while on duty."

Diana put both hands on her desk and stood. She gathered her things while I watched long fingers with even longer longing. They swept her hair out from under the collar of her jacket and she finally looked at me while tugging on each half of her coat, getting comfortable.

"Light his ass up." She said, while flipping the switch and leaving me in utter darkness.

Yes, ma'am.

Chicago, Illinois – 2007 – Trip

After Diana left, I found Roberts' file in the Captain's office. I figured I'd threaten him and see if I could scare him enough to at least stop the sexual harassment offences in later years. It took a few tries, but I finally found him on an old beat.

It took even more make-up this time to make me look like a teenager. I arranged myself in a park, bad posture with my arms crossed awkwardly over my chest, under some dim lights and waited for Roberts to cruise by.

"Hey!" he shouted from the driver's seat around 9 pm. "It's after curfew, you need to head home."

I feigned starting, jumping up, re-crossing my arms, and zipping off towards a group of houses. The car tailed me, rounding the corner to cut me off.

"Need a ride?" What a fucking chump.

"No thank you officer!" I squawked, walking faster. His car kept following me. I headed toward a secluded area of the park and grinned wildly in the direction of the trees when I heard a car door slam shut.

"Hey! You're being very disrespectful for someone out breaking the law."

I walked faster, drawing his ire out further, letting it curl around me like a thick fog, covering my transformation. Roberts caught up quickly and reached for my arm. I swerved deftly to the side and swung to face him, walloping him in the throat with my outstretched arm. He sputtered and I jabbed my knee into his solar plexus, knocking the wind clean out. Roberts fell to his knees choking pitifully and trying to curse me for eternity, but I spit out my poisoned words first.

"Shut the fuck up and stay down or I'll break your arms."

He glared up at me from his knees. I kicked him in the face with the bottom of my boot, shoving him all the way to the ground.

"You're being very disrespectful," I taunted, yanking his wrists behind him. He stilled, giving me enough of a pause to tie up his arms. Roberts thrashed wildly and I kicked him in the ribs, heel first, then tied his ankles and covered his mouth to muffle his grunting.

Roberts tried to roll away. I couldn't help but laugh. I stopped him while he was on his stomach and jerked his head back by his hair.

"Listen, you sick fuck. I know about all the women and girls you've been fucking with. That ends tonight or I'll do more than hurt you. I'll drag you down into my circle of hell."

I flipped him over, keeping a knee down to hold him still, and lit my brand. This was a special case. His scream cut through the cloth as I plunged the searing hot metal into his worthless flesh, right over his Adam's apple.

I stood over him, laughing wildly while tears of pain poured down his face, then blipped away.

Chicago, Illinois – 2018 – Trip

I took a few days off to wander the city, clear my head at the zoo. Chicagoans are fiends for sun, crowding any place where they can lap it up. The beautiful day hid me in the crowd. I let myself get lost in it. My ears drowned in ambient laughs and shouts. I thought about Diana there with me. She would probably walk fast and only stop at exhibits where animals were out, moving around.

For a few minutes, I let myself think about Charli. She used to only take me to the petting zoo, otherwise she'd cry over the animals being caged up, especially in the awful big cat house. Picture a city zoo at its worst. Black bars and fake foliage barely penning three hundred pound cats that stalked wildly back and forth, back and forth.

We used to joke about how our greatest fear was losing our freedom, peas in a pod. I wish I could ask her what that really meant for her, being trapped. What walls did she see? I was too naive. I just thought fear was universal when I was younger, like how when you're a kid you think that every family eats dinner together the same way and everyone's parents woke them up at 7:30 am on Christmas. I'll never know how Charli colored in her fears.

I riffled through a few cases when I got home. Things were still slow for me, so there were only four from the last week. The last one was fucking Marcelle again. I teleported to my favorite park just to scream into the ether and then teleported back home.

$$\Delta$$

We met in the same goddamn Panera at the same goddamn table. This time I was way better at acting like we'd never met. I listened to her entire story quietly, not even flinching when she said that this timeline's Officer Marshall Roberts tried to snatch Cassie into an unmarked car. Marcelle was afraid that he was trafficking teens, which was a visceral punch to my gut.

"Did you see him?"

"Yeah, he's bold. He got out of his car and tried to act like nothing happened. Flashed his badge at me. 'Official police business'."

"Did you notice anything on his throat?"

Marcelle lifted her eyes to the ceiling in thought. "Maybe? I think he had a birth mark on the front, kind of in the middle."

I guess this confirmed my theory that there was way more rot under this maggot. He couldn't be running a sex trafficking ring by himself.

"You know, Marcelle, I like your vibe. You're smart, you're sharp. Good heart."

She raised her eyebrow and brushed strands of hair from her right eye. I pulled some papers out of my folder and continued.

"This might be weird to say, especially right after what you just told me, but you should apply for the police academy. They need people like you."

She crossed her arms and leaned back, which I was prepared for. I shot her a finger gun – Jesus, I'm awkward – and chucked one last Hail Mary.

"And, I need people like you."

Her arms stayed crossed, but her eyes lit back up, searching my face for more details.

"Like, working for you?"

"Not really, definitely not for me, with me. This work takes a network, 'lot of secrecy and fragmentation. I couldn't do it without help. Keep your ears open. I'll give you a number to text with tips. You can also refer people to me. That's all par for the course. But would you also be open to missions?"

Marcelle bit her lip. "I would, yeah, but my sister and stuff comes first."

"Absolutely. Anyway, here's the number." I slid her a card with only my burner phone number on it and got up to go.

"And what about Marshall?"

I paused and grimaced. "Don't let Cassie go to the park anymore."

Chicago, Illinois – 2018 – Diana

I didn't love that Trip found me at my usual cafe, but at least she hadn't suddenly appeared in front of me. She gave me a weird, fake-cheery greeting. I sighed and motioned for her to sit down, since I'd been spacing out anyway. Maybe this was a sign.

She started chatting about the weather for some reason. Of course, when I want to talk shop, she acts like June Cleaver. I jumped in and a look of relief crossed her face.

"For once, I'm, well, not glad. I'm...it's okay that you're here." Trip leaned forward with interest and rested her hands on the table. "I think something really bad is going on in the precinct. I think some of the guys are involved in something shady."

"What guys?"

I was instantly annoyed. "Does it matter? It's not like you know them."

"I had a client come to be about someone in your precinct, so I know one. Two, if you include you." Back to being smug. Better than the weather, but not great. "Officer Marshall Roberts ring a bell?"

"Yeah, rings a lot of fucking bells. It's Lieutenant Roberts"

"Did he do something to you?"

"No, but he's roughed up some of the younger girls on the squad." I pounded my fist on the table in frustration. "I worked hard to get a few more women in the door."

"Well, what do you want from me?"

I uncrossed and re-crossed my legs and noticed Trip's eyes flicker to them, then back up. Noted.

"I don't know, but I was just thinking about what a mess this could be and how I couldn't talk to anyone about it, then you showed up. What did your client say?"

Trip grinned at me and I immediately wanted to put every last word back into my mouth.

"He tried to snatch her younger sister into an unmarked car."

"What the fuck?" My phone timer started going off. "I have to go. 1:00 pm. This table. Tomorrow."

∆

That night, I woke up at 3 am and watched the clock taunt me, minute by minute, then finally got up to make coffee around 4. My husband felt me stir and tried to pull me back in by the waist. I bit his shoulder gently and escaped, putting on my robe.

He followed me to the kitchen, lumbering and half asleep, and wrapped his arms around my waist.

"Go back to bed, I'll make you a cup and bring it to you."

"Oat milk, a splash."

"I know, baby," he said, biting my shoulder in a delayed return of violent affection.

He came back in with two steaming mugs of coffee and handed me my least favorite mug, something I'd never voice so I couldn't blame him, but had he ever seen me reach for it?

"Honey, can I ask you a philosophical question at 4:30 am?"

"You can if me answering will help you get some sleep."

I brought my top lip to the brim of the mug and let it steam up my nostrils. "How do you decide to trust somebody?"

He took some strong sips from his mug and smacked his lips. "Uhm, I guess I just base it on their actions. Like, my best friend in grade school. I trusted him and then he kissed my girl at the school dance, and I stopped trusting him. Easy. Or you, I trust you, right? That's because of your actions."

"Okay, but what if you don't have a good catalogue of actions to trust them on?"

He furrowed his brow in confusion. I picked at the comforter and tried to explain better.

"So, like, say you have a coworker and you're only friends at work. That's the only place you see them. Then they offer to give you a ride home one day. How do you know if you can trust them?"

"Trust them to give me a ride?"

"Yeah and to be a good driver or to not rob you."

He shrugged. "I mean if they've never showed up with, say, a broken nose from an accident or never robbed me before, then that's enough of a backlog of evidence to know I can trust them. I'm sure I'd be fine. I'm thinking of someone right now actually, this guy Ben at the office. We're cordial. I'd definitely let him drive me home."

"That's it? That's your only criteria?"

"Yeah, pretty logical. Do you do something different?"

"You know, I guess not." I kissed him deeply as a thank you for the coffee and went to shower. He sank back down under the covers to sleep another hour or two.

Δ

I arrived at the cafe early to find Trip already there, hands shoved deep into the pockets of her gray jacket. My routine was so ingrained that I almost pulled out my book and started reading after sitting down.

"Okay, here's the deal. If we work together, I'm going to be in charge." Trip said nothing, didn't even raise an eyebrow. "You have nothing to lose, but this is my job."

"That's fair."

Great. "Great." I opened my notebook. "So, could you use your powers, or whatever, to spy on this list of men I have." I slid a typed sheet of paper over to her.

Trip snatched it up hungrily. "Tail them, see what they're up to? Sure, that works. How'd you come up with this list? Also, do you have addresses? I can get them by breaking into the precinct but, seems like getting them from you would be just slightly easier."

This had to be one of the worst ideas I'd ever had. I sighed and pulled out the list with addresses.

"Can you copy these down? This is my list."

"Why didn't you just give me this first?"

"I don't know, Trip, lay off. I'm figuring this shit out as I go along."

"Pen?"

I tossed her a pen from the bag. "I wrote down some people he's close with and then some guys who just seem shady to me."

We sat in silence while she finished writing down the addresses. Unceremoniously, Trip stood quickly and turned to leave.

"Trip?"

"Diana, I know where to find you. I'll keep you updated don't worry."

"Sure, sure…how do you decide if you can trust someone?"

She put a hand on the rounded metal of the back of the chair and rubbed it softly with her thumb.

"Gut feeling."

"That's it?"

"Yea, I think so. I have to make a lot of quick judgements."

"But what about when you don't have to be quick or what if someone betrays your trust once, then what?"

She looked me over, scanning my eyes. "Still gut. People make mistakes."

"That's rich coming from you."

More measuring, like Trip was asking herself if I was worthy of a reply. She sat back down and leaned forward, dropped her voice to a gravel ground.

"Snatching girls into vans is not a mistake. Deliberately locking a bedroom door and forcing yourself on a girl who's been clear she's not interested is not a mistake. Spending hours every day making sure your partner is under your control is not a mistake. I don't punish mistakes, Diana," she said, curling her lips around my name.

"Okay, what about Forte? Maybe he missed some body language cues. The girl wasn't vocal enough. We've all done it."

That look again, assessing the value of spending her precious time talking to me.

"Speak for yourself. Keep pretending like sexual assault can be an innocent mistake and breeding more rapists I have to deal with. How do you decide to trust someone?"

Caught off guard, I hesitated. Trip waited patiently.

"I don't."

"You do. That's an inherent part of society. You can't drive six blocks without trusting dozens of drivers. Can't eat at this cafe without trusting the waitress to not poison your food. How do you decide?" she said, impatientience creeping into her voice.

"I guess gut. And routine. I don't think to not trust drivers."

"Yes, you do. You notice when someone slows down too fast. You smelled your coffee when the waitress brought it over, after eyeing her dirty apron. So, your gut tells you to trust fucking Michael Forte? I don't think so."

Trip left before I could answer. I spent the rest of lunch arguing with her in my head, getting absolutely nowhere.

Chicago, Illinois – 2018 – Trip

Diana gave an insane list of seven people to tail. I decided to do one a day and report back to her at the end of the week. Her instincts were right in suspecting all seven. I wondered if she had held back more solid evidence for her suspicion. They were definitely connected, but I didn't find any hard evidence of a ring. There were no secret meetings or notes being passed.

I needed Diana to do more. We needed to get into their phones. Technology did away with other evidence. These ssholes were probably blatantly texting each other everything. She wasn't going to like this.

I intercepted Diana on the way to the cafe and asked her to follow me to the park across the street. We shouldn't be seen together in the same place multiple times. Diana sat on a bench, listening patiently while I paced and reported out.

Roberts, Bowen, Rodriguez, O'Harrell, Dougal, Johnson, and Chen; one for each day of the last week. Many went home to wives, some children, too. I saw cash flashed, getting drinks with each other on the job, leaving to take phone calls in family restrooms, and letting people go. Then I followed those people they let go. A fake traffic ticket would be great cover for passing cash or notes.

"I'm brilliant, let's be honest. That hunch brings me to my hardest evidence. Two separate incidents of cops letting people go – one traffic, one jaywalking – by O'Harrell and Chen. Both guys they let off with a 'warning' live in the same neighborhood, in fact, only a few doors down from each other in Beverly."

"And?"

"Would take a lot for that to be mere coincidence, Diana. Plus, everyone knows each other in Beverly."

She brought her right hand up, curled her fingers, and rested her nose against them, pushing it into a snout. "Are you serious right now?"

I threw my hands up. "You asked for my help, dude. I'm not law enforcement. My evidence is different."

"Don't dude me. Also, evidence – hard evidence – isn't a subjective word and that's not hard evidence. That's wildly inconclusive, mildly interesting news."

"I said hardest evidence, not hard. Wait, you want to take these guys to court? Are you joking?"

Diana rolled her eyes. "Of–fucking–course. Did you really think I was going to put a hit out on them with you or something?"

"I mean, I didn't think you were dense enough to think it's a good idea to investigate seven police officers in your place of work and take them to court."

The eye roll turned into a full facial symphony, lip twitch, head tilt and all. "I need some evidence, then I'll pass it off. Or up."

Diana was fully delusional. As if I was going to let her fuck up taking down a child trafficking ring. There was no arguing with her, though. I had to play along.

"Okay, fine, whatever. That part's not my business. Here's my suggestion. We work together to get into one of their phones, find suspicious texts. That's hard evidence."

"Why do I have to be involved in this? You can literally teleport around. Do that."

"Swiping a phone is a two–person job and you work with all of these men. I need to know, like, exactly what phones they have, habits, openings, opportunities."

Diana argued that she needed time to think about this and decide. She also made a fair point; how would she explain herself when she turned the evidence over? I wasn't planning on actually letting her do that, but I did sincerely need her help for this. It would take me a long time to plan a break-in, and even then, most people slept within a foot of their phones. It was like trying to steal somebody's earrings out of their lobes.

"Okay, let's start here. Who's dumber: Rodriguez or O'Harrell?"

"O'Harrell, no doubt."

"Great, now we have a specific target. He's just an officer, right?"

"Yes, has a beat, comes into the precinct at the start, middle if he needs to bring somebody in, and end. Why don't you just mug him when he's leaving the precinct?"

"Because there are easily about fifteen things that could go wrong. And if I don't get it, he'll tell the other guys what happened and they might stop using their phones, smarten up, and get burners. Also, then you don't get your evidence."

Diana was running her hands through her hair over and over, distracting me. I sat down next to her and looked away to think this through. I wanted to stop all of this as quickly as possible and robbing people never goes well for me.

"You'll hate this, but I have an idea." I said, turning to her. Afternoon light illuminated the bags under her eyes and for one brief second, I felt some empathy.

Chicago, Illinois – 2018 – Diana

Trip was slumped defiantly across from me in my office. Her black eye was so well done that I wondered if it was actually real. Wouldn't put it past her.

"He's here."

I put my phone on the desk, within her reach, and went out to grab O'Harrell from his desk.

"Hey, can you watch this witness for me really fast? I need to make a phone call and if she runs, I'm screwed." I gave him "help me, sir" eyes and he stood immediately.

"Of course, Lendo. Anything for you," he said, which won him my best thankful eyelash batting.

I walked a third of the way into the room and caught Trip looking through my phone.

"Is that my phone? Give that to me, now!" I shouted while striding over and reaching for it. Trip leaned away and I accidentally knocked into the phone, sending it flying across the room. I ran over and crouched down, releasing a string of curses under my breath when I found it blank and cracked.

"What is wrong with you?" I demanded, my voice crackling with potential tears. "Jesus, what a day."

O'Harrell was looming over Trip, ready to slap cuffs on her.

"Shit, shit, shit. My calls in two minutes."

My white knight stepped up immediately; O'Harrell reached into his back pocket, not stopping to wonder why I wasn't using my desk phone.

I swooned over and took it, lingering a second on his hands.

"Thank you, seriously. Thank you, thank you!" I purred. "Code?"

"No code!"

Fucking idiot. I bounced out of the room into an empty storage closet near my office and closed the door, then took out my real phone to take pictures. This was unbearably easy. Cops make the dumbest criminals. Trip told me to look for unsaved numbers and take pictures of his messages from my phone. There were dozens of numbers. I quickly scrolled and took pictures, finding not only unsaved numbers but also text threads with other officers we suspected.

Nine minutes later, I opened the door and slid out. No one around.

O'Harrell had moved to sit on my desk, of course on some files I'd been looking through. His face lit up when I walked back in.

"I can't thank you enough. I got exactly what I needed to deal with this," I said, gesturing towards Trip and sneering.

"No problem at all, Lendo." He got up and strode towards the doorway, not noticing how many papers he'd knocked off my desk. I handed him his phone and looked up into his eyes, pasting placidity across my face.

Then I sensed someone staring at us from the pit. It took all of my strength not to turn towards the figure because O'Harrell was still talking, holding my hands while I tried to give him back his phone.

"We should get to know each other sometime. Maybe a drink after work."

"You're right! We totally should. I always mean to get to know the officers better. You just do so much for us."

"O'Harrell!" Both of us turned to find Roberts staring us down.

"Ah, well anyway, drink yeah?" he said, jogging away.

"For sure!" I said, walking back into my office. I closed the door and Trip and I went through the motions. I pounded on my desk a little, eventually letting her go after about twenty minutes.

I headed out soon after, waving my cracked phone at O'Harrell as I passed. "Nearest Apple store's a couple blocks down the street, right?"

"Yeah, I can print you directions or something?"

"That's okay but thank you!" I shouted behind me and ran out.

Chicago, Illinois – 2018 – Trip

We spent three nights in a row at bars, dim lit ones with enough diners that the wait staff didn't care about two chicks nursing shit beers in a dark corner. Diana sent me half the pictures of O'Harrell's texts while she took the other half. Working next to her was easy, almost blissful in a way. Silent and in sync, our hands flew over notes. She brought her laptop to check numbers in the database, which was an absolute goldmine of information and Diana's evidence ticket. She was excited how easy this was and mapped out a way to explain having the pictures to whoever she decided to tell.

Her story would be that she borrowed O'Harrell's phone – which three people could confirm happened – and saw a suspicious text from a number pop up when she went to use it. She then took a picture of the text, cross-referenced the number, and found out it was the cell phone of a convicted sex offender with no apparent relation to Officer O'Harrell.

Meanwhile, I was scouring the texts for more names of people involved, adding about five more to my list of seven hits, as well as getting all of their addresses from Diana's many databases on her laptop.

On the fourth night, we brought just our notes to a taqueria to look over and talk out, as well as have a mini celebration. I waited until she was full of burrito to stoke the argument fire.

"So, one quick flaw in your plan, other than not having decided who you're going to tell yet, you're only taking down O'Harrell."

"I thought about that. He'll squeal, trust me. Remember how I said he's the dumbest?"

I had two options: either I stopped her using time travel or I let her get crushed by the inevitable. Nobody was going to listen to her or follow up. And if they did follow up, it would be a classic CPD cover up where they'd fire one or two people and shift the rest around, retire anyone old. Or, I guess, I could convince her to work with me in taking everybody out.

It was going to be glorious. Each night I lay in the closet, listening to Lacrimosa on repeat and going over my plan. A hit one by one, each night like the twelve days of Christmas. I would start at the bottom, working my way through the ranks I'd parsed out, letting their fear build to a hysterical height.

I licked sour cream off my lips and sat back.

"What if they don't get taken down, Diana?"

She idly rolled the paper straw wrapper into a tight ball between her fingers and said, "I'll get there when I get there. For now, I'm happy."

"This is you happy? Yikes."

She smiled at my comment, eyes still on the wrapper.

"Working with you wasn't so bad. It's a shame you chose this," she said, sweeping her hands towards me, palms up.

"Back at you, Lendo."

She smirked and flicked her eyes up at me. "You're not putting up much of a fight. Should I be scared or relieved?"

"Whatever you do, whatever the outcome, I'm just going to erase it with time travel and handle things myself." Found my fourth option. "Sex trafficking isn't a mistake. I physically could not do it, not even at gunpoint or whatever's threatening to me. And I've killed people, but selling somebody into slavery? Never has even crossed my mind."

"How will time traveling do anything? This happened. You can't pull my memories out of my brain."

"Well, I kind of can."

Instantly furious, she snatched up her coat and strode outside. I tossed money on the table and scooted out after Diana. Her legs were unfathomably long. I had to run to catch her.

"Diana! It's nothing personal," I shouted, running up next to her.

She wheeled on me unexpectedly and caught me off balance. I had to catch myself on a sign post.

"Do you think I just don't fucking care? Of course I care people are getting sex trafficked but how are our systems going to get better if we don't use them? They need to be tried in court. They need to be examples so this shit stops. Women, victims, we need to use the law and make it work for us."

I didn't really care what she was saying, but I saw excruciating anguish in her eyes that made me gulp for air. She was yelling and causing a scene. Luckily there weren't too many people around, just cars driving through the intersection and someone walking their dog across the street. She wasn't saying anything that could catch us up.

I stood there letting her get it out. There was finger shaking and almost tears. I was getting cold standing around and shoved my hands deeper into my pockets. Her yelling drew the attention of the dog. It looked like an excitable breed. Diana noticed my distraction, threw her hands up, and walked into the crosswalk as the dog started running across the street, away from its owner.

The dog was dopily sprinting towards us while a car started coming through the intersection. It tried to hit the brakes and hit ice instead, skidding wildly towards the dog. I threw myself at the animal, grabbing it and shouldering into Diana right as I squeezed the gem and teleported to my safe spot, on top of a rock in Millennium Park.

Diana stumbled, not used to teleporting, taking me down with her in an attempt to stay upright. The dog ripped itself out of my arms and went running into the darkness. I was pinned in her tangle, unable to stop the dog.

She stopped writhing and went completely still, trapping me even more. I heard her start to catch her breath.

"You saved my life."

I was silent and still.

"Trip?"

"Yep."

"You saved my life."

"I did, yep. It's no problem."

Now there were definitely tears. This all was horrible. Her crying wasn't exactly loud but I could hear it, so I waited it out. Finally, she caught her breath.

"I can't believe you did that. Without even thinking about it, you just threw yourself at me."

She wriggled out away from me and sat up, taking my hands. They completely covered mine and were wonderfully warm. Diana looked deep into my eyes.

"Thank you. Seriously. I'm still shaking."

"Do you trust me now?" She must not have noticed the dog at

all.

"I do."

"Okay, then trust me when I say, the best thing we can do is take out everyone involved in this ring."

"That's a big ask."

I sighed. "What will it take?"

Diana rocked back, landing hard on her butt, and pressed her hands into the rock behind her, letting her shoulders sink in.

"Tell me how you learned to teleport."

Part II

Oak Park, Illinois – 1904 – Eloise

I know father doesn't think I understand or see much, as I am a quiet child, content in my own company. Every night, though, I hear his wet sobs. I hear him rasping long into the night, ragged with grief and mourning mother. Each morning, I see the red rims of his eyes as he absent–mindedly pats me on the head and heads out to work.

When mother was alive, she kept me entertained day in and day out. My days are much different now. Shortly after mother's death, father installed my grandmother in our sitting room to keep an eye on me. Memaw usually alternates between knitting and napping, while I have taken it upon myself to explore every nook of the house. Our home feels almost brand new to me, each room ringing with silence when before it had been colored by mother's booming voice. Her speed made it seem like she was in every room at once, dancing across carpets, running from front to back doors all day to receive visitors or deliveries or people in need. I was desperately trying to not be lost without her, grasping on to every scrap I found that could be traced back to her life.

My parent's room was first on my list. I swear I could smell the saltiness of father's tears in the air, mingled with the fading scent of my mother's perfume. The odor stung my eyes. I spent weeks just sitting in her closet, hugging her dresses to me and taking deep inhales. As spring blew through our windows, the breeze took with it my mother's floral, husky smell. The dresses' aroma faded, mingling with my own smell and the piling dust. I locked the garments in mother's trunk, vowing to only open it once a year to preserve her smell. It took me several trips to take each heavy dress down. I fell into mourning once they were all put away.

A few days of heavy sadness left me restless, so soon I moved on to her dressing table, still laid out like she had just gotten ready that morning. I sat in her chair and looked in the mirror, trying to see her in myself day after day. I pinched my cheeks, pouted, combed my hair the way she did. All I ever saw staring back were the same grief laden eyes my father wore. I soon grew sick of searching for a dead woman in my own cherubic reflection.

My searching became less about my mother over time and more about figuring out who my parents were, and theirs before them. I found dusty pictures, letters, and scraps from old notebooks. My mother's poetry in her winding script was so hard to read that it crossed my eyes. Two wedding dresses hung in the attic, each yellowed with age and fighting a losing battle with moths. To think, one day my vibrant mother met my melancholy father and was with him till her dying breath. Perhaps he wasn't as morbid back then.

The attic was by far my longest undertaking. Trunk after trunk lined the walls from years of family members living, moving in and out of the family home. I found old, Victorian looking toys and puzzles too swollen from humidity to fit together. Stacks of books with wrinkled pages. Old dresses and hats worn down from use. Working from front to back, one of my final chests was much more impressive than the others. It was full of fine things, like jewelry and silverware. I sifted through my inheritance over the course of a few days, admiring myself in the full-length mirror I had found, decorated in various combinations of necklaces and tea cups.

I believe it was a Tuesday morning when I sidled upstairs for the final time as a child. Light filtered in, illuminating swirls of dust as I bent over that beloved trunk. I pulled out a small, wood-carved case from the bottom and opened it slowly. The heft of it was from the thick ruby set atop a pillow of plush black velvet. I held the stone up to beams of sun and watched blood red patterns splay across the floor. It felt warm, as if it was generating its own heat. Absently, I closed my fist tight around the ruby and remembered father had left me a muffin in the icebox.

The next breath I drew was frozen inside of my lungs and I screeched, shocked by cold and darkness. I flailed indiscriminately and the door of the icebox flew open. I tumbled out, hitting the hearth hard and sending the ruby skittering across the floor. Still in a panic, I scrambled up to find a towel and picked up the gem, holding it as far away from me as possible. I found an old music box to shove it in and buried it in the trunk where I had put my mother's dresses. Memaw was dead asleep when I came back down. I picked up a book and started reading it under her feet, shaking uncontrollably.

Oak Park, Illinois – 1917 – Eloise

I finished my postal route slightly early and was surprised to find my father home. We had developed a comfortable friendship as adults, although he worked late most days, so we didn't spend a lot of time together. His way of coping with mother's death had been to throw himself into his job, rapidly climbing through the ranks of the police department. Tonight, he was idly smoking a pipe on the porch. We nodded at each other and I went inside to throw supper together.

I brought our plates outside to join him. We ate in silence, chewing meditatively and contemplating the road. After only a few bites, father set his plate aside and went back to puffing.

"You're home early."

"I am."

"Is everything alright, father?"

"Oh yes, yes. I did not lose my job if that's what you're asking. I just...I needed to think somewhere other than my office."

I kept my gaze on him, hoping he would go on. Father rarely shared details about his open cases with me. Perhaps he thought crime didn't interest me. He was dead wrong, if so. I saved all the articles about his solves, as well as those about other interesting murders. I picked up books my father read on crime the second he put them down. As someone who had never had a murderous thought in her life, I couldn't imagine what drove people like Lizzie Halliday or the Postcard Killer.

"Tough case?"

"Yes, possibly the hardest of my career. I'm sure several recent assaults are related. They have some thread running between them that

I cannot put my finger on. I'm worried if I don't get to the bottom of who the perpetrator is soon, someone will be killed."

"Do you have the file with you?"

Father looked over and raised an eyebrow.

"For?"

"I could take a look. Maybe fresh eyes would help." He looked unconvinced. "You know, I see a lot because of my job. Maybe I have noticed something that would be of interest to you along my route."

He trained his leaden eyes back onto the road and smoke came billowing out of his pipe, thicker than before.

"Perhaps."

Δ

Father was home again early the next day, his work spread out all over the kitchen table. He pulled up a chair and gestured for me to sit down when I walked in. I tossed my mail bag in a corner and started sifting through photos and witness interviews. I procured a pencil and paper to make my own notes, attempting to weave together connecting threads.

In the last seven months, five women had been assaulted by an unknown assailant. All were between seventeen to twenty-seven years old.

"I thought you said you did not know what all these cases have in common? All the women fit a similar profile, young and pretty. This many attacks in a short period of time in such a small town is alarming."

"They all have brown hair, too, but it is more than that, Ellie. Something else isn't sitting right with me. Also, that is a common hair color and not enough to go off of or set my alarm bells ringing."

"There is a big difference between, say, Judith's dark brown hair and Georgia's sandy blond." I picked up a page of notes and scanned it. "It seems that each one escalates in how violent of an attack it is."

"I noticed that, which is why I am concerned murder is next. It is as if they are gearing up for something."

"Where were they all attacked?"

"Close to their own property or on it. The location of their attack is listed on there, as well as their home address."

I pulled out a map and began plotting out the attacks in chronological order. They were in a loose ring, seemingly growing closer and closer to a center. It could be a random pattern, perhaps the criminal lived in the area, or it could be someone deliberately closing in on their prey.

It would be easy to pass through this territory on my postal route. I began mapping out a path to take that led me past the crime scenes, as well as the heart of the pattern. Father went out on the porch to smoke as I read through the victims' statements and interviews.

Georgia Pummel, aged twenty-one, was walking home from her waitressing job at night when someone came up behind her and hit her over the head. She fell like a bag of potatoes and lay quietly until she stopped seeing stars. The officers chalked it up to a failed mugging. Georgia saw and heard nothing of use.

Rose Comey, aged twenty-seven, was cutting through backyards on her way home from visiting her mother-in-law. She started to have a creeping feeling that she was being followed and picked up her speed to a jog. Branches began snapping behind her and when she turned to look, she saw a tall figure in all black racing towards her. Rose began sprinting but tripped over her dress and the attacker fell upon her, beating her with fists. Her screams drew neighbors, but the assailant escaped. Two witnesses saw a black-clad figure escaping but ran to Rose to help her instead of pursuing the attacker.

Martha Reever, aged seventeen, was sneaking back in through her back door from visiting her beau when someone came behind her and grabbed her by her hair. Martha was thrown onto the ground and paralyzed with fear. The assailant shoved their fist into Martha's mouth to quiet her and began groping her but was scared off when a light came on in the house. Her brother ran downstairs, but the attacker was gone by the time he reached Martha's sobbing, crumpled figure. Martha does not remember much, except that the attacker smelled like musk and mothballs and their mask was lumpy in a way that made her think they had medium to long hair.

Judith Thompson, aged twenty-four, had fallen asleep on her back porch late at night and woke up to a slap across her face. The attacker grabbed her by the hair and threw her to the ground. Judith was hit so violently in the head that she blacked out. When she came to her clothes were askew. Doctors confirmed sexual violence. Wool fibers and a few mid-length gray hairs were found at the scene.

Katherine Green, aged twenty-four, was walking home from her grandmother's early in the morning after spending the night when someone grabbed her from behind and flashed something metallic and sharp. The attacker punched Katherine in the head and kidneys from behind. Katherine fell to her knees, grappling the assailant down with her and felt a sharp pain in her thigh. She passed out and was found by a neighbor. The flesh wound was ragged, like whatever she was stabbed with wasn't very sharp.

All of the victims that saw the attacker confirmed that the figure was wearing loose black clothing and a mask that covered their entire head. They never spoke.

Father came back in a few minutes after I finished reading the reports. He said, slowly, "All of these attacks, they are very intimate, as if it was personal. They took nothing. I feel like the attacker may not be very physically strong since they seem to by relying on the element of surprise."

I did not feel queasy or fretful, just weary. I knew all of these women from growing up in the village. Perhaps, perhaps it was intimate. Although, isn't all violence against women intimate? Every attack is against what we stand for, how society sees us. A sharp knock when we step out of place. Tearing at what they can't have when we will not bow. Any glint in our eyes is a warrant for violence.

"Father, it does not take knowing a woman personally for another person to want to cause them harm to this passionate of a degree." Quietly, I added, "I did not know this happened to Martha. I have known her since we were children."

"I think they all feel some shame after being attacked. Maybe you should call on them."

"I am not supposed to know this information."

"Well, I am sure my most clever daughter can come up with some reason to see these ladies."

"Well, I am your only daughter. Most clever is not much of a compliment."

He smiled and stooped to kiss me on the cheek, in a rare moment of affection. "Oh, but it is."

Δ

The next day, I went around to several houses in the neighborhood under the pretense of collecting donations for the war. Georgia's house was my third stop. I knew that she would be home. I wasn't exaggerating when I told my father I would be an asset because of my job. Everyone's habits were well-known to me, due to my near daily mail route, on top of what I had simply sponged up from living in this village my entire life.

Georgia was alone and welcomed me warmly. Her hair fell in

soft, chestnut curls around her dimpled face. She had a reputation around town for being ditzy. I thought she was just kind and easy going. The sitting room was a little dusty, the furniture older, but comfortably worn in. I felt a pang of jealousy. My old house lacked the wear and tear of a real family, of real life being lived.

Georgia motioned for me to take the softest looking chair. "I know you just stopped by to collect donations, but I could use some company after being around a baby all day. Back to back days watching this child is exhausting, let me tell you, Eloise Scyra. What a little ball of energy. He makes me rethink wanting my own someday."

"Well, you are lovely with him." I sat down and admired the room, nodding along and answering appropriately while Georgia chatted and asked questions. Her brother's toddler romped around our legs while we caught up, his cheeks just as doughy as Georgia's.

"Ellie, I hope you are being careful along your postal route these days."

My ears perked up and I gave her my full attention.

"Why, dear?"

"Well, I'm sure you have heard by now about how I was nearly mugged." Georgia touched her head absentmindedly, her fingers grazing a spot near her temple. "I am one of the lucky ones, too. I have heard terrible rumors about other girls being attacked. It makes me feel so sad. What must one be lacking in their life to go around town hurting innocent girls?" Georgia scooped the boy up into her arms and held him close while he tried to wriggle away.

"I am so sorry, Georgia. I had heard you were hurt, and I should have stopped by to offer my condolences after. I simply did not want you to think that I was prying or nosing around."

"Eloise, no one would ever suspect you of prying." We both laughed at my expense.

"I hope you are feeling okay."

"You know, I am. My head was sore for a while and my memory was not great, but I am mostly healed. I feel extremely lucky that it was only a bump on the head. Sounds like the other girls had it much worse."

"Do you believe it was someone we know?"

The right corner of Georgia's mouth curled up in thought and she looked past me, racking her brain for the horrible memory.

"I truly do not know. Who in their right mind that knows me could do that? Although, I surely do not like that they came up right as I was getting home. The spot they chose, how many people could have known what time I was getting off work? I mean, I guess they could have been waiting around for anyone to come by, but it was so close to my home. It was not in some deep dark alley." Georgia shook her head, finally breaking the lock of eye contact she had been holding me in. "I do not know, Ellie. I wish I did though. I really wish I could help the police. Please be careful out there. I really mean it."

We caught up a little more and then I headed out with a can of beans from the Pummel family. It was perturbing to see someone as light-hearted as Georgia worried about my safety. I pored over my notes and told father Georgia seemed sure the attacker was waiting for her specifically.

Δ

I felt bad bothering Rose for donations. She was a young mother with a fresh marriage. Selfishly, though, I was looking forward to this visit, as Rose had babysat me after Memaw passed away. She had been my older role model, the swan to my duckling.

"Oh, hello Ellie! My, it's nice to see you." Rose's tall frame filled the doorway and two smiling babies took up residence on each of her hips.

"Hi, Miss Rose. Just collecting donations for the war and trying to do my part."

"Come in, come in."

"May I take a baby?" Rose smoothly handed one over and told me that she was named Posey. I cooed at her as Rose rifled through her cabinets.

"I gotta couple cans you can have. There's tea if you'd like to sit down a moment. I can put the kids in their pen, and we'll catch up. Little Ellie, I'm always blown away by how grown-up you are when I see you. Though, you were a very adult little child, prim as a princess, so it makes sense you'd turn into such a fine woman."

Rose's house was small and lightly furnished, likely with hand-me-downs from friends and parents. We sank into the sofa next to each other and she let out a deep sigh.

"Now, tell this old married miss what's new. I want all the stories," she said mischievously.

I laughed and told her about how Jed, the milk delivery man, had been getting a little too familiar with me. She asked after my father and I said he was well, forgetful as ever and work obsessed. At the mention of his job, Rose sat up a bit.

"You know, I'm sure you've heard, maybe from your father, that I was attacked. It was so nice to see his friendly face in a sea of police men. I always did appreciate him and how fiercely he loved you and your mother. Such different people, but he saw her and heard her and accepted her." Rose took a deep breath. "Yes, it was nice to be in your father's safe hands after something so horrible."

"I'm so sorry, Rose. I had heard something happened."

"It's alright. I'm just happy I'm okay and able to still take care of my babies. I heard Judith was real roughed up. Then Katherine, too. Although Katherine's handling it much better. She's practically a second mother to Judith's children at this point." She was silent for a moment, and then took my hand.

"All I could think of was surviving so I could see my babies. I swear to God if they ever find out who did this, I want a piece of them." Rose involuntarily squeezed my hand, almost too tightly. I felt the veins in her willowy hand bulging as her pulse sped up. She turned to me quickly and said, "You have to tell me, if your father has any leads, you better tell me, Ellie."

"He doesn't have any information that I can share with you. I'm sorry Rose." Her grip relaxed on my hand and she pulled hers away. I felt a draft of disappointment and relief release from her body. When you have tangible worries, just the thought of risking it all feels like a crushing weight. What fragile foundations the sanctity of our lives and ability to care for others are built on. Health, wealth, a sharp and flexible mind. It could all be snatched away by random events, sure, but more terrifyingly, by your own hazardous behavior. Rose would never risk her life confronting the attacker but that did not do much for her state of mind.

I picked Rose's hand back up and kissed the back of it. "I understand. My father will bring them to justice, and I think that will be enough for you."

Rose gave me a tight-lipped nod but allowed my touch. "I wish I could have given your father more information. I just was so busy fighting them off, and it was overcast, bordering on evening. They were in all black. I'll never forget the smell though. If you find those clothes, one whiff and I can finger the guy. It was so heavy and tangy. Like old face powder and mothballs." She closed her eyes and leaned back into the sofa.

"I think it's time I get out of your hair."

Her eyes fluttered open. "I'm sorry this became heavy. It was sincerely so nice to see you. Come back and visit. I'd love for my girls to get to know you."

We hugged at the door. I turned back partway down the walk to see Rose still looking after me, arms wrapped tightly around her.

I told my father about the smell later that night. I think it was hard for him to hear the added details about the attack on Rose. He went to bed early and I went to my own room to do more research. I wanted to throw on some clothes to try to estimate what the attacker had been wearing. Something black and shapeless. I didn't have much black, so I opened my mother's trunk for the first time in years. Father dragged it into my room when he finally took it upon himself to clear out my mother's belongings. Faintly, the garments still smelled like her. As I reached down deep with both hands to hug the pile closer to me, my right knuckle scraped against something sharp. There was some kind of box down there. I dug and found a small, wooden jewelry box but couldn't put my finger on where I knew it from until I opened it and saw a crimson glint.

The ruby set me back thirteen years. I usually believed my memory to be strong and reliable, but it did seem fantastical that the stone had somehow transported me to the icebox. Still, I was careful to clear my mind before holding it. It surged with a strange heat, warm on its own somehow and not just from my hands. I wanted so badly to ask father about it but didn't have the heart to wake him. I shut the box and climbed into bed, taking one of my mother's dresses with me, forgetting my original mission.

My dreams were tortured, black figures flying through the air, metal birds hurtling at unbelievable speeds through the clouds. I saw a thin woman with a shaved head barreling down on me through the alley next to the grocery store, but when I turned to run, I fell. In my hand I was clutching the stone. I closed my eyes, transporting myself awake.

Light was streaming in through my windows. I opened the box once again and held the stone in the palm of my hand. Just then, I heard a knock at the back door and thought "Oh, shoot. The milkman's here." Suddenly, I was standing at the back door. My hand was shaking as I reached out to let Jed in.

"Hello, Miss Eloise. How are you?"

"I'm okay Jed. I accidentally slept in so pardon my appearance."

"It's not a problem, miss. That's a lovely rock you got there. Family heirloom?"

He reached out to try to touch it and I snatched my hand away. Jed looked up, surprised at my speed and the look of horror on my face.

"I'm sorry, miss. I'm very sorry. I just...I'm sorry."

"Oh, no, it's okay. I'm sorry. I just clearly haven't woken up fully yet. If you'll excuse me, I need to get changed for work."

He gave me a sad look, disappointed he didn't get a chance to flirt with me today. I quickly closed the door behind him. My mind was all over the place after focusing so much on these cases, plus the mystery of this gem. Work would do me good. The walk, the monotony. I ran upstairs to quickly change, hide the stone, and run outside into the morning light.

I did not even have an inkling as to where that gem could have come from and why my mother had it. It must have frightened her, because I never saw her wear it. There was no way my mother's active mind had never led to a teleportation if she had ever held it. I was reluctant to tell father any of this because I did not want him to take the stone away from me. The only person I could trust with something that powerful was myself.

I chatted with people I came across along my route rather distractedly. My mind was focused on getting to the part of the route I had outlined for the investigation. There were ten houses that lay clustered in the center of the map I had drawn. I had been observing each household and their habits daily. Mostly, it was young families or aging couples, but there were some young men I did not like the look of. This stone opened the possibility of me being able to safely track them. Sandy Miller, Ethan Thompson, and Ned Trentley were all close in age and good friends. If there were multiple people conducting the attacks, that would explain a lot. They all worked regular office jobs, which was perhaps the reason for the strange hours of the assaults.

I came up to the Waterson's house lost in thought. Amelia saw me and ran outside to chat. She was a lively young woman, but her bitter, old mother kept a tight leash on her, so I hadn't seen much of her since she graduated from school.

"Good morning, Eloise."

"Good morning, Amelia. How have you been?"

"Doing alright. Business has been slow lately with the war. People don't have the money to spend on having someone else fix their clothes."

"I'm sorry to hear that, Amelia. That reminds me, though, father and I have some clothes that could use a mend. I've failed him in that domestic area. I never was good at sewing."

"Oh, wonderful! Would you like to drop by this evening, and we can sit in the yard and chat while I work?"

"Amelia, that's actually exactly what I need on this day."

We agreed upon a time and I left feeling relieved to have a distraction from the case. As I was heading in the direction of my next house, I saw Sandy, Ethan, and Ned walking home together for lunch. They all tipped their hats at me when I walked by. I nodded in return and hurried on my way. Once I was just out of hearing range, a peel of laughter rang out from their group.

∆

I brought a dress of mine and two pairs of father's trousers to be mended by Amelia. She ushered me into the living room and through the house. Amelia was a year or two older than me but seemed younger. She laughed easily, in a soprano ring, and her naivete came off as charmingly innocent. Her mother, Cheryl Waterson, had grown up here and scandalized the neighborhood when she became in the family way. Cheryl refused to name the father and worked long hours at the factory to raise Amelia all on her own. She inherited the tiny house when her parents passed away.

I saw little of Miss Waterson, but knew she was a bitter, bent woman. Her temper was short enough with Amelia to be heard by neighbors three houses down. Amelia was a catch, but her joy and freedom was reeled in by her mother's sternness. Perhaps she didn't want her daughter to make the same choices she did. All the same, it took a powerful amount of strength, or maybe spite, to stay put and give birth to a bastard in this little town.

Their house was dark and cluttered, piled up with decades of furniture and knick-knacks. The glass on the windows was old-fashioned and thick as a coke bottle, letting in sparse light. This was Cheryl's domain, as opposed to the rich, bountiful backyard that Amelia tended. We entered into a burst of blue sky. The grass was lush, and flowers bloomed all around us. I was effusive in my amazement and lingered at each patch of garden, stooping to touch budding tomatoes or smell a bush of roses. I desperately wanted to take my shoes off and feel the plush grass under the pads of my feet. Truly, I had never been anywhere this beautiful. Once or twice, Amelia had taken a group of girls through her garden, but she had outdone herself this season. I felt her personality straining at the seams of her confinement through each bloom. After days of wallowing in human misery, I needed this with all of my being, this expression of humanity and to see the great depth to which someone could care about an idea as fragile as life.

There were two trees in the middle of the yard, one old and one young. The oldest was an oak, strong around its core with bountiful, green leaves. I reached my arms around it, childlike in my awe. The second was heavy with some kind of apple, smaller than those at the market and paler. Fruit had fallen to the ground and been feasted on by creatures. Amelia reached up to pluck one off, handing it over with a smile that was appreciative of my admiration. I thanked her and we headed over to sit at the patio table.

We chatted only intermittently, as she was mostly focused on mending and I was content with silence. To my chagrin, our conversation eventually strayed to the string of assaults. I was reluctant to share case details, but Amelia was so isolated that I felt I had a duty to warn her and instill some fear.

"Who do you think is doing this?"

"I'm pretty sure it's someone we know."

Amelia looked up at me, startled, eyes wide with fear, and she exclaimed as she accidentally pricked herself. I warned her to be careful as she sucked on her wound.

"Oh Eloise, you know I don't get out much anyway."

I gave her a tight-lipped, sympathetic smile. "Can I get you something to stop the bleeding?"

Amelia examined her finger, probably poised to say no out of polite instinct, but saw blood gushing a little too fast for her taste and nodded "yes" my way. I went to the kitchen to fetch a dark colored dish towel. While bending over and rustling through the cabinets, I sensed a presence behind me and whipped around to face Cheryl a mere three feet away.

"Can I help you?" She coolly appraised me and the dish towel I had grabbed.

"Oh yes, uhm, Amelia hurt her finger and I was looking for something to stop the blood."

"You know, we can afford ice and tissue."

I was familiar with Cheryl's brand of callousness, reminiscent of the flint my blue-collar uncles carved their personalities from, and took it in stride. She reached behind me with calloused hands and sinewy forearms to open the icebox and then into the cupboard for some tissue. I took the items and hurried back outside.

"Thank you, El! You're a doll."

"No problem. I ran into your mother in there. I think she was a little annoyed to find me rifling through your kitchen."

Amelia looked off into the distance and sighed deeply. She glanced through the screen door to see if her mother was still in the kitchen.

"Let's take a turn about the yard."

I followed her through the grass to the far end of the garden. She stilled and then spoke almost so softly that I could not hear her, even though we were a few yards away from the house. I leaned in close enough to feel her breath hum on my ear.

"I'm worried, Ellie. Mother was all set to retire until the war happened. I was making a good living with my sewing. She was always a... a hard woman, but somehow, she seems even worse lately. I really don't know what to do. I hide outside from her all day." Amelia stooped down to examine a flower and beckoned me to squat beside her before continuing. I leaned in close, desirous of the intimacy and warmth of her breath on me again. "It's been driving me mad. I'm an adult at this point. There's no way of pleasing her and there's no way of living on my own. I'm starting to feel strangled. My marriage prospects are dim on account of me never being able to go out, for fear of mother, and who would want to date scary Miss Waterson's daughter anyway?"

"Amelia, don't talk like that. Any man in this town would be lucky to have you."

"I know that! But it's hard to convince them when I can't even be out long enough for them to remember my name."

We both laughed at her confidence in her own attributes. It was true. I personally thought Amelia was a dream. She was lovely and intelligent, strong and fiery. The plants blooming around us had been borne from nurturing hands. We sighed in tandem and then laughed again at our being in sync.

"Amelia, I'm sorry I haven't come to see you more. If I may be frank, I forgot how close we used to be in school. We spent lunch together nearly every day for a few years."

She patted my hand and stood up. "Lucky for you, there's an easy fix to that, El. Come see me whenever you like."

I followed the white billows of her dress back through the yard and noticed how dark it had gotten. Amelia noticed also and said "It'll be pitch dark soon. Come back tomorrow? I can finish darning everything then." She walked me to the door, and I left feeling lighter than I had in weeks.

∆

I awoke early the next morning full of strength, thank god, as today I planned on visiting Judith and Katherine. I also wanted to perform a few experiments on the stone. Walking home in near-darkness last night had given me an idea. As soon as father left for work, I took the stone out by using a cloth to hold it. I closed my eyes, squeezed the stone tight, and imagined the kitchen. Nothing happened. I emptied my mind again and carefully unwrapped the stone. Its heat lit my palm up and I once again pictured the kitchen. Instantly, I was standing in front of the refrigerator.

If I kept the stone carefully wrapped, I could be free of its power unless I really wanted or needed to use it. Maybe I could ask Amelia to fashion a pouch for me to wear around my neck.

It was time to steel myself for my visit to Judith and Katherine. Katherine was the vinegar to Judith's honey. When we were kids, Judith was bullied viciously. She has always been a delicate creature and an easy target. Her parents were much older and quiet, not very involved in the neighborhood, which made them outsiders. Infamously, Katherine stopped the bullies in their tracks one day with a wave of her fist and a few choice words. She was always a tough kid, the youngest and only daughter of five. Her father labored hard at the factory and her mother even harder at home, a slave to her many children's upbringing. It was shocking to see her throw herself in front of someone as feather soft as Judith. They had been inseparable ever since, the sisters they each never had. I think a lot of people were uncomfortable with Katherine because she was so open about never wanting to get married or have children of her own. Judith, on the other hand, had married a gentle man she had been going steady with since school days and had two children in quick succession. Both were welcomed more easily into the community after Judith married so far above herself, but they still mostly kept to themselves, happy and busy raising two children, while looking after the Thompson's house.

The two women had been the victims of the most violent of the attacks.. I had barely seen the two of them out in the past month and was reluctant to barge in on their healing. Hopefully, their minds were still fresh enough to give me details the officers may have missed to make this visit worth it for them in some way.

I walked up the Thompson's sprawling front porch. Their family money showed from the roof down to the very foundations of their home. It was one of the largest houses in the neighborhood, decorated with wood carvings on the banisters outside that were waxed diligently every year. The front door was heavy and solid. I used the forbidding iron knocker, a man's agonized face. Katherine answered, opening the door merely a sliver.

"Who is it?"

"Hi, Katherine. It is Eloise. I am stopping by to collect donations for the war." The stark whiteness of her one visible eye was magnified in the shadows and I witnessed it examine me as if I were a bug about to be brushed off her skirt.

"Come in, come in," she finally said, opening the door just wide enough for me to slide in sideways.

The inside of the house was much more welcoming. Stained glass windows threw shards of color across the many expensive surfaces of furniture, floors, and antiques. It smelled like old money in here, sharp cologne with wisps of tobacco.

Katherine hurried ahead of me, a broad figure whose temperament made it hard to tell if she was tall or her loom was pure personality. I heard infantile cries and briefly wondered if they were from Judith or one of the children. The kitchen was on the far end of the house. I had to nearly jog to catch up with Katherine.

I reached the kitchen, very slightly out of breath. "Katherine, I would like to offer my condolences, to you and to Judith. I am so sorry you both were hurt."

She leaned against the counter, arms folded. "Thank you, Eloise." Katherine paused and looked away. "You know what's funny? Not many people have been that frank. It is refreshing. People just dance around it. How simple is it to just say 'I'm sorry you were hurt.'?"

"Ah, folks don't want to bring it up and put you in pain all over again."

"Maybe I am less gracious than you, but I think it's because they are cowards, Eloise. Judith and I are practically pariahs because of something that happened to both of us. We did absolutely nothing."

"I would have visited sooner, I just did not think you wanted company, yet."

Katherine's posture softened, but her arms remained crossed. The crying became louder and she looked up, ready to spring on the problem. She glanced at me, then launched herself toward the noise. I followed swiftly behind, not dawdling to take the house in this time.

The nursery was a mess of toys and reeked of human suffering. The saltiness of tears and distinct sweet funk of grief permeated the air with its own version of humidity. Judith was sprawled defeatedly across a rocking chair. One child was reaching to put something in its mouth on the floor and the other was red from crying in the crib. Katherine grabbed the one crying, thank goodness, and I snatched up the second, along with whatever odd or end it was aiming to put in its mouth.

Judith couldn't bring herself to open her eyes until the baby was fully calmed down. She looked up, pleading silently, as soon as silence hit her ears and Katherine lowered the baby down into her empty arms with great grace and clemency, like a midwife giving a new mother her freshly swaddled child for the first time.

"To what do we owe this pleasure?" Judith asked softly without looking my way, one finger drawing across the babes pillowy cheek.

"I am here under the guise of collecting war donations, but if I'm being honest, I really wanted to check in on the two of you. It seems as if no one else has."

Judith nodded in agreement. It was like her vulnerability gave her strength. Katherine's help renewed her and fed her heart. Any other woman would be deeply ashamed at a near stranger witnessing such a scene, a new mother taken down by exhaustion who needed her friend to quiet her crying child. Maybe this is what it was like to live amongst only women. A robust serenity and acceptance of emotions and need. These children were lucky to grow up surrounded by this kind of power.

She looked up at me, directly into my eyes, and stood.

"Tea?"

"Tea sounds lovely," I said, handing Katherine the toddler I was holding. "I'll make it."

We all settled around the kitchen table and I poured when the kettle sang.

"Katherine and I appreciate your small kindnesses, Eloise. The spirit of your mother lives on through you. What a woman."

I bowed my head, slightly embarrassed. It had been a long time since I talked about my mother with anyone outside of my family. "I do my best to honor her memory."

Katherine leaned back in her chair. "You were so young. I suppose we were too, but old enough to remember her funeral. I had never seen so many people turn up to grieve together, really to do anything together ever. Not sure I've ever even seen a wedding larger than the party at your mother's wake. Surely, the entire town was there."

"You know there's no need to exaggerate for my benefit, Katherine. I'm a grown woman." We smiled at each other over the steam of our cups.

"It is a shame she didn't get to raise you. I think she would have taken great pleasure in watching her handiwork come to fruition," Judith added. It was all too much, this amount of simple kindness. If I blushed any more, I was going to blend into the pink, velvet drapes behind my head.

"You ladies are much too kind. I appreciate your warm words. Do you remember anything else about my mother? Any stories from when she was alive?"

They thought for a moment, reeling back into their own heads and memories. "Well, we were about nine or ten years old when she passed, but my mother was close friends with her. She helped out a ton with all of us kids. I think your mother actually used to babysit the boys, my brothers, when there were only one or two of them." I waited for Katherine to go on, hoping for more pieces of my puzzle.

"Her death really twisted mama up. She said Helena felt like home to her, always warm and inviting. I see that in you, but your own brand of it. Mama just threw herself into our lives after losing your mother. No more parties or social clubs."

Judith added, "Really, the whole town lost some of its vibrancy. Your mother organized so many activities and threw the best parties. Heck, even my old parents attended some of the get-togethers Mrs. Scyra threw."

We all went quiet, letting our minds wander into my mother's aura that she left dripping behind. All these years later, I felt the power of it. Her brilliance dappled my childhood with a light whose warmth I could still feel across my cheeks. She was all her, large, loud, and full of ringing laughter up until the moment she passed away. My mother was as clumsy as could be and terrible at comforting people with words. Even though I was so young when she passed, I remembered bits and pieces of her and in the rare moments father and I talked about her, he filled in the gaps. Father always said she owned her imperfections and made up for every single one with the sheer force of her striving always to live and act in kindness. Her titanic qualities were particularly stark when held up against the wall of quiet solemnity Oak Park put up. My heart ached and I slumped a little in my seat. It would have been nice to get to know my lovely mother for myself.

Judith reached out and took my hand. Katherine took the other and said, "Have you ever thought about taking up the helm? If it's not too bold of me to say, I hate to see how closed off you can be, Eloise. You would be doing this town a great service to share more of yourself with it."

I hesitated, thinking wearily about the amount of energy it must have taken to be my mother.

"Maybe, maybe in my own way. It has been nice to get to know the neighborhood better through my postal route."

"You could start with just us, spending time with us. Maybe we could have some kind of society for young ladies. We could name it after your mother! The Helena Society! I would be happy to host us here. We have plenty of room!" Judith exclaimed.

Katherine wrinkled her nose. "Helena Society sounds stuffy. What about the Scyra Society?"

I smiled. "I like that, "the Scyra Society" for young women in the Oak Park community to...to support each other."

"We need it more than ever, with all these hateful attacks." Katherine's eyes flitted to Judith to make sure her words did not have too much of a negative effect on her. Judith did not flinch. "Are there any leads?"

I was reticent to lie or be anything other than open with these two women after the way they had welcomed me into their home. "I can't tell you a lot. I do not know a lot myself, of course, but I am not sure. My father has not told me if they do or not." I paused and tried to read the room on how far I could go under Katherine's protective eye. "Any little bit of information helps, though. I'm sorry for bringing such a traumatic event back up, but have either of you remembered anything useful since the attacks?"

I watched each of their expressions fold in amongst themselves, sifting what they could and could not handle. It hurt me so much to ask. I had lived a life of immense safety and comfort. I could not imagine having that sense of security snatched away from me. Judith shuddered and wrapped her arms around herself. Katherine placed each of her hands palm down on the table and cleared her throat.

"Luckily, the wound I received was shallow and thus healed well. I cannot for the life of me figure out what could've done it. It was almost like someone scooped out a chunk of my skin..." She reached down and gently pressed her left hand to her thigh. "The only other thing I remember is how his flesh felt under the cloth. I was hard...mean. He is young, youthful strength." Katherine looked up at me. "Do you suspect anyone?"

I rolled both my lips inward in thought, surely making an ugly toothless expression. "I... I really don't like the look of those three boys that hang out together, Sandy, Ethan, and Ned."

Both women nodded absently in agreement.

"They have nothing against any of us, though," said Judith. "Why would any of them attack us so viciously?"

"Why would anyone in the whole neighborhood be attacking young women? They don't need a reason other than that do they, that we're young women?"

"I am of the same mind, Katherine," I added. "That's the only thing all of the people who have been attacked have in common."

"I truly do not remember anything, which is quite a blessing. Aside from my headaches, it's almost like it never happened."

"That's not entirely true, Judith."

Judith nodded at Katherine. "Well, yes, you're right. It's hard for me to be alone, since the attacker came right up on my porch. It is almost as if they knew I was going to be there or they had seen me do it before. Who else besides Kathrine and my husband know I fall asleep outside sometimes? As if the attacker was waiting for it to happen again, for me to be that vulnerable."

I let companionable silence fall as we all gathered our spirits. The children gurgled around us, unperturbed by our energy. Eventually, we chatted about more lighthearted topics like motherhood. I excused myself before it got dark. They stood in the doorway, seeing me off into the twilight.

"Hey, Eloise, I'm serious about this society! Round some ladies up and we'll all get together sometime next week, okay?" Katherine hollered when I was a couple yards away.

I shouted back "yes ma'am, how does Thursday of next week sound? Six pm?"

Judith cupped her hands around her small mouth and shouted, "That works for us! We'll host it here."

I smiled and gave them a final wave, then turned my back on the comfort of their home. Darkness was falling rapidly. I hurried, unnerved when I walked past that no-good trio of boys smoking their pipes on one of their porches

∆

My father and I spent a quiet, companionable morning together that Saturday. We ate our breakfast on the porch and then read, splitting the newspaper up into the sections each of us preferred. I was itching to discuss the case and there was no way my father did not sense how high of a frequency I was vibrating at. All these visits were weighing on me, and I still had one to go, as well as putting together a proper group for the women's meeting. I intended on inviting every woman who had been attacked while on my mail route come Monday, but I needed to cushion that with a few extras. I had several school friends I could approach that I knew liked me well enough and would likely attend at least the first get together. Hosting it at Judith's opulent home would be a major draw.

"Father, I am going to see Martha and then maybe we could review the case this evening?"

He glanced over and nodded silently. I rose to get ready and grabbed my donation basket. On my walk, I passed Amelia's house and remembered I had promised to visit her yesterday. Under my breath, I cursed my forgetfulness and decided to stop by after the Reever's.

Martha answered the door of the Reever's sunny home, her curly, short hair still mussed from sleep.

"Hi there, I'm collecting donations for the war."

"Oh, come in, Eloise! I'm positive my parents have some spare cans."

I followed her through the well-lit, well-loved home. It was brimming with evidence of life lived, toys, books open and written in, blankets thrown on furniture, and pillows around the coffee chair. They were a tight knit bunch, Martha, her parents, and her two brothers. I went to school with the middle brother, Robert, and socialized with her eldest brother, Stephen. Martha was always with them growing up, just as rough, just as rowdy. She sped into the kitchen so fast I almost had to jog to catch up. I did not catch the first part of what she was saying when I came in on her tail, as she was already head and shoulders in a cabinet, rustling around.

"I am sorry, what did you say Martha?"

She turned to face me and sat on the floor, legs sprawled. "Oh, sorry. I was just saying it's so good of you to do this! If they'd let me, I'd absolutely sign–up."

"There are jobs for women, nurses and such."

"Yes, sorry, I meant they as in my parents. They don't trust me to travel that far alone and I need their permission to enlist. It's driving me nuts. Stephen is going in a month or two."

"I had not heard. Are you upset?"

Martha scrunched up her face and stared hard at the wall just above my head. "I suppose I will be. For now, I'm just jealous."

"Did you graduate this past spring?"

"One more year left, then I'm out of here. I need to explore."

I smiled as she turned back to the cabinet, now on all fours and pushing boxes aside. "Martha? Would you like to join a little group I am putting together? It is a social group for some of the young women in the neighborhood."

Her voice muffled, she said, "Probably! When? Where?"

"This Thursday, at 6 pm. Judith Thompson's house."

"Ah ha!" Martha shuffled backwards, bringing several canned goods with her out of the cabinet. "Yes, yes that sounds great! Let me write it down, or would you? I'll find you some paper."

This time I actually did jog to keep up with her as she zoomed out of the kitchen and wove through different rooms in pursuit of paper and pen. I almost ran right into her when she stopped abruptly, waving a stray brochure and pencil. I took both and wrote down all the details.

"This sounds great, a woman's group. I need something like that. I've been feeling a little...a little restless lately and nothing is solving it. Usually, I could just ride my bicycle or do some gardening, read a great book, it would go away. It's really been ever since that horrible woman attacked me, I just can–"

"Woman?" I interrupted, turning my full attention to Martha.

"Yeah, didn't you hear? I expect your father told you."

"Yes, I just thought it was a man."

Martha trained her eyes past me again, thinking out loud. "I guess sure it sounds like something a man would do? But I just really felt like it was a woman. But I guess I'm not sure why I thought that."

"Will you let me know if you figure out why you got that sense? It may be helpful."

"Sure! Yeah, I'm really not sure why." She refocused her eyes in my direction, piercing through me with sudden anger, bright hot, a lightning bolt through my heart. "I'm not sure who it was but I'm sure about what I want to do to them. I swear if I ever, ever came across them I would rip them in half with my bare hands." She raised her trembling fists in front of her. I reached out and put my hand on her arm. She went slack at my touch and let out a deep sigh.

"I'm so sorry, Martha. I truly can't imagine what you're going through."

"I appreciate the sentiment, Eloise. I'll see you Thursday." I took that as a dismissal.

Δ

I stopped by Amelia's on my way home to pick up my sewing and invite her to the first women's group meeting. "Scyra Society" made me blush; I could not bring myself to refer to it as that. Cheryl answered, looked me up and down without a word, and called for Amelia, who bounded through the halls to me.

"Ah, Amelia, I am so sorry I forgot to come by yesterday. I was with Judith and Katherine much later than I thought and did not want to be out at night."

"No need to apologize at all! Come in, we'll have some iced tea on the porch while I finish the last few stitches."

I had not planned on staying, as I was eager to get home to father, but I was pleased to enjoy the flourishing back yard for a second time in three days. This time, I did take off my shoes and felt the grass rise up to lick the curves of my feet. Amelia pointed me towards the most fragrant flowers, and I beckoned her over to join me in smelling them. She also took off her shoes and then picked her way carefully across the yard. I grasped the stem of a large bloom and gently bent it towards Amelia. She stooped down to take it in, wrapping her hand around mine holding the stem. Her warmth jumped my skin into goosebumps and her scent mingled with the flowers'. I laid back into the grass, feeling completely at peace. Amelia ran to get her sewing and then sat down beside me in the grass, chattering about her future plans for the garden.

"Amelia," I said without opening my eyes. "Could you make me a small satchel I could wear around my neck?"

I felt her quizzical gaze on me but all she said was yes, of course. I also invited her to the Scyra meeting. Amelia pursed her lips but said she likely would be able to make it. Her mother would just have to deal for once. She finished up the sewing much too soon for me and I headed home to talk through my visits with father.

He was ready, documents and maps spread across our dining table. I brought out my notes, debriefs from my visits with the victims and sketches attempting to tie the crime scenes together. Our heads bowed nearly together, we examined each other's new findings. We sighed and mhmm'd while moving around the table like hikers picking their way across rugged terrain. I brewed coffee and tried to open up a conversation, but father held up a hand. Leaned back in my chair, I sipped and pondered the smell recollections from my interviews, the smell of moth balls and face powder. That could be found in every other home on the block. Perhaps, though, if we found the perpetrator, they could be positively identified by their scent or the smell of their home.

Finally, father sat down and looked at me after giving his eyes a rub reminiscent of my friend's toddlers close to nap time. "So, what have you found?"

"I think, most importantly, that you need to expand your investigation to women." Father raised his eyebrows, as if that thought had been stewing, looking for words. I had found the letter, the words, the evidence. It made me feel sick to my stomach, but everything except the actual crime felt feminine. I could smell her, I could see her form. I felt the strength of her body and arms bearing down on me in the shadows. The victims had painted a gorgonic picture. I feared even more for all of us, if we were truly at the mercy of a brutal, feminine intellect. Where was she lurking now? In wait, watching her next victim?

He let silence wrap us, to my fury. At this point I felt that I knew more than him, having had intimate conversations with the victims. Shouldn't he be picking my brain?

"Father, I take that back. The most important step right now is watching those ten houses. I feel that the victims were hunted, and the criminal is currently watching someone."

"Ellie, your map really is not enough evidence to set a police watch on those houses."

"Sure, but so many of the victims told me they felt like it was planned, like they had been watched and attacked at the most opportune time for the attacker."

"I understand these are your friends, but I do not think that is compelling enough to use up so much police officer time. We are a small community, people are always walking out and about. How far away are we measuring as close to home? What counts as watching? You yourself said you are familiar with the habits of all the people in our community. That just feels like women's society to me. You're seeing things through a female lens, ascribing feelings as facts."

My face remained still, his did not. He was speaking with the help of his hands now. "I'm not opposed to opening it up to investigating women as the suspects, but even that is going off of slim evidence, physical descriptions from when we first interviewed the victims. I appreciate your help, Ellie, but none of your notes give me a real, actual lead."

From my own father's mouth, betrayal. For all my work, betrayal. The folly of man was going to get somebody killed in our very own neighborhood, under the nose of my idiot father, who would not lift a finger based on women's word. I was tired, limp as if the air was suddenly at full humidity.

"Well, then we have nothing else to discuss." I felt his eyes on my back as I retired. I have never liked being told no.

∆

We passed sullen days together. I refused to lift a finger for my father, making only coffee for myself and eating hasty meals. He reached for things I usually put out for him, coming back to his body empty handed. I'm not sure how miffed he was, dour as ever with his nose in his work. A daughter who never asked for anything and this one time he refused. Well, now I would embody refusal and he could watch its power work.

The only thing I had to look forward to was our first women's club meeting. I invited some women along my route here and there, mostly girls I went to school or grew up with, in addition to Amelia, and all of the victims. Martha was the only one who could not make it, as her family was out of town on vacation for the week. I expected around ten to twelve women to show. I wrote down a rough agenda, hoping no one else had done the same. We would talk about war efforts, how we could support each other and the community, and then set the next meeting date. I wanted to open with half an hour of chit chat, socializing and snacking. Most pressing though, I desperately wanted to suggest a neighborhood watch. It felt like a big ask, to do a police man's work, but well worth it if we stopped another attack.

Thursday's morning light came streaming straight into my eyes. I was up and dressed by the time Jed knocked on the back door, but in a hurry as he was a little late. I tried to do a quick hi and bye, but he stuck his foot in the door before I could close it on him.

"Awe, Ellie, it's been so long since we caught up."

I scanned his face, unsure how to take this, as camaraderie or aggression. Either way, manipulating him with docile, lightheartedness was the only way out of this situation.

"Oh, Jed! You're the one who's late today, flirting with other girls on your route?" I shot him a winning smile, hoping he would take his foot away. Instead, he pried the door further open and moved to step in. Goosebumps prickled across my flesh, feeling his raw strength open my back door that I had every right to close in his face. Just then, my father wandered into the kitchen, likely expecting coffee.

"Oh, hello Mr. Scyra," Jed said, jerking back out of the doorway and releasing his iron grasp on the frame. Father looked up in time to see Jed's guilty, awkward movements.

I said, "Well, see you tomorrow!" and closed the door in his face. To my father, I turned and said, "Did you see that? He was trying to force his way in here."

Father pursed his lips at me and frowned mildly. "Has he done that before?"

"Usually, I chat with him a bit but have not had time to in recent weeks. This week he was late, so when I tried to do a quick hello-goodbye, he started shoving his way in."

Father's mouth puckered more, from tart grapes to lemon slice. "I can accept the milk from now on."

"I appreciate that. You will have to be here in the morning to receive it and will not be able to dash off early."

"That's doable, Ellie."

I gave him a quick smile, more just a pull of the lips, and turned to leave as he added "You know, I'm not a monster." I pointedly ignored his hysterical comment. No one ever said or implied he was a monster.

My route was lively today, all the ladies in attendance and those who could not attend wanted to chat about the meeting, my mother's legacy, and what this get-together meant for the community. I basked in its warmth, stark next to the chill I was cooking up in my own home. My last stop before the meeting was Amelia's. She met me at the door, glanced behind her, and closed it firmly as she stepped out into the sunlight. We hugged, lingering slightly, as we had not seen each other since last week.

"I made you something," she said, while pulling back and handing me a velvety pouch with a slim cord.

"Amelia, it's perfect! I really appreciate it. Here, let me grab some money from my pocketbook."

She stopped me by taking my hands, gently peeling them open, and placing the bag in them. Her two closed around my two, a reverse flowering, and she looked up. "It's a gift, El. No need to pay me." We smiled at each other and loped off towards the Thompson's.

The house was already buzzing when we walked in. The ladies had almost all arrived early in their excitement to not only be inside the Thompson's lavish home, but also to catch up with everybody. Amelia and I were immediately drawn to the sweets table after giving out nods of hello. We parked ourselves in a quiet corner of the drawing room and mostly listened. I wanted to conserve my social energy for running the meeting. Judith and Katherine were lively hosts each in their own ways, Judith like a warm summer breeze and Katherine a crisp spring billow. I was lucky enough to be sandwiched between both for a time. Strange how much I was enjoying attention recently. I never thought I needed much, but perhaps that was less about who I was and more about self-preservation in the vacuum mother left. Katherine and Judith approved my agenda, including the neighborhood watch portion.

Eventually, Katherine called the meeting to order and gave me the floor. I let everyone know my tallies on canned goods since I began the project and we brainstormed other ways to support the troops. Jane, a former classmate of mine, suggested writing letters to soldiers and volunteered to get addresses from the war office.

"I am in, as long as my pen pal's a single man," Georgia chimed in. This set off titters and side jokes. I laughed and then cleared my throat when their voices died down. "Next, I think we should talk about what we all personally need and if there are community needs that we are aware of. It is okay if we can not think of any now but try to bring some ideas to the next meeting."

Some of the girls offered to babysit for others. Amelia mentioned her sewing business, in case anyone had forgotten, and that she checked in on her neighbor, Mrs. Dredd, once a week to make sure she needed anything. Judith suggested we all think of someone we could check on, of any age. Katherine chimed in that if we all made it a habit of the community, it would not be seen as being imposing or presumptuous. I felt this was a good segue into my big ask, so I interrupted the flow of conversation in order to bring up our next topic.

"Yes, we could all do more to look after each other, in our neighborhood and town. I, myself, am particularly concerned right now about the women of our community." Their faces all dropped from light to somber, so I knew none of this would be new information. "I am sure all of you have heard. There has been a string of attacks. I am sorry to bring this up, but I also feel that we need to be aware and to do something about it." I paused, gathering my thoughts, trying to reel in my anger at my father.

"Unfortunately, it does not seem that there will be an arrest made any time soon. I am deeply concerned for all of you and your well-being." I decided to be generous, remembering my father immediately stepping up to shield me from Jed. "It has been a difficult investigation. I think, though, we could do something very small and simple now that we have all come together. I would like to propose starting a neighborhood watch. Each of us could pair up. There is a certain area of the neighborhood that is most vulnerable—" I paused, feeling that I needed to explain, only a little, but still somehow explain "It is most vulnerable due to the way...the way the houses are laid out."

They all nodded along, willing to follow my lead. My heart swelled in that moment, witnessing their trust in me in action. "I think as long as we are in groups of more than one, have flashlights, and maybe a weapon, such as a heavy stick, we should be okay." There was more nodding. They all seemed eager, ready to sign up, like troops off to war. "I think two shifts, one from dark until perhaps midnight, everyone should be in by then, and then very early, 4 am until about 7 am. Hopefully, we can find other women to join. Two shifts is a lot to ask of the spare amount of people in this room."

"Could we find some gentleman to help us?" Rose asked.

"I do not think that is wise for now." The ladies nodded in agreement, a bit wide-eyed, but willing to take the Police Chief's daughter's word for it.

"I think that is a wonderful idea, Ellie," Katherine said, smiling broadly at me. I smiled back, knowing that if Katherine was behind it, everyone else would be, too.

I brought out a notebook and had everyone who wanted to take a shift come sign-up for the week. I had already put my name down for the debut shift. Amelia came up first, put her name beside mine, gave my hand a squeeze, and went back to her seat. I passed out maps of the patrol area, checked in on who needed flashlights or a weapon, and jotted down what houses to drop supplies off at. It felt good to have gotten that ask over with. My body felt exhausted, now that the adrenaline had left it.

It is hard to put into mere words the tranquility of my mood that night as I lay down to sleep. A blanket of communal, feminine energy tucked me in. I dreamed that Amelia and I were children, walking hand in hand through a wild field. Just ahead, my mother bounded. Each time I looked at Amelia, she grew older, and then back at my mother, who grew farther away, until my mother was a speck and Am was withered. I looked down at my free hand and found it to be wrinkled and spotted. Suddenly, I felt so tired and motioned for Amelia to lay down beside me in the grass. She took my head into her lap and I closed my eyes, listening to her breath and light hum, as she wove her fingers through my hair.

Δ

The next few weeks fell into a steady rhythm. We recruited quite a few more women, so that no one was doing more than two shifts a week. I covered one evening shift with Amelia, one morning with Katherine or Judith, each week and then filled in whenever someone needed to back out last minute. My notebook never left me, nor did the gem I now kept around my neck in the velveteen pouch. It was deeply enjoyable to spend one on one time with Amelia, Judith, and Katherine, as well as nearly every other woman who stood with us.

News of our society and neighborhood watch spread like wildfire throughout the neighborhood. Many people stopped me along my postal route to praise the watch and make suggestions. Day by day, I think we all felt a little safer that the attacker likely knew we were watching out for each other, giving them less room to breathe. Neighbors left their lights on for us or stayed out later on their porches than they normally would have in solidarity and as extra protection. My father said neither praise nor criticism but pursed his lips in concern each time I went out.

Scyra meetings grew to fifteen, twenty, and then hovered around thirty attendees each week. Off shoots spawned, book clubs, best friends, nannies. Amelia's sewing business was booming so much so that she usually worked during meetings, her deft movements setting a beat when I spoke. I talked into their rhythm, never getting more comfortable with the spotlight despite leading the group most weeks.

In addition to our night shift, I often stopped by Amelia's for a half hour or so after work. I so enjoyed her company, particularly our silence in her extraordinary backyard. Night shifts were for chatter, secrets and, after a while, fictions, making up stories together or dreaming about what the rest of the world was like. We bounced adjectives between us, trying to pinpoint the solitary joy of a single, perfectly ripe cherry, or just what about the elusive scent of a thorny rose we found to be so intoxicating, so just out of reach. A smell that your nose lost itself to in familiarity almost in the same second you took a whiff.

The only thing we didn't talk about was my gem. I felt that it was a burden to know and did not want to weigh her down, too. I was glad to have it just in case, God forbid, we ever were attacked. I wondered if I could transport more than myself and what it took to do so. There was no humane way to try, although I did very briefly consider using a baby. Luckily, I thought through the many pitfalls of that, such as just I transporting and the infant free falling through the air or arriving at the next destination holding only a chubby arm or leg. How would I explain that?

It was hard, though, to keep that piece of myself from Amelia. I had no idea how freeing it was to share yourself with others, or with someone special, so completely. My most vulnerable moment with her was confiding in the cover of night my father's reaction to asking him have police officers guard the neighborhood. To my utter surprise, I felt tears stinging the dry lenses of my eyes, burning away pent up rage and pain. Amelia brought me to an unlit porch and let me cry. Heaved up through my eyes, my mouth, my lips, were years of resentment that I had until this moment felt too embarrassed to acknowledge. I had never wanted anyone, anyone ever, to know they could affect me or have power over me. She murmured soothingly into my hair until I calmed down and felt better. With my heart, free now from tears, Amelia's aura melted my desire to maintain my walls into another, one to be seen and heard and understood. I felt so light these days, I swear I bounced from door to door. So, this is what it was like to feel alive.

Δ

Fall started encroaching on our watches. I didn't mind the nip in the air, especially after Amelia surprised me with a scarf. The other women complained little, still happy and fulfilled by keeping watch over our community.

The only problem was that it was starting to get darker earlier. Soon, I would have to risk walking home in the dark when I stopped by Amelia's after work. There was the gem, but I couldn't help but daydream all the ways that could go wrong. I would be in so much danger if people found out I could time travel. We had learned about the Salem Witch trials in school. I was already encroaching on spinster territory; an additional title didn't need to be added to my reputation.

We were wrapped in blankets and rocking gently when I brought it up. Amelia pursed her lips in displeasure and kept her eyes on her sewing. I waited patiently for her to digest her thoughts. Her skin was particularly dewy that evening. She was always running at a higher temperature, as if her body generated extra heat to keep everyone else comfortable. It was a wonder to me that her extremities stayed warm enough to sew outside comfortably.

She sighed and said, "It's going to be a long winter, isn't it, El? Sometimes I wish we could just move in together. We get along so well."

I wrapped my blankets up higher to cover a creeping flush, flattered she would want to live with me. I had the same thought, often, especially when the rooms of my house rang with steps instead of laughter.

Amelia put down her sewing. "We should make the most of the light we have left from now on. I won't sew anymore. There are plenty more blankets in the house we could lay out on."

Before I could answer, she was buzzing around inside gathering blankets and snacks. So that became our routine most weeknights. Our intimate conversations that were previously reserved for night watches moved into the light of day. Each time, she found things to say that made me blush, such as that I was her best friend.

When we weren't talking and telling stories, she clipped blooms at their peak, as well as leaves and pieces of bark, or different fruits from the garden. Amelia dropped them onto the blanket between us and we took deep inhales of floral, oaky, green; fresh, dry notes. Our adjectives were limitless. We started pairing different buds and bits together, making each other smell the latest and greatest combo every five minutes. Sometimes we just lay there holding hands and watching the clouds or braiding flowers into each other's hair.

One especially beautiful autumn day, after we had laid out our usual nest of blankets, I told her I had something to say. I'll never forget her face as she looked at me expectantly, the breeze ruffling her curls that I knew smelled like lavender and basil, her lips slightly parted, her gaze peaceful and at rest, but entirely on me.

"I was too shy and flustered to tell you when you said it, but you are also my best friend. Really, the best friend I've ever had. I made you this, it's kind of silly but you'll probably love it."

I made her close her eyes and I put into Amelia's soft hands a lock of our hair braided together, with a dried flower woven in between. In my head, this moment after, from when she started opening her eyes, lasts for as long as I want it to. I spliced it away from the disaster and grief that followed so it could always exclusively be ours.

Amelia's eyes softly fluttered open, plush lashes curling up to the sky as she looked at my gift in her hand and then at me. Later, years later, she described to me my face, laughing generously at my intensity. Although she laughed, I knew that my look pierced her heart so thoroughly that next she leaned in and pressed her lips to mine, petal soft, billowing across my mouth. So much made sense in that moment, my desires, my choices, my destiny. I kissed her back, locked into a passion fiercer than any I had ever felt before. She leaned forward, wrapping an arm around my lower back, and deepened her kiss, just as we heard an unearthly wailing rise from the house.

Amelia and I pulled apart, whipping towards the noise as a black-clad mass pummeled towards us. My first thought was that it was a demon, coming to drag us down into hell. I was so sure for half a second, I could almost smell sulfur. I threw my body across Amelia, ready to protect her from anything, only to realize it was Cheryl, still wailing. She flung me aside and grabbed Amelia's arm, dragging her back towards the house. Am struggled to get to her feet after being dragged halfway across the ground on her knees. Now we were all screaming and wailing, Amelia and I in pain, Cheryl in fury. I danced around them, not wanting to hurt Am by prying her from her mother's grip. Cheryl told us we were disgusting. She told us we could never see each other again. She told me I was vile and corrupted her daughter, that she should have known and never let Amelia get so far away from her. I was galloping, skipping, reaching to get just a light brush against her skin and let Am know it was going to be okay, but Cheryl was effectively keeping her body walled between us and shoving me out of the door. She slammed it in my face, and I pounded on it over and over. Cheryl was screeching still at an ungodly pitch.

My body was shaking with rage and I ran home, suddenly afraid the entire neighborhood heard us. I locked myself in my room and was immediately doubled over in full body gasps, trying to get air in between sobs. Blinded by tears, I felt around for my mother's trunk, unlocked it, and pulled out dress after dress until I was buried underneath the fabric. Deep breaths of my mother's aged, but recognizable scent calmed me down. The skin around my eyes and each breath that hit my lungs felt raw. The memories of Cheryl's unmitigated hatred renewed my anger and I ripped the dresses off of me and beat my fists on the floor. I had to get to Amelia. I started pacing to help me plot out my next move.

After a few minutes, I stopped, suddenly remembering the gem around my neck. It would be wrong to teleport into Amelia's house without her consent or knowledge of the gem. Somehow, I would have to get a note to her and one back telling me when I should visit. I also needed to convey that I could covertly get to her, without explaining too much, lest the note get into other hands. My body was finally draining itself of all of the adrenaline and trying to recover back to a normal state. I felt wholly exhausted and passed out in the pile of dresses into a black sleep.

Δ

Waking up was tough. I did not remember the night before until I opened my eyes fully and saw that I was nestled into a pile of dresses. My next hour was pure madness, scrawling furious notes and plans, dashing around the house to pull everything together. I needed Jed and I needed to appear blasé to Jed to communicate with Amelia. The routine of getting ready for the day calmed me down some. I ran into father on the way down and told him I would handle the milk this morning. He raised an eyebrow but did not argue.

"Only this morning and probably the next, though, then please take it back over." He nodded, headed to the door, then hesitated.

"Eloise, I'm just going to wait here until he's gone. If you don't mind." I shrugged sheepishly, touched by him being protective.

Jed knocked on the door shortly after. I greeted him warmly "Hello, Jed. It's good to see your handsome face!" Internally, I cringed, hoping my father had not heard that.

Jed's face lit up at the sight of me. "Ellie, it truly has! You've been hiding from me." He laughed and I matched it.

"My darn boss changed my route up, so I've had to leave the house earlier than usual. It's such a shame. I'll get to see you today and tomorrow though! Have to cover milk duty for father, busy week. Chief of Police duties far outweigh postal."

"Ah, Ellie, don't sell yourself short. Mail's pretty high up on the list of important jobs."

"Hey, so is milk!" I added, as well as a fake laugh. We chatted mundanely for a little bit longer and just as we both turned after saying goodbye, I called him back, feigning forgetfulness. "Oh, Jed, could you do me a favor?"

"Sure thing, Ellie. Anything for my favorite customer."

I smiled and tilted my head to the side. "Could you bring this note to Amelia Waterson? Silly me forgot to tell her the time of the next meeting and I don't have a moment to drop it off today."

"Yes, they're at the end of my route. Happy to help, Ellie." I gave him about five more smiles and thank you's and finally shut the door. Father nodded at me and left, no questions asked. All I had written on the note was tomorrow's date and then "11:00 am, meet you at home and walk over together? Main agenda topic is leaving and arriving safely". I felt that was vague enough in case anybody intercepted it. Hopefully, Amelia understood and wrote back consenting to my visit tomorrow.

I raced through my route so I could go home to practice with the gem and visualizing Amelia's house in general. The backyard was probably the best place I could land. It was the easiest place for me to see in my mind's eye. I was so frantic to get to Amelia. I lay on my bed for hours going over as much of her house in my mind as I could. My imagination laid down thick blankets of grass, planted each garden, arranged furniture, painted bark onto the two trees. I transported quickly from room to room in my house before father came home. It was thrilling to have control over time and space. I felt invincible which was really just the attitude I needed to face Cheryl's wrath.

My dreams that night were feverish, pitching between joyous and terrifying. Black figures surrounding Amelia and I enjoying a picnic in the field. We fended them off back to back. I was terrified, but so sure, so reassured to feel the pressure of her backside protecting my own. Our midnight fights found me awake early and entirely tangled in my sheets.

I paced around the kitchen while waiting for Jed. Father was silent in the living room, keeping to himself and his thoughts. My lunge at the door when the knock came was a little too much. I paused to breathe, hand on the door handle, and pulled it open gently, transferring that soft touch to my tone as I greeted Jed warmly. The light banter was much harder to pull off this time around. I was getting impatient and ended up interrupting his story about being chased by Ms. Henderson's dog.

"Really quick, Jed, before I forget, did Amelia write back?"

"Oh, yes! It's here in my wallet," he said, pulling out a note and waving it just over my head, clearly expecting me to playfully get it from him. My stomach sunk. I felt sticky playing along with him as he teased me. There was the shadow of his past forcefulness hovering over my head. Finally, finally, he relinquished and gave it to me. I practically shut the door in his face, entirely over his antics.

Amelia's note simply said "I trust you". I clutched it to my thunderous heart, took a deep breath, and tucked the piece of paper into my gem pouch. My plan was to run through my route as fast as possible, take a quick break to teleport to Amelia's, and then be out of there by noon. Cheryl would certainly be at work. Even if she wasn't, I was going to teleport into a dark corner of the garden and then check in the windows to make sure the house was empty, aside from Amelia.

11:00 am was soon upon me. I ducked into my home's foyer, crouched into a ball, clutched the gem, and imagined the vegetable garden. Sun hit me, and soon after a shrill screech. I awkwardly scrambled up and found Amelia merely feet away, shrieking. I was upon her in no time with my hand clamped over her mouth. She took a few calming breaths and I removed it.

"Eloise Scyra, what in the world did you just do?"

"I'm sorry, Am, I told you I'd be here!"

"First of all, you kind of told me. That note did not properly convey that you were going to just appear in my garden. Second of all, I figured you would hop the fence like–" She shook her head, trying to wrap it around my sudden appearance.

"We have much to discuss. Is your mother gone?"

"Yes, of course, she's at work."

"What if she checks up on you?"

"She's not going to. She can't, El. She's a factory worker. She doesn't get to come home when she pleases like your father."

I blushed and nodded. "Yes, yes, you're right. Okay well I suppose most pressing for you is how I got here." Amelia gave me a frenzied nod. "Okay, well, I teleported."

"El, I gathered that much with my own two eyes."

"Okay, yes, right, yes you did. I teleported using a gemstone that I found when I was a child. It was after my mother died. No one else knows about it. I assume it was my mother's, but I'm afraid to ask father in case he takes it away from me."

Amelia's eyebrows were knit together but she nodded and said, "That's understandable."

"Yes, and I haven't used it or really touched it until recently. This is the farthest I've ever gone with it. I came from my house."

She smiled into my eyes and took my hand. "Let's go sit down on the patio." The tension in my body melted the second she touched me. I had been so worried she was angry or regretful after what happened. We sat in our usual spots. She pulled her chair closer to mine, but never let go of my hand, even after she settled down.

"Can I see the gem?"

"Yes, but please don't touch it or else you might teleport. It's scarily easy to use. You just hold it – it has to be touching your skin, which is why I asked for the pouch – and picture where you want to go." I reluctantly let go of Amelia's hand to take the pouch from around my neck. She leaned in as I opened the bag. I tilted it so a beam of sun hit the gem, throwing a red glower up onto Amelia's face. She saw what I had seen years ago, that it was no ordinary stone. Her face reflected an enchantment I recognized. For moments, it was just her and the magnetic gem, eyes and colorful beams dancing. I clapped the bag shut. Amelia blinked up at me.

"Eloise."

"Amelia. I know."

It was nearing time for me to leave and resume my route. We made plans for me to take my usual lunch break with her from now on. She consented to me appearing in her garden, same spot, same time, no more screaming.

The best part was that she kissed me goodbye like it was no big deal. We just made sense. Me, Eloise Scyra, and her, Amelia Waterson, were in love.

Δ

It had not been too hard to find women to help cover Amelia's usual shift with me, but one day did go unfilled. The girls from Scyra were worried about me, but I managed to assure them. I was becoming more and more used to using the gem from my lunches with Amelia. If there was any trouble, it would be easy to disappear. I practiced teleporting to my bedroom in case of an emergency.

The night was chilly, one of the coldest so far that autumn. Every porch was lit up and many rocking chairs were occupied by watchful neighbors. It was enjoyable to patrol by myself. Socializing as much as I had recently was moderately draining to me. I stopped and chatted with people along the way, but mostly ambled around the usual path. Spending time with Amelia had attuned my senses to the natural world around me. There were more kinds of trees in my neighborhood than I ever could have imagined, bushes that before blended together for me, and evidence of animal activity that would have previously passed right under my nose.

With only an hour left to go, the neighborhood had gone quiet. I was deep into my own head and not paying attention, wandering through dark patches with my head down. Suddenly, I heard rustling clothes behind me and turned just in time to see a black–clad figure bearing down. There was little time to think. Just as they reached me, I grabbed my gem and teleported to my bedroom. My body folded down into a stricken heap trying to process any detail I could. I scrambled for paper and tried a sketch, tried writing down every adjective I could think of. There wasn't much to put down. A figure in black had ran towards me, maybe smelling of rotten fruit and moth balls.

I couldn't sleep and eagerly awaited lunch with Amelia to tell her everything. She was very still throughout my tale, which bothered me into telling the story more and more energetically, until I was waving my arms around frantically by the end. I finished and sat back into my seat with a huff.

Amelia asked, "How are you feeling?"

"Oh, I feel fine, really. Nothing actually happened."

"I'm worried you're still in shock. I know nothing happened, but it was close and that's pretty disturbing you were attacked. That means someone has been watching you."

I blinked in surprise. "That's...that's true. True and very interesting. A lot of the victims have said they felt that they had to have been watched before their attacks."

"You're so worked up. It's very unlike you." She wrinkled her nose at me. "Don't make that face. Your arguing face revs up before you even open your mouth."

I stuck my tongue out at her. "What face?"

"Like an angry cat that's either going to run away or strike." I stuck my tongue out even further at her and we both laughed.

"Yes, okay I'm definitely worked up. But I feel okay. Aren't I allowed to be okay? I don't have to be a wreck."

Amelia took my hand, opened it, and stroked my palm softly.

"You don't have to be. I just want you to know I'm here if you are and it's okay if you are."

I smiled and nodded, then stood and leaned into her seated body. I wrapped my arms around her shoulders, nose pushed into her hair. It smelled like hay and blossoms. I took one of her hands and kissed it, smelling her fingers, stained and scented from picking and canning fruit from her garden. I leaned in and kissed her forehead, then reached for my gem just as Amelia started to rise from her seat. My fingers jammed against the gem.

I knew we had teleported but could not bear to open my eyes, sure that Amelia had been harmed or fragmented. During the time lapse of a few deep breaths, I felt Amelia's arms tighten around me, so I knew she was at least alive. I peeled my eyelids open reluctantly. We were in my kitchen, fully embraced.

"Amelia, love, I'm so sorry, but we're in my kitchen."

Her lashes ripped open, bewildered.

"Eloise Scyra, what in the world!"

"It wasn't on purpose." I started sobbing with relief. She was all there.

"Eloise, Eloise it's okay. I'm sure it wasn't, it's okay."

She held my trembling body for almost twenty minutes, until I could finally talk and bring her home. We walked briskly. I didn't dare use the gem. Closing her front door behind us, I broke down again behind that barrier.

"Amelia, Amelia, I thought I hurt you. I'm so sorry."

"You're okay, you didn't". She gathered me, fingers, arms, legs, head, folded me into her lap and held me much longer than I should have stayed. My route could wait.

Δ

Being able to not only teleport, but also teleport two people was a paralyzing amount of power. I took ill, my body likely overwhelmed, and was forced to stay in bed for a few days. Father brought Amelia a note for me to let her know I was sick. He came home that night with a basket full of blessings from Amelia's garden.

I was almost in tears with hysterical laughter, picturing my father trying to drop the note off and immediately leave, while Amelia yelled at him to hold on and rushed around her kitchen. The shawl she used to cover all the goods was rich with her scent. The basket was essentially a do-it-yourself bowl of soup, homemade broth with dried vegetables and canned beans, as well as a few different jams for bread.

The next day, I felt well enough to have dinner with father. We worked together in the kitchen, side by side, making the soup Amelia sent us. I think it was the first time we ever made a meal together. It was definitely the first time in a long time I had eaten with him. We enjoyed each other's company more than usual because we avoided the topic of work. I think my relationship with my father had for years been a holdover from my youth, hollow affection from growing up with him. Our falling out destroyed everything we had so that it could begin fresh. I was feeling much more affectionate toward him lately because I had actual reasons to. I appreciated him saving me from Jed, silently supporting my neighborhood watch, and bringing notes to Amelia. I didn't just like him because he was my father and I had to. Now, I saw him with adult eyes. That night, I felt his eyebrows raised in surprise under my chin when I kissed him on the forehead goodnight before heading to bed.

On the third day, I was well enough to be up and about. I answered the door when Jed dropped off milk. Feeling generous on this morning, I chatted with him for a long time and asked how his grandmother was doing. He said she was getting very old these days, likely not many years left in her future. I offered to stop by and ask some of the girls to, also. His grandmother was an odd bird, a little witchy, but warm and generous, always willing to chat, kind of like Jed. He pushed away my offer. I brushed it off in my mind. He probably felt uncomfortable receiving help, but I wanted to see his grandmother and she was probably suffering from at least a little social neglect. I knew Jed spent a lot of his time down at the neighborhood bar in the evenings. I decided that I would stop by after my route tomorrow.

I spent time on the porch, well-wrapped in blankets, reading and just watching the neighborhood pass by. My father had taken another note to Amelia to let her know I'd resume work tomorrow and stop by to see her. He came back with a basket of food that we made for dinner, root vegetables and chicken breast with day-old homemade bread.

The gem was tucked into my dresser upstairs. I hadn't touched it since the incident, except to remove the pouch from my neck. My fear had waned to empowerment. It was nice to know that if I absolutely needed to, I could also protect Amelia.

It was pleasant to resume my routine. People were happy to see me, and I blushed, reminding them I had only missed two days. I was most excited to spend lunch with Amelia. She was waiting for me in her garden and sprinted across the yard to leap into my arms the second I landed. We hugged each other for a long time. I nestled my nose into the fuzz of her neck as long as she could stand still for. Eventually we moved to our usual spot on the grass, Amelia bounding over while I followed well behind.

As we were eating, she brought up resuming her watches with me. I furrowed my brow "Amelia, how is that going to work? Your mother absolutely lost her mind."

"Yes, but, that's all she did. She can't keep me locked up here through sheer words and will."

I smiled at the mention of her mother's strong will, an admirable family trait. Amelia left me to my silence. The consternated expression on my face told her to wait for me. After a while, I came back to the present.

"I suppose, also, if your mother becomes unbearable, you could live with me. It wouldn't be that out of place, and even if people did gossip, my father's reputation and station would protect us."

Amelia picked at the grass. I added, "You are not obligated to stay with and support your mother. In fact, honestly, you aren't even obligated to love your mother."

"I am not," Amelia replied, softly, into the breeze.

I left it there and we talked about getting Scyra back on track, how to sneak Amelia to meetings, and what future topics might be. As I tried to get up to prepare to leave, Amelia suddenly thrust her arms around and hugged me fiercely. I breathed deeply into her hair until she let go. I took her face into my hands and looked her in the eye, hands on her soft cheeks and forehead until I really truly, absolutely had to leave and finish my route.

After I delivered my last piece of mail, I rushed home to eat hurriedly before heading out to see Jed's grandmother, Alma. Her house was only a few blocks over from mine, but much smaller than my family's home and those around it. Jed's family was wealthy and prosperous long ago. The house was considered roomy and swanky when it was first built. I believe one of his great-great — perhaps greater more — grandfathers was the mayor of Oak Park. Over time, their family lost much of their money from bad choices and other family tragedies. Jed's father died when he was very young in a factory accident, leaving his mother, but mostly his grandmother, to the task of raising him. You would think he'd be more of a gentleman after spending so much time being loved and taken care of by women. I'm not sure how men and their attitude towards women remains impenetrable by proximity.

Jed lived in his own apartment in the little downtown area of our province. I had no idea how much he stopped by to see his grandmother, who was now left almost utterly alone after the recent death of Jed's negligent mother. I knocked, waited a few minutes for Alma to have time to get to the door, then knocked again. After about fifteen minutes, I hesitantly and slowly pushed open the door. The smell that greeted me made me think Jed inherited his mother's carelessness. It was a bearable smell of decay, molded food, mothballs, dust, and accumulated human scent. I breathed in lightly through my nose to grow accustomed to it while shouting, "Hello, Alma, it's Eloise Scyra!"

Alma was in the living room. She saw me, but luckily did not start, and attempted to rise. I rushed forward, assuring her that she did not need to get up. She plopped back down heavily and gave me a toothy smile. Her plump, paper-thin hands reached up to take mine as her voice box creaked out a few words too quietly for me to hear from a standing position.

"Hold on, dear, let me bring over a chair to you. I stopped by to see how you were doing and see if you could use anything or need any errands run for you."

Alma nodded peacefully, waiting to speak again until I was settled and close enough to her mouth to hear her.

"Eloise, it is so nice of you to stop by. How are you? How is your father?"

"We are well thank you for asking!"

I chattered on about father and I, then about current events in the neighborhood, trying to dominate the conversation so that I did not have to awkwardly strain to hear her. While she was physically fragile, her face was still expressive and she listened intently, reacting appropriately with coos and sighs, while still stroking my hand. I knew her affection for me had not been won by me personally and she was mostly seeing my mother reflected in my face. Both her and mother were lifelong members of this community and crossed paths a lot. I made a mental note to ask father, but I was pretty sure that Alma was close to, perhaps even best friends with my maternal grandmother.

I wanted to drink from her well of grandmotherly attention and softness for a little bit longer, so after running out of town gossip, I started telling her all about the Scyra Society. Maybe it was just projecting my heart's wish, but I swear her eyes absolutely lit up as I explained what it was and what we've accomplished thus far. It was also the first time I stopped to feel proud of all of us and of myself. I realized I had lost track of time and it was already getting dark, without me having even stopped to ask Alma what she needed or poke around myself.

"Miss Alma, I'm going to see what kind of groceries you need and pick them up. I can stop by later this week also to freshen up your place a bit." She nodded and smiled. I was relieved she assented to my help so easily. Her cupboard was so sparse that my blood pressure rose in anger. Jed had plenty of time to flirt with every woman in the neighborhood and poison himself with alcohol every night, but not feed the woman who raised him? The audacity; I resolved to return tomorrow morning with food before I started my shift and then clean in the evening. The thought of bringing Amelia flashed across my mind. I would have to use the gem. It was not an emergency, but I could use the help cleaning up this house, as well as rearranging it so that Alma could move around better. The furniture looked depressingly heavy and would probably take two people to even push to a different spot. At least, while not life-saving, I would be using the gem in the name of service to another person, not just my own heart.

I put together a quick dinner for Alma, then said goodbye,

repeating several times that I would be back in the morning. I went out the front door and ducked into the bushes on the side of the house to blip home, as it was very dark by that point. The familiar smell of my bedroom was delicious, and I took a few moments to just breathe it in, years of home cooking baked into the slats of our home, mixed with my perfume and wisps of cedar from my trunk. It made me suddenly miss my father. I went downstairs to say goodnight, knowing that despite the cold of impending winter, he would be smoking his pipe on his porch.

After hugging him goodnight, I hesitated before releasing him.

"May I... try a bit of your pipe?"

He jerked a bit in surprise, trying to look at me through the wreath of my embrace.

"What has gotten into you?" he asked lightly, smiling and handing me his pipe.

I pulled the smoke gently into my lungs, slowly inhaled, and exhaled it back into the crisp night, where it dissipated along with the warmth of my breath.

"I don't know," I said slowly, "happiness?"

He looked at me thoughtfully. "Those baskets from Amelia were thoughtful. She's grown up into a really wonderful young woman."

"I heartily agree, father," I replied and turned back into the warmth of our home, smiling at this increasingly common moment of quiet approval from the only family member I had left.

Δ

The next couple days left me exhausted each night. I rose early, worked my route straight through without taking lunch, then brought Amelia over to help me at Alma's so I could return her before her mother came home in the evening. Most nights, I went back to Alma's, after dropping off Amelia, to chat for a bit with my newly adopted grandmother.

I learned how to angle myself so that I could hear her light voice, a cheerful sing-song quality left still in its breathy cantor. Unlike most people her age, Alma had never smoked and so she spoke quietly, but her voice did not grate across its chords. She always clutched my hand, clearly thrilled to have company.

All this made me so glad I had begun the work of repairing, well building really, a relationship with my father. In my most bitter moments, I had relished at the thought of leaving him all alone. Isolating yourself by choice was power; being left all alone was a gut punch. My heart wrenched at the utter silence of Alma's house every single time I entered. Being abandoned, is it even really in our control to avoid? Maybe not, but it was in our control to look around ourselves, like my mother always had.

Unprompted, Alma told me many stories about my mother. She was always ready with one when I arrived to sit with her in the evenings, knowing how much it meant to me. I felt my face alight with joy at the mere mention of mother's name. She was a fierce child and lorded over a pack of rowdy kids. Mother's parents were busy, her mother being a socialite and her father a city banker, which left her up to her own devices. Her mixed-sex pack of friends defied social norms at the time, and honestly even those now. Their friendships lasted through adulthood and grew with marriages and children.

The most surprising story was about how my parents met. I knew they grew up together but never thought much about their union, especially since my father was so reserved.

Alma told me that my father was one of the founding members of my mother's social group. He was a shy kid, content to sit at the back of the class and daydream. Mother was drawn to his solemn intelligence because it set him apart from all of the other children and their frenetic energy. For years, she pined for him but never felt that her feelings were returned, so she let it go as they grew up. Her unrequited love put aside, the wall it built between them came down and they became best friends. Mother told father everything, even about who she was dating and interested in. Unbeknownst to her, the closer they grew, the more in love my father found himself.

I had to go to my father for him to fill in the details. I wanted to know what made him love her and was too enthralled by this new information on the history of our family to be embarrassed to ask. I went home early that night to make dinner and then join my father on the porch. Vibrating with curiosity, I brought it up before his bottom even reached his chair.

He hesitated, then leaned back deeply and a wide, peaceful smile spread across his face. He reached for his pipe and lit it before speaking.

"I thought you knew this story, Ellie."

"I knew you two grew up together, but no one ever told me it was a story. I just thought your parents set you up and it happened to work out well."

"Love is always a story. No, our parents were very pleased, but we came together all on our own."

The smile still had not left his face. He took a deep drag and went on "She teased me to no end about not noticing her enormous crush on me, but how was I to know? She was so social that I didn't know her attention to me was any different than what she paid others. I also thought I was only a part of the group because my childhood best friend was your mother's cousin and next-door neighbor. Anyway, we became close when we were around thirteen or so. One day she scraped her knee pretty badly while we were playing, and I hung back to tend to it. My mother was a nurse and I had picked up some first aid skills. I took her home to my house to bandage it. Then we ended up chatting for hours around my kitchen table. She even stayed for dinner. After that, we were fast friends. I couldn't help falling in love with her. It wasn't sudden by any means, but it did grow each and every time I saw her until I was absolutely sick."

He took a deep inhale and watched his breath mist the air in front of him. "I made myself physically ill just thinking about all the ways I could lose her. If I didn't tell her, then I would have to watch her end up with someone else and it wouldn't be appropriate for us to be such good friends anymore. If I did tell her, she could reject me, which was hard but okay, or we could date, and it could end up not working out. That was by far the worst option. I knew I could and would love her forever. I didn't think she felt the same way. I couldn't assume she would."

"Just wanting someone around you for as long as possible, that feels like the purest form of love," I said.

"It may be, maybe, pure but I know for sure it was overwhelming and I wasn't smooth when I admitted my feelings. I walked her home one night after a friend's Christmas party. We said our usual goodbyes on, well, the porch we're on now."

My heart fluttered a bit. No wonder father sat out here every night.

He took note of me sitting up straighter, alert to mother's presence, and then continued. "I turned, took three steps, turned back around and said to the back of her head something like 'Helena, I love you. So much, with all of my heart, and right now I couldn't bear to go home one more night without asking you if you would be so gracious as to let me kiss you and to maybe also take you on a date as soon as you're free next.' I forget a lot of things, but I'll never forget how her entire body was perfectly still, except for her head tilting backwards, snowflakes catching on her eyelids. I think that's when I knew I really loved and knew her because I knew that stillness, that gathering of her essence was her taking me seriously. I stepped forward one hesitant step and she turned, then I rushed the last two."

Father stopped abruptly, likely too embarrassed to narrate their first kiss. I released my breath after realizing I was holding it hostage in my lungs. We let the silence enwrap our thoughts. I wasn't sure how I was going to convey through words how happy I was that he had shared that story with me. It was surely the longest he had ever talked about something other than work.

Father was not much of a story teller, sticking to facts and figures, rushing towards the conclusion. There probably weren't many people who had heard about that night with my mother from his lips. Maybe my mother told it so many times to other people that it colored his telling, fluffing it up far past his capabilities. Or maybe it was the one story he told himself so often that he had time, years and lonely moments aplenty, to think through each adjective. I choose to think it was his and only his, a version he told my mother on cold nights or those last months of her illness when he was at his most indulgent and desperate. My heart sunk a notch at the thought of him working so hard to please her that he wrought this story out of his soul and fine-tuned it to her specific pleasure.

Father turned and studied me in the moonlight. "I'm sorry it took me so long to tell you that. I should have talked about her more."

"Yes, and you should talk about you more."

He nodded solemnly and said only "that's fair," breaking his loquacious spell.

I stood up, stretched my arms up out of the blanket I was swaddled in and let the cold brush my fingers. "Thank you, thank you, thank you. Promise to think of another story?"

"I promise," he said, smiling up at me as I kissed his forehead goodnight. I took one last look before going inside, noticing how far the gray in his temples had creeped up, and felt a last pang in my heart over lost time.

Δ

Amelia and I were getting bolder in our rendezvous'. She relayed that she could tell Cheryl was suspicious and sensed Amelia was leaving the house nearly every day. There was no way for her mother to check up on her though. Getting off early or even a day off from the factory was unheard of. After some begging on my beloved's part, I started using the stone to teleport her to meetings, as well as continuing our usual route. She arranged pillows under her sheets to look like her sleeping figure and continued to use "what is my mother really even going to do?" as her argument. I had nothing to argue against that with, especially after offering Amelia a place to stay if she ever was kicked out.

Of course, I also relished every moment with Amelia and was deeply pleased to have her by my side again. We still had so much to learn about each other. At night, while I lay in bed, I could pull from memory the exact lines on each of her palms, the right and the left patterns being to me as different in their ridges as a dandelion flower and pappus. Each of her many scars scattered along the length of her legs was a story. One day we charted out our family trees and drew terrible sketches of all the family members we'd known personally. I destroyed the one I made of my father, as it was offensively bad, demeaning his face and my usually mediocre talent, but not before Amelia laughed at it so hard that tears streamed down her face.

We continued to stop by Alma's. At first, I had been afraid of Jed finding out and being furious with me, but that was overtaken by indignance at his neglect. Sometimes there were groceries in the pantry Jed must have dropped off, mostly items that were difficult for his grandma to prepare and eat, solidifying my opinion that he was awful, utterly thoughtless. Amelia and I supplemented Alma's rations by bringing over home cooked meals and leftovers. We kept the house clean and spent a lot of time chatting around, across, over, and sometimes to Alma, while cleaning and exploring. Her home held many lifetimes of family treasures and had a strong undercurrent of feminine influence. Everything was handmade, from the furniture to the blankets to the paintings on the wall. Throughout our many conversations, Amelia and I figured out that Alma's family had born daughters for decades. We privately mourned the female flame being nearly extinguished, blown out by Jed. We also worried about what would become of the house when it went to him.

As for the attacks, I was at a loss for leads, as was my father. Both of us felt strongly that the assaults had stopped due to the Scyra Society's watch and how our group had spread awareness to the community better than the police department. Father and I spent many nights chatting on the porch, despite the increasingly bitter cold. He started bringing home whiskey and I made hot toddies for myself with it, until I grew bold enough to sip the drink plain. It was unexpectedly magical. In the serenity of those dark evenings, safe and in good company, my tongue was able to parse out the smallest flavors of leather, vanilla, even, I argued with father, blackberries. We opened up to each other in our own ways. I kept him up to date on Scyra activities, which he continued to quietly encourage. He told me more stories about his childhood, many including my mother.

On Saturdays, Amelia came over for a few hours for breakfast and then coffee on the porch after, while her mother was at work. A peace fell across us, like the comfort of bringing a family all together. I didn't want to think about anything bad. For once, my mind was quiet enough to enjoy the gift of being loved and thought of and accepted. I ignored the storm that was potentially brewing in Amelia's household under Cheryl's growing suspicion.

One Saturday, we suddenly realized it was much later than Amelia usually returned home. We walked briskly, arriving just before Cheryl was due. I came inside with Amelia so that I could safely blip home, as it was already dark. Amelia kissed me goodbye and tucked her downy head into the nest formed by the intersection of my neck and shoulder. I leaned down with closed eyes to fully take in one last whiff of her floral hair, looked up and let out a low moan at the sight of Cheryl bearing down on us from the hallway. Amelia nuzzled closer and I was fully paralyzed on the spot, how could I make this less worse? Disappear or run out of the front door? I don't know why I let Amelia stand there without warning. Perhaps to let her have a few more milliseconds of happiness.

Cheryl let out a harpy's screech and snatched Amelia away by her thin shoulders. We locked eyes, her face in shock, mine at a blank loss, and I closed my fingers tightly around the gem, blipping out of the house and into the hush of my bedroom. Usually when people say they did not sleep a wink, they're exaggerating, getting snatches of rest, moments of a silent mind throughout the night. I lay awake truly the entire night, perfectly still on the outside, while punishing my idiotic choices on the inside. I couldn't even begin to wrap my mind around how much worse I just made things on Amelia by magically disappearing from her hallway. That decision was my first real scar. I knew it was something I would have to live with, suffering with my mistake for the rest of my life, no matter how many times Amelia told me she would forgive me. There was no absolution ahead of me.

Δ

I rose with the sun, dressed, and quietly watched the clock until it was the hour that I knew Cheryl left for work. Luckily, Amelia and I had discussed what we would do in case Cheryl ever caught us together again, agreeing on an exact location for me to blip to. There was a small shed Amelia kept her gardening tools that her mother never stepped foot in. I teleported there. I don't know how long I waited for Amelia to open the door, but it was much longer than I expected.

The door was finally flung open and the sun beat down into my eyes blinding me, but I smelled Amelia before her arms reached my trembling body, and I knew I was safe. After holding each other a long, long time, we gathered up the blankets Am had brought out, but flung aside to embrace me, and closed the door of the shed. I took her in, noticing the red rim under her eyes, and brushed the delicate skin, dry from being bathed in salt. She was vibrating with energy.

"El, you should've seen me. I ripped myself away from her and grabbed a pot to keep her back. She was screaming that you were a witch and threatened to lock me in the house, tie me up to the bed, so I couldn't see you. You know what I told her? I would tell your father if she tied me up. That's entirely illegal. I'm not her prisoner. She was stunned, I wish you would have seen the look on her face."

I looked down, irked by her inflated mood up against my foul, solemn one. She let me sit in silence, ever gracious. If I were her, I would have been furious at me being so quiet and sour. That silence gave me time to refocus my thoughts on her and what she needed.

"I am so sorry this happened and especially sorry that I teleported away."

She waved her hand, dismissing my remorse.

"It's not like she'll ever tell anyone. Who does she have to tell? And who would ever believe her?"

"Yes, but she could hurt you, physically. I'm afraid of your mother. She's a brutal woman, and fiercely strong."

Amelia took my hands and leaned her head close to me to look deeply into my eyes "You and your father would never, never let that happen."

I nodded and brought my hand up to her face. "What now?"

She smiled. "We continue as if this never happened. And if one day I don't show up, you teleport over and save me." I sighed into Amelia, letting all the tension I had been holding in my body melt out in the ether as I pressed it into her. It crossed my mind that I should probably be holding her right now. Oh well.

So, we continued as Amelia asked, and I worried, but I kept

that to myself. She was an adult and, as her partner, I feel strongly that it was my job to treat her as such. Many times, I asked her how her home life was going. She brushed it off with either a wave of her hand or by saying everything was as it always had been, quiet and tense. Even though sneaking Amelia out so much worried me, I figured it was better than her being completely cooped up inside her house now that it was too cold to garden.

My favorite time spent together was still our patrols. Sometimes we held hands now, figuring it wouldn't be too out of place for women to hold hands in the cold. In the absence of any more attacks, we relaxed our guard substantially and often varied our route in accordance to different trees Amelia wanted to see. She had recently checked out books from the library to learn more about gardening, then branched into arboriculture, so we not only went in search of diversity, but also for trees that may need help. We spent many nights bent over bark samples and leaves, examining them to ensure they were in good health.

One night, we were poring intently over leaves, unsure if the rot was normal fall deterioration or a growing disease we should worry about. I noticed Amelia shiver and immediately took off the bright red scarf and hat she had knit me, wrapping it around her myself and adjusting the hat. She stood deathly still, aside from her face softening as it looked into my focused expression. I took a little extra time to arrange her curls perfectly under it and then kissed her lightly on the tip of her nose. Amelia wrinkled her perfect nose at me and smiled even wider. I sighed contentedly and bent down to collect more leaves, looking for a quick way to be rewarded again with that smile.

There were some excellent specimens in the area I searched, and I stood up fast, turned around, eager to show Amelia.

"Amelia, de—"

Behind her was a figure, black clad and bearing down quickly on us. I saw something flash in the moonlight, potentially a weapon in their hand. The figure was closer to her than I was. I screamed and hurled myself forward, hoping to throw my body in between them as a barrier. Me and the attacker collided. Strength for strength matched, we all fell into a heap struggling against each other, tangled in our winter garments. Amelia was screaming; I started screaming for help and trying to push the attacker away from us. That's when I noticed they were flailing to get away, waving a knife around in their struggle, and I was not quick enough to stop Amelia from thrashing directly into the blade.

Her screaming turned to low moaning and it took everything for me not to retch right there. I wailed Amelia's name and the figure between us also started howling after realizing what they had done. I rolled away, having to rip my coat off in the process to untangle myself. When I stood, the attacker was kneeling over Amelia's body. My fury exploded and I grabbed them by the head, ripping them away from her and in the process, removing the veil-like garment that had been covering the assailant's face. Cheryl's dark thick hair tumbled out and down her shoulders. Her hawk like profile was ghostly pale, stunned, stunned, stunned. We all were stunned. I struggled not to faint, to focus on staunching the blood that seemed to be pouring from Amelia's side.

Thankfully, people heard us shouting and came rushing out at the noise. Somebody called the doctor, someone else brought out bandages and helped me to carefully wrap up Amelia. Cheryl tried to help, and I swung viciously in her direction, screaming for someone to arrest her.

It was a tragic blur that I hate recalling. I was grieving before the scene was over, before Amelia was even struck. All this never needed to happen. The crushing weight of violence took my breath away.

Δ

Amelia was my main and only focus for the next month as she recovered. Luckily, the knife had only slashed her side open, missing any organs, but putting her in a massive amount of pain. The wound was wide and took a long time to heal, to not be sore or weep. When I wasn't at the hospital, I was preparing a room for Amelia at my house. I did not discuss this with father, nor did I plan to because, in my mind, there was not a single other option or path.

She was kept in the hospital for three weeks. I begged the nurses to keep her there until I was sure that her mother was in custody and the state was taking action against her, as well as keeping her behind bars during the trial. Amelia was quiet, exhausted from healing and the beat of hospital lighting, and mostly slept or held my thigh in comfortable silence as I knit. I'm glad I kept so busy or Amelia's grief-stricken silence would have melted me into despair. She was limp and tepid, hardly eating, pale as a tombstone in the moonlight.

I brought her home to a spare room decorated with her things. When we walked into the room, she crumbled into a sharp heap and inconsolably wailed. I couldn't bear her grief, surely caused by seeing her things from home. I should've warned her. I crumpled, too, wildly clutching her and pulling her into her lap. My father was home at the time and I felt his breeze stir the air behind me, looking over our bodies to make sure we were physically safe, then leaving us to our woes. Most nights, I snuck into Amelia's bedroom after the lights went out and tucked myself into her warm body, which she gladly accepted, sleepily rolling me tight into the nest of her arms and stiff knees. I didn't mind them in my back, the pain a reminder that we were still here at the end of each somber day.

After a few weeks, she started gaining strength and meat back onto her body. Color rose in her cheeks. We were both starting to become bored, but not ready to talk. Like a low hum of a motor growing closer, I felt her energy vibrating at a faster and faster rate inside her. I knew the dam would burst, but in what direction, I could not tell.

Father gave me minimal updates and only when I asked. Cheryl was being charged with Amelia's assault, but the case was not yet in court, as she was being investigated for the other assaults. I felt a dull surprise. I never suspected Cheryl, but with her aura of cruel menace, I could picture each and every assault at her hands. Father was gathering evidence slowly from the Waterson's home, which is how I was able to migrate so many of Amelia's things into our house. He graciously went through Am's room first so that he could release her items to me as soon as possible. I didn't tell Amelia any of this and she didn't ask.

When she was sleeping, I examined my old case notes over and over. My daydreams were spent on picturing Cheryl as the perpetrator of each attack. I spent hours piecing together every assault. Her motive simply seemed to be jealous rage, or maybe something more unhinged and religious. My stomach churned at the thought of how hateful a person had to be to attack not only innocent young women, but also her only daughter. I let my thoughts churn endlessly, stewing in my own form of rage.

On top of my father's small and quiet kindnesses, the women of Scyra came together to take care of our every need. Many visited us in the hospital and stopped by my house to clean or leave food while I was with Amelia. Katherine and Judith often came over in the evening to sit quietly with me, when visiting hours were over and I felt the empty vacuum of Amelia's absence. Once I brought her home, I refused to leave Amelia alone in our house and needed someone to check in on Alma.

Three weeks into Amelia being home, I received a call in the afternoon from Katherine.

"Eloise? It's Katherine. I need you to come to Grandma Alma's."

"Katherine...isn't it Martha's day?"

"It is."

I hesitated. Katherine's tone was deadly serious, but I was deeply reluctant to leave Amelia alone.

"Is someone free to come over and stay with Amelia in my absence?"

"Eloise, I don't mean this harshly, but I think she will be fine. I need you to come immediately."

I rubbed my face with my free hand, massaging my temples, not even pondering just standing blankly. Katherine said impatiently after twenty seconds of silence, "Eloise Scyra, let's go. Amelia is fine!"

"Okay, yes. I'll be there in fifteen minutes."

Amelia was asleep so I left her a short note saying that I was running food over to Alma's. No need to make her worry if she awoke before I came back. I threw on my coat and a hat, then rushed over.

When I entered, Katherine was standing in the drawing room to my right with Martha seated, her face deathly pale, a few feet away.

"Where's Alma?"

"The kitchen, eating supper. Please come have a seat." Katherine motioned to the couch cushion nearest Martha. I hugged them each before sitting down.

"Martha needs to tell you something."

Martha sighed deeply. "This is all so silly really. This is my first time coming over to help Alma. I'd never been in this house before. When I walked in, it just smelled so familiar, but I didn't know why. I mean, you have to admit it's kind of a distinct smell in here, not just like any old person's home."

Me and Katherine sniffed the air. I knew what Martha was talking about. It wasn't a bad smell, but definitely unique and identifiable as belonging to Alma.

Martha continued, "I didn't think too much about it, just kind of said 'huh' to myself and then went on with the checklist you had sent me. The last item on the list is to fold clothes and pile any that need to be cleaned. I sat Alma down to eat and went upstairs to poke around. I found some items on her bedroom floor, picked them up to see if they were clean enough to refold and put back, and the smell really hit me. I–". She stopped speaking and shook her head, then stood up and paced a few steps.

Martha wheeled around suddenly to face us, gripping each of our arms and pulling us in.

"Her clothes smell like the person who attacked me. I'm absolutely sure. But Alma physically could not have, obviously. I called Katherine because I started to panic. She said she doesn't have a good enough sense of smell or memory to confirm if that's what her attacker smelled like, though."

Katherine nodded, "Yes, it's not bringing back anything for me."

"I believe everyone said the attacker was wearing all black, did you find anything black that could be what they wore?"

"I didn't look."

"Okay, no problem, Martha. Let's head up, if you're both okay with that, and poke around."

I said hi to Alma, leaning over to give her a kiss on the forehead. She looked up and was puzzled to see me but didn't say anything. I headed upstairs. My body was trembling with adrenaline, but my mind had not yet caught up to processing this information. We found many articles of flowy, black clothing, and compiled them in a lump on the floor. We hung over the pile, thinking our own separate and racing thoughts.

"Should we bring these to your father?" Katherine asked.

I replied instantly, "Absolutely not. Smell is not evidence."

"Yes, but what if there's blood or something on these."

"That's not evidence either. It could be anyone's blood."

Katherine and Martha nodded in acquiescence. I looked up at them.

"So, it was Jed all along." They nodded again, with much more vigor.

"Gross," Martha said, our faces all mirroring that sentiment.

I bagged up the clothes in case we needed them and made sure Alma would not be at a loss without them. We finished the chores in silence together and made sure Alma was comfortable, fed, and would be fine the rest of the day. It was only two o'clock; father would not be home from work for hours, so I brought Katherine and Martha back to my house.

Amelia was awake and puttering around the living room. I was caught red-handed. Her face was immediately accusatory. She probably already suspected my note to have been a lie. Why would I suddenly leave the house after staying with her for the last few weeks, day and night? My aura of firm leadership vanished, and I just stood staring at her. Katherine and Martha bumped into my abruptly halted form and we all gracelessly tumbled into my foyer.

"Uhm, hello, Amelia, hi. I have some news if you want to sit, I'll grab tea, ladies please make yourself comfortable. Please don't start talking until I'm back," I said, then rushed into the kitchen.

I smoothed my skirt and rubbed the back of my neck, taking deep breaths. The tea kettle boiled faster than I would have liked, and I joined everyone in the living room. Katherine and Martha were sitting like living dolls, stiff with discomfort in the presence of an injured soldier.

I let Georgia and Katherine explain. Amelia listened thoughtfully and we were all much more relaxed by the time they finished their explanation. I went to the kitchen to put together a bite of food while the women asked Am how she was feeling and to see her wound. When I came back, Martha was pitched forward in her seat, eyes piercing through Amelia's skull.

"The attacker must have been Jed then, not your mother. I hope that's some comfort to you."

To all of our surprise, Amelia scowled and said, "What do you mean? Of course, it wasn't my mother." She looked around at our shocked faces. "Oh my god, you all have been thinking it was my mother? Does your father think so?" she said accusingly in my direction.

"Uhm, well, he's been investigating her."

Amelia groaned and leaned back in her chair. "My mother would never just attack random women, are you all serious? That's so stupid."

I felt a flush creep across my cheeks. "She viciously attacked us, dressed as other victims had described, at night. How is that a stupid conclusion to come to?"

"First of all, she clearly did not mean to actually hurt either of us. She just wanted to frighten us. Secondly, she had motive, not a good one, but motive to attack us. What in the world would be her motive to attack Martha and Katherine?"

"Beyond her natural cruelness and clear jealousy of you, a young woman?"

Our voices were raised against each other. "I'm her daughter. I know her. She doesn't care about anyone else! She just wanted to scare us away from each other. My mother has never hurt me, and she never would on purpose. You don't even know her, Eloise. You're so afraid of her you can't see past your own bias."

"Amelia, that woman stabbed you!" I screamed, viciously. Everyone was taken aback at my tone and I was immediately ashamed.

Amelia was not to be cowered, though. "You've been keeping things from me. I'm not an invalid. What is going on? Where is my mother?"

"She's in jail, Amelia," answered Katherine. "They originally were going to charge her for attempted murder against you two, but the police are collecting evidence against her in all the attacks. They've called all of the victims in to be interviewed all over again."

Amelia's ire turned on Katherine and Martha. "What did you two say about my mother?"

"As far as I know, nobody had anything new to add to their original statements. I think we were all at a loss as to why Cheryl would have done any of that, but like Ellie said, although a bit harshly, it wasn't a far jump to think it was your mother."

"I guess we'll just all have to agree to disagree, but you're all idiots to have thought that. Again, why in the world would she do that? She was clearly just desperate to scare me so that I'd stop...going out."

"Okay, but if my father wanted me to stop going out, he would give me a stern talking to, not dress in all black and chase me and my best friend in the dark with a giant knife." Katherine and Martha nodded in agreement.

"My mother is a weird, mean, shut-in, sure, but she's not a merciless sociopath out attacking neighbor girls. Her cruelty comes from fear. Look at how she grew up. Poor family, probably berated for that in this area. I mean, Eloise, look at your home compared to mine. Then she was ostracized for getting pregnant with me and had to work in a factory her whole life just to get by. My mother doesn't get to live in the world or the nice society you all live in." Amelia crossed her arms and sat back hard in her chair, wincing at the pain from her wound being rattled. I saw her agonized expression and flinched, too.

After readjusting, Amelia went on. "Anyway, the most important thing now, other than getting my mother out of jail—"

"Amelia, she stabbed you."

"Eloise Scyra, it was an accident. Anyway, we need to get Jed. He's a menace to society. I never liked that man. He's a sleaze."

I sighed, "First, I need to review my case notes, then we can get everyone together and make some kind of plan. This bag of strongly-smelling clothes is not arrest-worthy material. I've already had this argument with my father when I first started looking into things."

Katherine and Martha raised their eyebrows at me. "Oh yes,

well I didn't do much. I really just know about the cases."

There was silence. I hoped they'd forgive me for sneaking my way into their lives, but it wasn't really pressing right now. They got up to leave and we hugged for a long time, reluctant to part. Katherine agreed to call around and have everyone come to my house tomorrow afternoon. She would warn them that it was about the attacks and let them know that their kids, of course, were welcome to come. I was making a shopping list when Amelia came into the kitchen. Even behind me and out of view, I could sense she was still hot and bothered.

"El, you're done treating me like an invalid. I cannot believe you didn't tell me they were investigating my mother. She would never, ever do that to all those women."

"You keep saying that and all I can remember is her waving a knife around at us. That's unhinged."

"She saw us kissing, El! Of course, she was frightened. Aside from her own prejudice, she probably was picturing us going through the same social shunning she went through."

"That's just... that's so silly. She already keeps you locked up, or thinks she does, so what shunning could you be subject to?"

"I'm not saying it's right or logical, I'm just saying I see it."

"Okay well, you do what you like Amelia. I get it, she's your mother, but I don't have to like it or her. I was there, too. She not only could have stabbed me, but she actually stabbed you and I love you so goddamn much."

Amelia's face softened and she reached out to try to touch me. I brushed her off and went to the grocery store. That night, I lay awake for such a long time that I gave up and slid into bed with her. I slept a few hours and slipped quietly out at the break of dawn, before she awoke.

I spent the next morning reviewing all of my notes, writing down anything that could help us catch Jed. The only commonality I found across each account of his attacks were the black clothes. If he still had them at his home, that could be evidence, but we would have to get the police to investigate it somehow. The other fact that drew my attention was that the cops never found the weapon he used to stab Katherine. If that was found with blood on it, as well as the black garments, that may be strong enough to bring him into custody. I didn't feel good about it and was not looking forward to our meeting, other than seeing all of my friends after a long, cold, couple months. I had missed enjoying the first snow and we were now coming quickly upon the beginning of spring. Would warmth bring more attacks if we didn't stop him?

Amelia and I worked together to arrange the living room and prepare a play area for the children. Luckily, they were all small and not old enough to absorb our words, so I wasn't worried about having them around us while we talked. I put together some food in the kitchen and set the coffee on a warming tray along with cups so that people could come and go as they pleased.

Katherine and Judith arrived first, with no children in tow. Judith looked strong and I hugged her tight, feeling a plumpness that had not been there months ago when we first reunited. Martha and Georgia came together. The two had become close friends the last few months, being younger than most of us and also without children. Rose came in a little late and flustered. I assured her it was fine she was tardy and joked that I wasn't exactly eager to get started. She didn't smile, just bit her lip.

Rose was probably the most out of the loop. She attended meetings but didn't have the capacity to take on helping out around the community. We all pitched in to watch her children, letting her leave to grocery shop alone, a luxury for a young mother, and take a little extra time to visit shops. I pictured her fingering goods she couldn't afford, not with longing or desire, but with admiration of their craft and interest in what was new in our rapidly changing world.

Amelia and I each took a baby from her. Our goal as a group was usually to not let Rose hold her babies even for a second when we were all together. They were just beginning to crawl. We baby proofed the room and blocked off exits. Jaq and Posey took off the second we set them down, puffy legs propelling them at top speeds all over the carpeted floors.

I had written down what I wanted to say, making it as concise and transparent as possible. There was no easy chatter this meeting. Everyone was silent and apprehensive. I stood up to speak, nervous to my core. Amelia squeezed my hand assuringly. I welcomed everybody, then let Katherine and Georgia tell them what happened yesterday.

Rose was so furious she stood up and began pacing. "It must have been Jed then. It had to have been. That makes so much sense. We all always said that it felt like the attacker knew where we were. His job gives him easy access to that information, getting to know all the households in the neighborhood, as well as the lay of the land."

Georgia cut in, speaking slowly like she was still sorting through it all, "It does, really does seem likely it's Jed, but we cannot say that for sure. Can we?"

I shook my head "No, and we definitely don't have police worthy evidence. Not even enough for the police to search his apartment."

"We could search his apartment," Amelia said. Her tone held a slight challenge directed towards me. I ignored her. I was obviously not going to bring up the gem to this group.

"Aren't the police going to need a motive, too? Can anyone think of one?" asked Martha.

"Jed had no reason to lay a hand on me. I don't even know him, beyond sometimes paying him for the milk," said Judith, as she shifted, rewrapping her shawl tighter around her chest

Everyone talked at once, sure that he had no reason to come after them.

I chimed in. "I think he's just entitled. That's motive enough. He was aggressive towards me once because I was in a rush and not in the mood to chat with him, like usual. My father witnessed it, too. I would happily be a character witness. I can't be the only one he's been like that with." I paused to see if anyone had something to add. No one spoke up. I went on. "The reason I wanted to have this meeting is to be able to decide on a course of action to eventually stop this man. I'm not really sure how we want to do that or how even to."

"I liked Amelia's idea. Let's break into his apartment and see what we find," Katherine said.

"Or we could send someone, lure him into a trap where he brings someone over?" suggested Georgia.

"Absolutely not. That's too dangerous. Eloise, don't you have a way to get into his apartment?" Amelia asked.

"Yes, I do," I said, quietly.

The women looked at me, waiting for me to go on. "It's not that risky either, as long as someone has their eye on him or knows a time when he'll be gone."

"Amelia and I can figure out logistics later. What do I need to look for then? Black clothes. Katherine, I hate to bring this up, but maybe the weapon he used to stab you. May I see the wound."

She nodded and lifted up her skirt so that we could see the scar on her thigh. It was oddly thick and curved upwards, like a smile.

"It wasn't very deep, and the doctors said whatever the weapon was, it was dull. I'm sure it was made of metal. I don't think he meant to stab me, either."

"It doesn't really fit in with the other attacks. Everyone else, it seems he was trying to knock-out. Maybe it was something heavy and he meant to hit you over the head with it," I mumbled.

"So, you're going to find evidence, Eloise, then what?" asked Katherine.

I knelt forward, elbows on my knees, and covered my mouth with my hands. "I don't know. Let's just start with making sure he's the attacker. Amelia and I can handle that on our own, probably within the next two days?" I looked at her to confirm and she nodded. "Within the next two days, then we can reconvene."

Everyone left quietly, likely deep in thought. Amelia and I put the living rooming back together and cleaned up quietly. She grabbed my hand in the kitchen. I let her pull me into a hug.

"I think you made everyone feel left out," she said softly into my ear. I pulled back and looked at her.

"How do you know?"

"I don't. I just feel it. You were very 'end of discussion' dismissive. A tone I recognize well and have, myself, been unhappy with." She said this with a playful smile and brushed back a piece of hair from my face.

I bit my lip, surprisingly not angry with Amelia for picking at me when we had something terrifying to quickly accomplish. "I'm just trying to protect them and get this done."

"What do you think you're protecting them from?"

I shrugged, "More pain?"

Amelia pulled me back in and patted my head. "Let's get to work."

It felt good to be a fully functioning team again, our wounds either brushed over or healed. Time would tell. I was still off work, giving us the luxury of time. We planned for me to blip into Jed's while he was delivering milk in the morning. Amelia would leave early to check the names on the mailbox and figure out which apartment unit was his, then watch his house from afar, making sure he had left and was running his route. She then would come home, and I'd head out to search his apartment.

I woke up well before her and paced in the morning's light, letting it wash over my feet as I drilled peace into my body, bottom up. Amelia finally awoke, got ready, and left quickly, allowing me only one long forehead kiss before scurrying out. She was well wrapped so that people wouldn't notice her, as it was her first time leaving the house and nosy neighbors were bound to ask questions.

Two hours or so later, she burst through the door and told me the unit. I was deeply anxious about attempting to travel somewhere I'd never been, but there wasn't time to think. Every minute that passed was more time for him to get rid of evidence or attack someone else. I hurried to the apartment, as well wrapped as Amelia was when she left hours earlier. The doors were glass. I looked through and blipped inside. With light feet, I walked daintily up each creaky step until I reached unit three. I crouched down and tried to look through the gap under the floorboards. I couldn't press my face flat enough to look through.

There was a noise downstairs. I looked around desperately for an escape route; there was none. The front door opened. As a last-ditch effort, I stared at the unit door for as long as I could before the steps of the person below sounded to close. I pictured the door without the number on it, less lit, closed my eyes and clutched the stone. The steps became muffled. I opened my eyes slowly, looked right and left, and found myself in Jed's apartment.

Three deep breaths slowed my trembling enough for me to move. I found photographs and some mail to confirm it was Jed's apartment, then began searching. The front door opened up to a dark, sparsely furnished living room. There weren't even books in there. It took me less than a minute to search. Next, I went to the room to the right. His bedroom was cluttered, brimming with clothes, shoes, and dirty dishes. There was too much to search. I would have to move everything and potentially leave a trace of my visit. I turned back to examine the two rooms at the other end of his apartment. The bathroom was filthy, but at least sparse and easy to look through.

The other room's door was closed. I opened it slowly. The room was furnished as an office, a heavy oak desk pushed up against the back wall. There wasn't much else, furniture odds and ends such as two side tables and an antique lamp. In the corner was a pile of black clothes. My heart started racing. I leaned down to smell them. They were musty, a pungent smell of mothballs rising up to greet my nose. I gently pressed on the pile hoping to find more evidence. My fingers pressed into something hard and I carefully peeled back a layer of clothing to reveal a gardening trowel, crusted with something dark.

Before my eyes flashed Katherine's smiley–face shaped scar and I started to retch, imagining the pain of that being dug into her flesh. I caught the bile in my mouth and swallowed it back down, then pulled myself together enough to pull the black cloth back over the small shovel. From a crouching position, I reached over and gently pushed the door closed, then blipped back into my room at home.

Amelia was sitting on my bed. She screamed, not expecting me so soon, and I screamed, too, extremely startled by her reaction, and hurled again. She ran to me immediately and apologized for her reaction, saying she had been deep in thought. Am undressed me gently, put me into bed, and cleaned up the puke. I was breathing raggedly, deeply disturbed and unable to speak about what I had found.

Amelia crawled into bed with me and held my body tightly to her. I felt bad later about how frightened she must have been, imagining that I found a dead body or something worse. Once I stopped feeling so queasy, I hopped out of bed and got dressed. Anger at Jed's absolute audacity to have all of that incriminating evidence simply laying around in his room was starting to rise in my throat. I finally told Amelia what I had found. My voice was shaking with rage. She looked at me with eyes round in wonder. What were we to do?

"I'm going to tell my father I went over to Jed's and found something strange."

Amelia's eyes somehow grew even bigger and her lips puckered, sourness pouring forth from her heart.

"He's never going to believe you."

"What motive would I have to lie?"

"Maybe to get Jed in trouble after he was so aggressive with you?"

We went back and forth heatedly, not angry with each other but full of steam we needed to spout off.

"Ooo I've got it." I snapped my fingers. "I'll say I was picking up something for Alma."

"What about when Jed says you're a filthy liar?"

"It's my word against his."

She raised an eyebrow "Exactly. I don't want to find out who would win."

I crossed my arms and lay down on the floor, knees drawn up.

"Why don't we just take care of him ourselves?" Amelia said softly.

I rolled over onto my stomach and reached out for her left calf, which was resting against my bed. "Absolutely not. That's too far. Also, you're the one who said that we need to involve the others." I squeezed her leg, letting her know I wasn't judging her, but had the same thought. "Do you mean permanently?"

"I'm not sure what I mean. Or want."

I nodded in agreement.

"I think that you underestimate the power of the gem, El."

My hand automatically went to the velvet pouch around my neck. I could feel it's warmth even through the fabric. "I don't. I just– I can't let myself go there." Amelia waited for me to go on. I rolled onto my back again and looked up at the ceiling.

"I don't want to abuse it and do something that I can't change. I don't know how much guilt I could live with. I mean look at how sick I was over you getting hurt, and I didn't hurt you or have anything actually to do with you getting hurt, but it didn't matter. My mere existence, my involvement with you and...my choices. That was enough for me to obsess over. To still obsess over."

"Yes, but what if he hurts another woman? How will that feel? If you could have stopped it. We're sitting here worrying about hurting somebody who clearly hasn't thought about his effect on people once."

It was a fair question and something I needed to face, this weird power. I couldn't see that in the moment, though. I made a noise of disgust. "I'm not God all of a sudden. All I can do is teleport. I can get places quickly. Should I really be living my life as if I'm special?"

"Yes," Amelia said, immediately, "without a doubt."

"Well you get to be sure. You don't actually have the gem and have the choice." I walked out of the room to go cool off and start dinner. Amelia stayed behind, thinking so hard behind me I could sense the air shifting around her, thoughts cast across the sky like light beams.

Dinner brought more hard questions. Father gently asked Amelia if she'd like to visit her mother and she nodded yes. They arranged to go over together in the morning. I couldn't bear to ask her if she wanted me to go, feeling deeply ill at the thought of disappointing Amelia as well as the thought of seeing Cheryl.

Oak Park, Illinois – 1917 – Amelia

El's father woke up early with me so we could arrive right when visiting hours began. We moved around each other comfortably, working together to put together a light meal. When we sat down to eat, I put my nose close to the hot tea and breathed in deeply, letting the steep coat the inside of my nostrils. I surprised myself by eating everything on my plate.

I wasn't sure what to call him yet, this gentle, solitary man who had taken me in without question. In many ways, Eloise and I had lived mirrored lives. Long stretches of being in the echo chamber of our own thoughts, never fully interrupted by the restrained parental figures also haunting our homes. She saw my mother as a monster, I know. I did not and so I was able to see the similarities.

The only difference was that my mother got outwardly angry. Mr. Scyra just turned in on himself, boundless folds of emotion that would never be beat out in the light of day. Hence, El's deep discomfort with emotion, particularly rage, while I could easily let it rush around me while I stayed undisturbed, a trunk in a gale. That was for Eloise, dearest El, to discover about herself on her own, though. I was onto other things.

The prison was small and gray. My skin began to tingle before we even walked in. I hate being trapped and the worst part of all of this was knowing my mother was under lock and key, unable to make almost any choice for herself.

Mr. Scyra brought me to her cell. His entire demeanor was unceremonious like it was every day he brought me to visit Cheryl Waterson, the woman who stabbed her daughter. I appreciated that he didn't give me a pep talk or do something weird like hug me, even though I could feel his own nerves rattling around. I gave his hand a quick squeeze before he walked away, to comfort him, then turned to my mother. She threw herself against the bars to try to touch me, her eyes pawing at my form to try to see if I was okay, which clearly, I was, as I was standing there in front of her. I reached up to press my fingers into hers and looked her in the eyes.

"I'm okay mother, the wound is healing well." She nodded and sighed in response, closing her eyes with deep relief.

"I'm glad that you're okay, Amelia. So glad."

"I told Mr. Scyra it was an accident and that you just meant to frighten us. You'll probably still have to serve some time, but they're lowering the charges. I'm not sure to what. I don't know legal lingo. Will you be able to get your job back?"

"I believe I will be able to." Her eyes were on the ground, fingers still laced with mine. I moved to sit down, and she followed suit, then stuck her hand back through. This was the most sustained physical contact I'd had with my mother in years. Before this, it was me puttering around her skirts as a child for the rare hours she was home, clinging to a leg when I could. That was as tender as she got as a mother, allowing me to be under her feet.

"How is the house?"

"I don't know. I haven't been home since I was injured. I've been living at the Scyra's."

She recoiled her fingers fully and body partially.

"Mother, I'm not putting up with this anymore. I'm an adult. You don't get to have any say over me."

She scowled at these words and opened her mouth to speak. I held up a hand.

"This isn't an argument."

We sat in silence for a long time. I was in my own thoughts, wondering what to do about Jed. Mother stared openly at me. After a while, I stood to go. We touched fingers briefly before I left. I considered stopping by the house, but my garden would have been the only reason, and it was deep in hibernation at this point. I didn't want to go home yet. Eloise was not yet back at work and though she would not explicitly ask questions, I would feel her thinking them and be annoyed. I walked for hours and fantasized about ways to hurt Jed. I wanted to crush his soul, grind it into tiny bits then scatter them into the wind. I didn't feel like reigning in my desires after all the years of being cooped up. I wanted to drag El into this with me, get our hands as dirty as Jed's. If he could live his life clean-conscienced after what he did, so could we.

Δ

The meeting with Jed's victims was just as tense as before. There were no children, just women and our fraught nerves, each displaying their fray differently. From stony to hysterical, laser-focused to vague exhaustion, shock to tranquil expectation.

Eloise was nearly limp with emotional wear. I wanted to hold her and stroke her hair, but that was too intimate a gesture for this crowd. Everyone was arguing, in side conversations, as a whole, loudly, desperately, blithely. Usually, I would be the silent supporter behind El as she sorted through this mess, but like every single other person in this room, she was just fighting because she didn't know what to do. I sighed and cleared my throat.

"Okay everyone, let's take a moment to have some tea. We have to finish this meeting before Mr. Scyra comes home and I'm sure we all want something to come out of this." I waved my arms around big and vaguely. "This, this is not working. So, let's calm down and I'll go get a pen and paper."

The level of agitation remained the same but everyone did at least listen to me. I found a pen and paper easily in the home of these sweet, bookish folks. Seated in the middle, I waited for everyone to sit back down and then began.

"Let's write down our options on dealing with Jed. One, do nothing to him and continue our patrols. What else?"

"Convince the police to search his apartment," said Eloise. I nodded and wrote it down.

"And hope he gets arrested and then sentenced," added Rose, grimly. Eloise frowned at her.

"Let's just do actions right now and talk through outcomes after. Okay? Three, scare him somehow and hope he never hurts anyone again," I said.

"Four, kill him," said Katherine. We were all silent for a long time, thinking either about the consequences of that choice or if there were any other options.

"Five. Maim him," added Judith, quietly.

"Like rip off his...doodle?" said Georgia, wide-eyed.

Eloise said "maybe" thoughtfully before I could laugh at Georgia's inability to say penis.

"Anything else, ladies?" I asked. Most everyone nodded no. I couldn't think of any other options either.

"Should we vote?" asked Eloise to the group, sounding like her feet were finally on the ground. I knew a list would calm her down and give her a sense of control.

Everybody voted to kill Jed. I was shell-shocked. It was one thing to fantasize it on a walk, another for a group of seven people to vote to kill someone, and surely a completely other to actually go through with it.

The room erupted with everyone's grand ideas on how to kill Jed.

Martha's voice rose above the din. "I have an idea! I heard from my brothers that Jed owes a decent amount of guys money from playing cards. We could spread that rumor around enough that it gets back to the police."

"If it's a lot of different guys, too, then the police won't just suspect one person and we don't have to worry about someone else being thrown in jail for it," said Rose excitedly.

It was closing in on when Mr. Scyra would be home. Eloise set a time to meet Monday. I reminded her that she started work again then and she shrugged, then set the meeting for lunch time and asked Judith to host. Monday it was.

Amelia and I cleaned up silently and quickly, both eager to talk to one another before Mr. Scyra came home. We sat in the kitchen, close enough to the door to hear her father come in. We were both starving and dug into the scraps left over from hosting. I waited until Eloise's mouth was full to spring my thoughts on her.

"We're going to have to handle this ourselves."

Eloise furrowed her mighty brow, always in strong contrast to the softness of the rest of her face. I loved it most. "Maybe, we'll have to talk through it all with the ladies but I'm sure we'll have to be the ones to do it."

"El, that was not a question for the table. That was a statement. We have to handle this."

Her confusion deepened, stirring my heart further. I rested my foot against her calf. "Why do you say that?"

"Because murder is... insane?"

"Oh." Her forehead went from parallel lines to a trench of angry v's. "We cannot do that to them. I'm not taking away their choice. If you want, persuade them, sure. I'm not just handling things. That's unfair. We weren't even attacked, they were."

"Counter point: we don't have time; murder is unacceptable in so many, many ways; we have to execute this anyway so it should be up to us. Our conscience, our decision."

"Amelia, this really isn't like you, I'm appalled."

I was instantly furious. "Oh, I wasn't aware you knew me that well Eloise."

She moved her head like I slapped her, slammed to the side and down. We heard the door rattle and rose.

"We're going to finish this argument, let's go to my house."

"Goodness, Amelia, you want to go there to argue? You haven't even been back since…"

"Since my mother stabbed me? It's okay, El, you can say it." I don't know if I was being hateful or being honest, that line as fine as lisianthus petals. "Hurry up, take us there."

She obeyed just as the door opened and we landed in my living room. We both coughed at the dust. I was instantly disgusted at the smell. Somebody must have left food somewhere. I searched floor to ceiling, looking for the source of the smell.

"Am, what are you doing? What are you looking for?"

"The smell, why does it smell like that? There must be some leftover food decaying somewhere."

Eloise looked alarmed and I paused my search. "My love, it smells like your house always does. Maybe you're just not used to it anymore."

"Why didn't you ever tell me?" I said, frantically.

"That would be extremely rude, Amelia. Also, it's not bad, it's just different. Different than mine or, for example, outside."

"It's not different, it's gross. It's so stale."

El lips pulled back straight across her face awkwardly. "It is a little gross."

"Was I dying in here?" I reached out and pulled Eloise to me.

"You were not, Am, but something was. Hope? Joy?"

"That's very dramatic." We both laughed, mine muffled by her breast. I took a few deep breaths. "Okay, let's argue. I feel better. I'm sorry I said you don't know me. I think after being caged up for so long, I was angry you tried to do it to me. You do know me, but I want there to be more."

El pulled back to look at me. "I understand. We're very young."

I blinked a bit. That statement somehow felt heavier than our impending argument about murdering a member of our community. I was not to be distracted, though.

"Well, back to the topic at hand. We are not murdering anyone."

"My point still stands, Amelia, you will have to convince the group."

"Our next meet up is five days away and you'll be back to work then, probably tired since you're not used to walking as much after being on leave." I brushed some hair back from her face as I said this. We were still standing awkwardly. I was reticent to sit on the couches, still unused to the smell, and it was far too cold to go outside.

"Are you that concerned he'll strike again?"

I bit my lip. "I suppose I'm concerned he'll attack someone else and then the rest of you, your suffering will deepen even more."

"We could come up with a plan right now and go around to the women tomorrow individually."

I nodded enthusiastically. "Then maybe there won't be such a mob mentality if we get everyone alone."

Eloise grimaced with what I hoped was shame and went to search for paper. I cleared off the dining room table and dusted off the chairs. It took El a long time to find a pencil and paper, giving me time to brainstorm alone. She sat heavily and waited for me to speak first.

I spoke slowly, anxious that Eloise would rebuke my idea. "I think you and I should scare Jed and threaten him. Bring a weapon, wave it around, tell him we know what he's been doing."

El nodded and said, "And what are our reasons for not murdering him?"

"Are you serious?"

"Deadly, Am. Reasons?"

My sigh shook the flimsy chair. "This is ridiculous. First of all, what if we get caught? All of us know and are co–conspirators. It would be incredibly stressful. Second of all, I'm not letting all of you have that on your conscience forever."

"What if they say that the stress and guilt is worth making sure no one else suffers like they have?"

"I don't know. I don't know, Eloise. Do you honestly think you could murder somebody? That's probably the best argument I have. I just can't do it. I know that."

She slouched in her chair and sucked air through the gaps in her teeth, the most unladylike habit you'll ever catch El indulging in. "I suppose not. It sounds messy. Blood gushing everywhere. Your wound got blood truly everywhere. I was sure you were dead and very shocked when the doctors later told me it was not that deep of a cut."

It was unbelievable to me that she was sitting in front of me saying that her biggest issue with murder was the blood. I just knew it wasn't true, of her or of anyone else involved in this. I was determined to protect her from her future self. This level of denial was clearly out of her control.

"So, neither of us could execute it, and we obviously have to be the ones to handle this since we–" oops "since you have the gem. I think we should blip in, in the middle of the night, maybe three am, when he will almost definitely be home and asleep. We'll need weapons. Can you travel and carry things with you? Or does he have things we could use?"

"I think we should bring weapons with us. He doesn't own much."

I stood up and Eloise followed suit. We went out to my shed. I picked up a small axe and brandished it for Eloise. It was dull, perfect for threatening with. El took it from me, lifted it a few times to feel the weight in her hand, then reached for the gem and teleported across the yard. The axe went with her. She walked back over to me with a giant smile on her face. I was grinning, too, mostly at the confidence of her walk, hair loose and blowing fiercely in the wind as she carried the axe at her side.

"Wonderful. Did he have any knives? We'll both need something. I'll take the axe, if you don't mind, since I'm used to handling it."

"And I'm used to handling knives?"

"Well, you are the better cook."

She smiled again. Twice in an hour, it was like hitting the girlfriend lottery. "I am and I did see knives. I noticed because I was ready to use one in case he came in."

"Oh goodness gracious, when did you become such a cowboy? May I please have my El back, the one who spent all summer weaving me flower crowns?"

She stuck her tongue out. "What do flower crowns and self-defense have to do with each other?"

I smiled and kissed her once, pulled back, then a few more times for good measure. We walked into my house and I carefully wrapped the axe in my scarf. It was dark now, but we had to walk home. Surely, Mr. Scyra would notice if we were suddenly upstairs.

We spent the rest of the night formalizing our plans and what we would say, then Eloise plotted our walk to hit every house at a time the women would be home. We slept soundly that night, Eloise curled under me in a bath of cold moonlight.

Δ

I spent all morning prepping El, getting her fired up about my plan. I knew the women would be easily persuaded if she was firm. Each and every one listened without interruption, nodding along solemnly, as I sat back and observed, tended to their children, filled up coffee mugs, and, once, answered the doorbell. We walked home like women with a plan, ready to execute, ready to punish someone. That night, we practiced our roles and lines, fine tuning it so that we were in and out, so that our weapons flashed menacingly. The next day was agony. We were so restless that Mr. Scyra broke his usual equanimity to ask if we were okay. El was quick to blame it on being tired of being cooped up in this cold, which he accepted without question and went back to his porch–sitting, newspaper reading, and general weekend puttering with no more comment.

As soon as El's father went to bed, we started practicing again and brewed a pot of coffee. Our clothes were laid out, black sweaters and trousers, scarves and hats to hide our faces. We braided each other's hair into two flat plaits and then held each other for a long time. At two am, we got dressed and started rehearsing again in the dark, so that our eyes adjusted quickly when we got to Jed's apartment. I unwrapped the axe and tapped the blade lightly. At the last minute, Eloise thought to find a flashlight we could blind him with. 2:59 am, I took Eloise's hand and placed it on my heart so she could hear it thrum. She took my face in her hands and we took deep breaths together.

I whispered, "readier than ever" and we blipped into Jed's spare room. Teleporting always dropped a calm across me. Sometimes I worried it was like a small death. We landed so softly, breath even and slow, hearts steady. I went out first, brandishing the axe and walking slowly, to give Eloise time to grab knives from Jed's block. She took two, the chef's and a small paring knife. I mentally hesitated, not liking the look of a blade in her hand but exhaled the distrust on my next breath. What was I going to do if she killed him? Stop loving her?

We creeped towards Jed's sleeping form. I was to do most of the talking since he didn't know me. A few feet away, we stopped, and I inhaled, ready to make my voice gruff, but not too loud that a neighbor would awake.

"Wake up!"

Jed stirred and I said it again.

"I said, wake up!"

Eloise turned on the flashlights and Jed bolted up, tangled in his bed sheets. He moved to stand.

"Stop right there!" I said in my best cop voice, stopping him cold.

"We know what you did, Jed," I said, shaking the axe at him. "We know you attacked those women, Georgia, Rose, Judith, Martha, Katherine. You're sick. If you ever do it again, we will destroy—"

Jed lunged for Eloise on my right and she stumbled backwards, dropping the flashlight and skittering hard across the floor on her bottom. A knife flew forward, and I saw Jed notice and reach for it. He flung his body off the bed onto all fours, crawling desperately for the knife and then for Eloise next, who was struggling to stand. I turned sideways and was standing over his prone body. I swung, bringing the blunt edge of the axe down on Jed's ankle closest to me. His howl followed a sickening crunch. I clutched the axe, trying to keep it to my side and ran over to Eloise, who had finally shakily come to a stand. Jed was begging us to call a hospital and we ignored him, looking for the knives and making sure we had everything we brought. I took one last look around and made a split decision to take the knives. Eloise pulled me tight to her, and we teleported to my living room. We had decided to land there to compose ourselves before returning home.

I sat down shakily and set the axe on the kitchen table. Eloise lit a candle, then bent over to stretch while rubbing her tailbone. When she stood, she looked at the axe on the table and let out a deep moan.

"Amelia, Amelia, it's bloody."

"What? Your back?" I stood up, deeply alarmed.

"The axe. The axe is bloody."

I wheeled around. The sharp edge of the axe was dripping. I sunk to a crouch with my head in my hands.

"Oh my god, oh my god, oh my god." Bile rose in my throat as I heard the sound of my axe grinding through his bone over and over. Eloise crouched down and grabbed my face.

"We don't have time for this. He could be dying. We need to hide the evidence."

I just kept moaning. "Eloise, can you deal with it? I feel so sick."

"Okay, stay here. I'm going to take his knives and the axe and take them to...to the farthest place I've ever been. Let me think about it. We used to go to this farm in southern Illinois when I was younger."

My groans deepened. "Eloise, that's dangerous. You can't just teleport somewhere. What if there's a barn there now or something?"

"Okay, father took me into the city a few months ago and we went to a restaurant. I could teleport there and throw this stuff into a dumpster. We need to get rid of our clothes, too. Give me yours now. Run to your room and find us outfits."

I obeyed, stripping right there and then running to my room, still gagging down the threat of vomit. Eloise was pacing when I returned. She got undressed and shoved all of our clothes into a bag, as well as the knives and axe. El then used my scarf to wipe up the blood on the table, checked for drips, and shoved the scarf in the bag.

"A neighbor surely has heard him and sought help by now, yes?"

I nodded silently.

She went on, "We don't have to get rid of this bag tonight."

"Yes, we do. Please, please get rid of it."

She looked up at me and came over in two long strides to hold my face.

"Of course, of course Amelia." We stood there like that for a long time, thinking about what to do. "I'll just take it to the dump. I know the perfect spot to land.

El tied up the bag, kissed my forehead, stepped back and teleported away. I went to the back door to open it and breathe in some fresh air. Eloise was back relatively quickly. Or I was so out of it that I had no idea how much time was passing. She immediately blipped me back into my bedroom where she put me to bed and went back to her room. I fell into thick black sleep almost immediately, only waking when the sun began beaming directly into my eyes. I laid there until well past breakfast. It was Sunday, so we had to be around Mr. Scyra.

Eloise knocked softly and came in, closing the door behind her.

"I told father you started feeling unwell last night. Also, I know you say I'm a terrible actor, but I swear I did a fantastic acting job this morning feigning confusion about why Jed hadn't dropped off our milk delivery yet...I might have to attempt a career on stage now."

She came over and stroked my hair. I covered my eyes and started up my groaning again like I'd never stopped or slept.

"El, I chopped a man's foot off."

She smiled down at me. "I know. After all that fuss about murder, a man knocks me over and your swift justice is amputating his foot. I'm very flattered."

I removed my hands from my face. "Why are you in such a

good mood?"

"Well, father received a call this morning about Jed from the station. He's alive and alert. A neighbor found him. He will likely not keep his foot. And he's saying it was a robber, one whose face he did not see because he was blinded by the flashlight. I was able to toss the evidence in the incinerator. And Jed will be crippled for the rest of his life, unable to chase innocent women through alleys and yards. Also, the love of my life unflinchingly chopped off a man's foot to protect me."

I curled my body around her lap and buried my face in the thickness of her thighs. "How are we going to tell everyone?" I said, muffled by her leg.

"I'm not sure we need to hurry on that. News will get around fast. I think everyone will be pretty pleased. They can all start spreading the rumor about how he owes several people money." Eloise kissed me on the forehead and rose to go downstairs. A little bit later, she returned with a breakfast tray. I sat up and she yanked a brush through my hair, humming softly.

"El, this isn't the end of something. This is the beginning of many decisions."

I felt her pause behind me, suddenly fully alert.

I went on, ticking each thing off of my finger "My mother is still in jail. We'll have to decide if we want to keep up patrols. We have to feel this out to make sure your father does not suspect anything. The victims will probably have a lot of emotions to sort through. Oh, my goodness, Alma! We'll have to start taking care of Alma full time and buying her groceries. I have to handle the affairs of my home, depending on the verdict. That will be an entire process. What if she doesn't receive jail time? What if she does, but it's only a few years? I'll have to get rid of that radish smell, throw out a lot of clutter. I'll need to make it mine."

"Make your house yours? You would move home?"

I placed the tray of food on the side table and turned to face Eloise.

"Of course. I can't live here forever."

"Oh." Her face twisted away in pain, lips rounded on that small "oh" long after it was done being pronounced.

"Eloise, I am deeply indebted to you and your father's kindness, but living here for what? Forever? That's just not reasonable." I turned back around. She said softly, "Yes, of course. That would not be reasonable," and shortly resumed brushing my hair.

Part III

Oak Park, Illinois – 1950 – Eloise

The first thing I did when we got home from the doctor was write to Amelia. Her and my father had grown very close, particularly as he'd gotten older and more gregarious. We built the enclosure over the front porch together a few years ago so that even in his precarious state of health, he could spend every day year-round out there, rocking, reading, smoking, and meditating.

  I hesitated towards the end of the letter, unsure if I should hint at or tell her some news I recently discovered about our gem. Part of me was worried that if I didn't mention it in the letter, I would never tell her in person. After a few moments, I decided against mentioning it at all. She was in India last time I heard, investigating a blight that had befallen acres of fig trees, with a smarmy professor. I prayed the only address I had was up to date and she would receive my note as soon as possible. It would be a long way home.

  Father was in the kitchen having a light supper of stale coffee and mini Bundt cakes from Rose. When her children grew up and moved out, she took up baking as a way to fill up her time, but it soon became a passion, and then a business. The rush at her store on Sunday mornings was so overwhelming that I helped work it, checking out customers and restocking shelves. It still shocked me how many faces I didn't recognize. The war had rendered our town aboom with young families.

  I kissed father's forehead and let him know I'd be back in time for dinner. I wanted to bounce some ideas off of him about what to do about my employment. My boss was over a decade younger than me, a quick talking father of four little girls. We had a good rapport with each other. I won him over years ago after offering to babysit his girls once a month so him and his wife could go see a movie or have dinner alone. All those years of helping out with children through the Scyra Society gave me ample experience in entertaining a small, but powerful mob.

I decided to check in on a new neighbor, Samantha Beckett, to see how she was getting along. The gossip around the neighborhood was that her husband secretly brought home another woman from the war. Samantha found out about his two-timing shortly after realizing she was pregnant, picked up her life, got her own house, and moved to Oak Park. I'd been too busy lately to get to know her, but I wanted to bring her under my wing to make sure she wasn't ostracized for being a single mother.

The air smelled of spring. I made a note to stop by the Waterson's old house. When Amelia started traveling more than she was home, and after her mother passed, she sold the house and her prized backyard to Judith's daughter, Emmaline, now grown up and a fitting apprentice to Am's legacy. I usually helped during planting season and looked after the garden when Emmaline and her husband went on vacation.

I had been in Samantha's house once or twice for get-togethers at the former owners. It was a small place, but comfortable, and the perfect size for a mother and child. Before raising it, I took a minute to admire the strange door knocker. It was a horse, bucking its body wildly. Even weirder, it was not flat but a fully carved 3D horse whose thick belly hit the door to make a ringing pound.

Samantha greeted me warmly. Her eyes crinkled nicely when she smiled. I introduced myself as her neighbor, Eloise Scyra, dropping by to get to know her. She waved me in and brought me to the kitchen, where she was in the midst of unloading groceries. I tried to help, but she wouldn't accept assistance and settled me at the kitchen table with a cup of tea.

"It's so nice of you to stop by! I've met a handful of people but haven't had the time to properly socialize. The baby keeps me so busy, and it hasn't even been born yet!" Samantha said, her back to me as she floated around the kitchen.

"When are you due?"

"At the end of August. I think it's going to be a girl. I feel it," she said while turning to wink my way. She put the last box away, added some milk to her own cup of tea, and sat down lightly across from me, ankles crossed, elbows on the table.

"I'm happy to help with absolutely anything. I only work part time these days. I would also love to introduce you around town. I've lived here my whole life and haven't managed to break into the new circles forming amongst the many new young people, so my social circle is mostly old ladies, but we're always happy to have a fresh face around. I actually run a women's group that meets once a week or so, if you're interested."

"That would be fantastic! Let me find a pen and paper to write all this down." She sprung up and bounded into the living room. I heard drawers slamming and idly wondered if perhaps her new weight had given her even more balance. There was an evenness to her movements. She had to have been a dancer. Movement that fine tuned is not an inherent talent. She came back in waving a pen and old envelope. I told her the date and time of the next meeting and she scratched it down while talking.

"I could definitely use some friends. It's been a little lonely. I had only ever lived in the town I grew up in, a little spot just north of the city, before moving here, plus I have a huge family to keep me busy."

"Do your parents still live up there?"

"They do, as well as my husband's. They've all been very supportive – I left him and moved here – but it's a bit far so they can only come every so often. I'm glad, though. This is my little adventure. I want them to all be the fun, spoil-my-child-rotten-but-not-raise-them type of grandparents that I roll my eyes at. It would drive me mad to have them fretting over me and Cha– uhm over the baby."

It sounded like all the gossip had been accurate, except for the town's speculation that Samantha was crushed by her husband's infidelity. I was already struck with warmth for this breezy young woman. Half an hour together and I would have thrown myself in front of a car to save her. Amelia would be amused. We chatted for a long time, mostly about the preparations she was making to become a first-time parent. Her parents were wealthy, inheritors of her grandfather's lumber company. They were supporting her and helped buy the house. Samantha did not bring up her husband again, but I figured I would find out more in time.

I shared a little, telling her about my involvement in the community and my family background. She didn't ask me many questions but did listen intently when I spoke. At one point, I asked to touch her belly and she comfortably declined, saying she did not like to be touched.

When I got home, father was waiting for me on the porch. I

greeted him by adjusting his blankets to cover him better then took my usual spot, a wicker chair flush with pillows. He looked up at me, affection in his milky eyes. There was something about the mobility your face gained as you got older. At first, I had thought that these warm facial expressions of his were new; him becoming more emotional as he got older. Now, I had a theory that they were always there, but the slackening of his skin emphasized them so that I noticed the crinkle around his eyes more, the softening of the muscles around his mouth at the simple pleasure of my company.

He patted my hand as I sat down next to him and I moved to readjust the corner of his blanket, now exposing his arm after that movement. He made a gesture for me to stop. "Eloise, I want to talk out a few things before we sit down to dinner."

"Yes, I have a few things to discuss with you also, about my job."

"Mine first, dear. I want to talk about my death."

I raised my eyebrows and stayed quiet.

"I have a will. All of this will go to you, as well as the money I have in savings which is a fair sum. Once we go inside, you can find the latest bank statements in the safe in my bedroom. I think you should hire a nurse. I can't stand the thought of you devoting all your time to taking care of me."

I nodded, acquiescing to his request because I didn't want his last year or so to be spent on worrying about such a small thing as how I spend my time. "Is that all?"

"That's all."

It was my turn to pat his hand. "Sounds good, father. I'll ask around for a recommendation. I think Judith said the nurse she hired for her husband after his accident was excellent. Okay, my turn. My boss brought me into his office two days ago and told me that while I absolutely do not have to, I could retire any day and receive a decent pension. I was miffed at first. I felt like he was calling me old, but let's be honest I am old. Too old, probably, to be carrying mail. I swear I have a dent in my shoulder from carrying that bag for decades. Then I could also spend more time with you."

Father chuckled, "El, we've lived together for fifty years. What more could you possibly learn about me?"

I didn't laugh. "It's not for that. I just enjoy your company. It's very peaceful these days, now that you're old and helpless. It's not just about you, anyways. Then I could help Rose in her shop more, plus I made a new friend today with the neighbor two houses down."

Δ

Over the next few months, I saw Samantha near daily. She became fiercer as her due date approached, which I encouraged. Motherhood was going to be difficult despite the monetary support from her parents. I met her and her husband's parents a few times. They were lovely, unremarkable people, with not a trace of Samantha's enthusiasm.

Father was still sharp, but rapidly physically deteriorating. It was nearing time to bring him to a hospital. I feared that I should have taken him to the hospital long ago and my selfishness was keeping him at home. Samantha helped out as much as she could, her enormous belly not stopping how light she always was on her feet.

I tried to take her around and make friends, but it didn't come easily to her. I think people were uncomfortable with her intensity and she knew it and accepted that gracefully, while refusing to compromise any of her self or her many desires. Calling her spoiled would not be fair. Her attitude was never one of entitlement. I don't think she thought anyone deserved anything, good or bad, right or wrong. She was just like any other willow tree, growing in every direction possible to reach the best nutrients or sliver of sun. The effects of her roots barging through someone's water pipe or into a well-established ant tunnel were the problems of critter factions, not her singular majesty.

Samantha did make every Scyra meeting and acted appropriately, probably cowed by my disapproving looks. Or maybe she just respected me. It would be surprising if she feared me, fear being something I had never seen flit across her face, not even when she confronted me about my father's health. She was growing rounder by the day and couldn't help my father as much physically anymore. He was starting to have accidents. Samantha was worried that we were affecting his dignity at the time in his life where it was most valuable to him.

I admit, I was angry at her prying, but then again, I had invited her in by asking her to help me. Father's eyes did something akin to lighting up when I broached the subject with him, and he was in the hospital within a week. I never let Samantha see how much she had offended me, knowing that following her advice would secure her trust in me.

The following week, I went to see my father about an hour after visiting hours began, just as I did every day and would do for the rest of his life. He liked to sleep in a bit. June was heating up day by day. Trousers had still not caught on for me, but I regretted my heavy, layered skirts by the time I reached the hospital. My thighs were swiping against each other, lathering the moisture into an unbearable stickiness.

I entered his hospital room in a fury, upset by my discomfort, but stopped suddenly upon seeing a slim cut figure in the window, sunbeams laying artfully across her square shoulders. Her back was to me and father was still asleep. I could have stood there forever, this bittersweet moment roasting like coffee beans, the tender, burnt aroma lifting my soul just a little out of my heavy, corporeal form.

"Eloise, when are you going to let me buy you a sensible pair of pants?" she said without turning. I came up softly behind her and rested my chin on her shoulder, angled at the perfect height to accommodate me.

I tilted my head to whisper up into her ear, "Despite your immediate attempt to annoy me, I still desperately want to wrap my arms around you forever."

The corner of her mouth I could see curled up. "Why don't you?"

"And give my already dying father a heart attack? No, thank you. The way I would hold you would be undeniably romantically charged. He could not continue to live in oblivious bliss. Anyway, for the first time ever, we have the house to ourselves."

She whirled around "I hadn't thought about that."

It took all of my strength not to reach up and stroke her face. "I have, daily," I said, softly.

"Amelia?"

She turned towards my father's croak and I reached down to smooth my skirts, giving myself a moment of composure. When I turned to look, Amelia had her arms wrapped around his shoulders. I watched them until she finally moved to sit down and reached for his hand. I saw her face, perfectly placid. It took many years, but I finally learned this was Amelia's most pained face, carefully arranged to betray nothing.

I excused myself to give them time alone for a while and did some shopping, stopped at home, then returned to the hospital. Am had settled in and was waving her hands around, talking about her most recent adventure. We sat enraptured for hours, letting her weave details in and out of our brains, across our palms, under our noses. Many lonely voyages had helped her to hone her narrative voice.

We left father when visiting hours ended, promising to be back the second they started again tomorrow. Amelia zig-zagged, doubling the time it would usually take to walk home, which was okay now that we had street lights illuminating the path and the neighborhood was more populous. She wanted to not only look at everything, but also run her fingers tips across it all; mottled bark, railings on houses that old friends used to live in, downy hair coating the heads of children who were still playing outside, defying their parents beckoning every ten minutes for them to come in. I trailed behind, enjoying her eternal childishness. Physical restraint was usually an early sign of maturity. Amelia skipped that step, jumping straight to a world-weary hardness that repulsed me when she first started traveling for long periods of time.

What she surely left out of the stories she told my father was the suffering she witnessed. Amelia traveled to solve problems. The industrial boom removed many people in the United States from having an immediate relationship with flora. While I bought nickel cans of vegetables, Amelia was helping to restore people their livelihood by diagnosing plants that could not communicate beyond physical symptoms.

I brought her up to my room and gave her a few minutes to unpack before launching into my news.

"Amelia, I have something incredible to show you."

She didn't look up at me, just continued to unpack, expecting me to go on.

"This is important."

She stood and looked at me. "El, you're practically vibrating with excitement and I'm so damn tired. Seeing your father took it absolutely out of me. Just tell me." She went back to putting her things away and turned her back to me to reach into the closet.

I frowned and crossed my arms. "Okay. I time traveled with the gem."

She threw aside the dress she had been about to hang, strode over to the bed, and flung herself onto it, stomach down, head perched on bent arms. "Spill."

I told her about how I gave away my trunk, forgot, and pictured my bedroom with the trunk when teleporting home one evening. My eye for detail drew my attention immediately to the trunk and I was deeply puzzled, sure I'd given it away. Just as I was about to open my door to go downstairs, I heard someone coming down the hallway to my bedroom. Confused and scared as to who it could be, I hid in the closet so I could observe what they did. The person who entered my bedroom was me. I almost passed out, completely overwhelmed by seeing myself, but held it together. It was late, so the other me got into bed and fell asleep quickly. I decided to go back to where I had been before I teleported home, a quiet wooded spot Amelia and I often visited as young women. I landed there and ran home. There was no second me there.

"Have you tried it again since?" Amelia asked.

"No, I've been too afraid to. I couldn't stand for something to happen to me, leaving father all alone."

She scoffed, "He would never be all alone."

"I know," I said, crossing the room to join her on the bed and pet her head. I'd forgiven her for her earlier attitude with me. It must have been very hard to travel all this way and find my dad shriveled up in a dank hospital room. Amelia rolled over to put her head into my lap and smiled up at me. I traced the wrinkles on her face, mirroring my own in placement, but where my crow's feet were deep, her laugh lines were merry furrows.

I went on, "I have a list of things to talk about, but I'll save it until morning."

"Written down?"

I gestured vaguely towards my desk and laughed with mild embarrassment.

Amelia laughed, too, and dragged me down to lay next to her.

We slept heavily and late, only waking up because the sun was in our eyes. I dressed quickly and urged Amelia to hurry, not wanting father to wake up without us there. He was awake, well-rested and eager to hear more from Amelia. I stayed for a bit and then left to run errands. It was a relief to know someone was there with him. Spending all day at the hospital was excruciating. I was deeply bored. It was nothing like sitting on my own porch. Part of me regretted moving him there, but I couldn't afford the amount of care he needed.

Samantha was outside her home when I passed by on my way to drop off some things before returning to the hospital. She waved me over anxiously.

"How is your father? I miss him so much." I wouldn't let her visit so close to her due date, for fear of her catching an illness from the other sick patients.

"He's well, no different. Amelia arrived yesterday, so we'll probably split our time there and I can visit you during the day again."

"Oh! I'm dying to meet her. Can we all have dinner tonight?"

I hesitated and then said, "Sure. I'm sure that will work."

"Wonderful, I'll make it. Don't worry about a thing. Just come over at 6:30."

I nodded and squeezed her hand goodbye.

Amelia was at father's side, just like the day before. He seemed tired but determined to enjoy every moment with her. I told Am I'd take over and asked if she had some things she needed to do today. She rose obediently and kissed my father on the forehead. I walked to the front with her.

"Our new neighbor invited us to dinner tonight. She's very excited to meet you."

Amelia smiled at me, amused. "And why is she so excited?"

"I don't know, it's not like you're interesting or anything," I said.

She blew a raspberry at me and ran away before I could hug her goodbye, then yelled back that she'd see me at 6:30. Her perfume blew back at me, something foreign and earthy, in stark contrast to the heavy.

Father was already asleep when I returned. I brought items to darn to pass the time. My fingers were clumsier than Amelia's but just as fast after much practice and training. In fact, I had replaced her in town for a while as the go-to person for clothing repairs during her long absences.

Amelia was not at home when I finally returned, which disappointed me. I had so much I still needed to discuss with her.

It was always awkward when she first came home. It felt like coming up for air and I couldn't breathe her in enough. I immediately started depending on her, seceding much of the emotional work I did on a regular basis to her until I felt full enough to take over again, but I always felt a hint of resentment. So, one could imagine how high my blood pressure rose when I walked into Samantha's kitchen and Amelia was already there, a cup of coffee resting in her hands and down to its cold dregs.

We locked eyes. I gave her a filthy look, unable to help myself, then behaved for the rest of the evening. Amelia had already dragged the entire story about Samantha's absent husband out of her, something I refused to ask about. Am told me later that he had brought home a woman from the war, bought her a house, and lived as if she was his wife, knowing his family would not accept their relationship because she was foreign. Samantha suspected his solution to keeping up appearances was to court her and have her be his public-facing wife, while he continued his relationship with the other woman.

I had told Samantha bits and pieces about Amelia, what she did and how she traveled, but hadn't talked about our own history. Amelia told her stories about me as a young woman and a watered-down version of how Scyra came to be, as well as our friendship. I beamed internally, deeply pleased that Am talked about us more than she did her work. It may have been her way of making up for her intrusiveness, but the reason didn't really matter. I was more relaxed than I had been in a long time. To round out a perfect evening, Samantha asked me to be present for the birth of her baby.

The next few months followed a similar pattern, hospital to Samantha's, Samantha's to hospital. Amelia and I enjoying the house to ourselves, like blissful newlyweds.

∆

The impending birth did not distract me from noticing the light slowly fading from father's eyes. Now, most of our time was spent in comfortable silence. He was too exhausted to talk or listen for most of the day. Every night, I fretted that there was something I should be doing or talking about or asking him while Amelia just listened, knowing there was nothing she could say.

There was nothing to do but wait for him to die. I don't know who this waiting was hardest on, me or him. We agreed without discussion that the energy he had each day would be spent on Amelia's interrogations. She brought her diary and asked mostly about cases during her absences, even though father had been retired for nearly fifteen years now. These scraps of hours hopefully distracted his still whole brain from counting each and every second he still lived, painfully aware.

Samantha had begged me to let her see him before he died, but it was impossible to tell when that was coming. We were all waiting for his organs to finally give out, cascading him into unconsciousness. His slow death was horrific and normal and part of life and I wished, and I wished for it to be all over, for him, for me, forever. I made Amelia promise to die after me because I knew she could handle it. She just shook her head and walked away, never one to be indulgent.

The first thing I thought when Samantha called to say she was in labor was that we were going to lose our lovely evenings together, eating and playing cards. My next was sixteen hours later, as I held Charlotte Becket, struck dumb by her miniature perfection.

Oak Park, Illinois – 1952 – Amelia

Our routine for the past few months was to hiss at each other over the same thing until one of us broke and touched the other, a hair tousle, a passionate kiss, a silly hug. This time I rushed El's rigid body and swung her around in a crushing hug until she laughed and begged me to stop.

I set her down and joked, "Till next time, then."

Eloise went somber all over again. "I'm so tired of this. Also, we're very late to meet Samantha and Charlotte."

"I'm surprised you're making us do this. The winter has been astoundingly frigid."

"Well, it would be fine if it was just us two, but Samantha said she was coming, and you know there's no room for discussion with her."

"At least we get along otherwise," I said, smiling. She smiled back and kissed the tip of my nose. After her father passed away and the house became hers, I decided to stop traveling for long periods of time, and when I did leave, El usually accompanied me. After all these years, we got to be together, as much of a real couple as we could be. Nobody batted an eye at us living together. Two old, dear friends and spinsters living together was nothing new. Nobody cared about relics in this booming post-war town.

We dressed each other in warm clothes, ensuring our scarves and hats and mittens were firmly in place to defeat a chill. Eloise still looked contemplative.

"I do hate having this fight–"

"It keeps things spicy," I interrupted, tugging on one of her braids playfully.

"I wish we could get someone else's point of view on what the right thing to do is."

I rolled my eyes "We cannot. You would never stop worrying if someone else knew about the gem and it is not a moral argument we're having." She opened her mouth to protest and I tapped where my watch was, buried under three sleeves. "We need to go. Poor Charli's probably all bundled up with nowhere to go and absolutely losing her mind."

Samantha was waiting placidly while Charli bounced around the hallway. She was a good mother, solid and strong, but not very warm and nurturing. I figured, though, neither was my mother, and I turned out okay. I swung Charli over my head. I was in my 50's but still rippling with muscle. Long gone was the flesh Eloise used to grip onto at night when she'd sneak over to my room in our youth.

The cemetery was as silent as a rural street during the first snow of the year. I held El's hand the entire time, knowing how bitterly his death still sat in her heart. She was out shopping when he died, leaving me alone to hear his last words. I told her a million times how easy it would be for her to travel back using the gem. No one had been around except for him and I. I think she was deeply angry at herself for being so afraid of its power, but she'd never admit that. Our personal forms of stoicism never matched up. I had to speak my fears and learn to control them, learn to sharpen my mind instead of letting it cloud over just to survive some of the environments I had traveled to.

For Eloise, fear to her was weakness and likely always would be. Samantha was the same way. I swear that's what drew them to each other. They respected each other's invincible walls of self-containment.

Later, we ate at Samantha's. I helped her set the table until she yelled at me and I sat down with a warm cup of coffee while Eloise played with Charli in the other room. Samantha had been oddly quiet; clearly something was on her mind.

"Spit it out, dear."

She turned around and looked at me vaguely. "Hmm?"

"Usually you ask me about a question per minute. This whole day your rate's only been about one question an hour. What's wrong?"

She pursed her lips. "Well, I hope you don't take offense to this, but I was wondering, honestly for some time now, and I swear this won't change anything or how I think of you or Aunt Ellie or anything, but do you have feelings for her? Are you in love with her? It must be very awkward living together if you are." Her face was twisted in consternation.

Just then, Eloise came into the room behind me. I turned slightly so I could see her and reached up my left hand.

"El, Samantha would like to know if you know that I'm in love with you?" I said and glanced slyly at Samantha. She had her full attention on Eloise, like this was some great moment in all of our lives.

El came up behind me and wrapped her arms around my neck, smiling softly. "I do. It's all very awkward, me trying to go about my business while Am follows me around like a lovesick puppy. I was actually thinking about pawning her off onto you, you have a spare bed, right?"

I smacked her arm lightly and laughed. "I'm sorry, Samantha. I suppose we thought you knew, and it was just an unspoken thing."

She pouted at us. "Am I the last to know? Does everyone else know? Do Aunt Rose and Judith and..."

Eloise cut in, "Oh, Samantha, absolutely not. Nobody knows. It's not like we're trying to waltz down to the courthouse and get married for all the world to see. It's not acceptable. You can't tell anyone, promise us."

She promised and then went on to interrogate us throughout dinner, only interrupted by communal coo's over Charli when she did something adorable. We answered most of her questions, although it did feel very intrusive. Eloise and I didn't even talk about our relationship when we were alone, or the many years we, mostly I, spent entertaining interest from other people. It had just kind of quietly worked out for us. There wasn't much explanation for that.

We went home very late, around 9 pm, after keeping Charli up well past her bedtime Samantha kindly but firmly kicked us out. It was lovely to see Eloise in such a good mood despite this afternoon's activity. It made me reflect on how happy the last two years really had been. My life with Eloise was deeply peaceful and I enjoyed my age. People left me alone, which is all I ever really wanted.

Shortly after we got home, I heard Eloise answer the door and usher somebody in. I glanced at the clock and walked into the living room, deeply curious. It was probably someone who needed assistance and was recommended to us by a Scyra member, which happened on occasion.

The young woman in the living room was completely bald so my first thought was that she was ill. She had sharp eyes and a lovely nose, large and well–carved. Her clothes were strange, almost futuristic, maybe imported from Paris. Eloise was bustling around in the kitchen, probably making our guest a cup of tea, giving both of them a moment to get comfortable.

I walked up and extended my hand. "Hi, I'm Amelia Waterson."

She seemed nervous but took my hand and shook it firmly. "Olivia."

"Olivia, what a beautiful name," I said. "What brings you here?"

Olivia uncrossed her legs and leaned forward. "I think I should wait until...until Eloise comes back."

"Okay, sounds good," I said and leaned back in my usual chair.

We waited in silence while I openly observed Olivia. Her ears had many piercings, including some at the tip, which I had never seen in the United States before. She must not have grown up here, maybe went to school abroad. She was in her early twenties, her skin giving off waves of supple youth.

Eloise bustled back in with a tray. I worried about her carrying things around, as she refused to accept trousers into her life. I sighed internally as I watched her feet kick around her layers of skirts.

Once we were all settled in, Olivia cleared her throat and began, her voice even and rich, deeper than you would expect to come from her small frame.

"I hope this all doesn't come as too much of a shock to you two. A close friend of, of yours, both of you, sent me here to talk."

We both nodded at her to go on.

"I am actually part of the Scyra Society, from the future actually. Eloise, well I call you Ma, a future version of you asked me to come back and talk about time traveling."

I smiled broadly. My heart was pounding. Eloise was sitting very stiffly.

"So, you come visit a lot, Olivia?" I asked.

"I started visiting you all when I was about 18 and I try not to, too much, but the guidance is priceless. I mean, there's no one else to talk to about time travel with."

She smiled shyly.

"How old are you now?"

"I'm twenty. I inherited the gem from my teacher, which was not you two. I've never actually met you guys."

"What year are you from?" Eloise asked.

"2014. I can't tell either of you much. I don't want to mess up any timelines, but you, Eloise, asked me to just come explain time travel because I'm the one who has done it most out of everyone who has ever used the stone."

"I suppose that makes sense." I glanced over at El. She was still board-straight in her chair. I thought about reaching over and taking her hand to relax her but left it alone.

"So, I think you both already know you can time travel, not just teleport. Yes? You do it the same way as teleporting, by picturing the location, but you have to anchor it with something specific."

Eloise nodded. "The one time I did it, it was an accident. I pictured my room with a trunk in it that wasn't there anymore."

"You can't go into the future. It feels like a wall almost, it's just impossible. Also, I'm pretty sure that time traveling makes you age faster, but I'm not sure at what rate. Anyway, you, future you, didn't really give me a reason for doing this. I think that's all I can share."

We sat in silence. While I wasn't in shock, I wasn't prepared to ask questions about time travel.

"Will you come see us again, Olivia?"

"Yeah, you start keeping a journal of when I visit and pass it down."

"That's helpful. You said it's still called the Scyra Society?"

"Yep, I'm a member of it. I can't answer any more questions. It takes a lot of action or actions to change the future, like talking and having conversations doesn't influence much. People are gonna do what they're gonna do, no matter what you say or tell him, but if you like, cripple somebody, chop their leg off, that can change things. I do my best to do no harm, but I'm also pretty cautious. I never let my past self see my current self and I don't bring the gem out or look at your gem."

"Do you have it on you?" El asked.

Olivia paused and went on cautiously. "I do, but please don't take yours out or anything. I know where it is."

Caught, Eloise brought her hand down from the pouch around her neck she had been worrying almost this entire conversation.

"What do you think will happen?" I asked, allowing myself just one more question. My curiosity was rising out of my throat, making me hope Olivia would leave soon so I didn't lose control and start interrogating her. I mean, for goodness sake, just tell me when I die already.

"I really don't know. It's just kind of superstitious on my part but I don't see any reason to not do it." She glanced at our clock. "I need to head out. I'll stop by again, well a lot. I don't know when though and I don't know if I visit you in order. Actually, I do know I don't because I've already started visiting you out of order. Can I leave from your kitchen?"

I stood, followed by Eloise. We both embraced Olivia. She was stiff and awkward about it, clearly not much of a hugger. Neither of us followed her to the kitchen immediately, but waited a minute or two then went in.

I turned to El and waggled my eyebrows. "A message from future you, how chic."

"A message?"

"El, that was obviously your way of telling you that time traveling is okay." She frowned at me.

"What makes you think that?"

I rolled my eyes and patted her condescendingly on the head. "It's hard being the only living expert on Eloise Scyra."

Her frown turned to a scowl and I laughed and pulled her to me.

"I'm sorry, I'm so sorry dear. You're just so goddamn serious."

Oak Park, Illinois – 1965 – Eloise

I was making a checklist in preparation for a month-long trip to Chile with Amelia when Samantha called. It was our longest trip together and my farthest from home. Of course, Amelia planned to pack the night before, whereas I had a full packing and shopping list. I still wasn't used to all the new stores and fancy, brightly packaged objects in them, but I had to admit everything was much easier and more convenient than when I was younger. I couldn't begrudge progress that made it easier to be elderly.

I was so focused on my list that the telephone ringing confused me for a moment; I wasn't sure where that darned noise was coming from. After two rings, I snapped out of it and ran over to answer.

"Hello?"

"Ellie?" Samantha asked, her voice deadly calm. I was immediately concerned. Lately, when she called her voice was pitched high and snappy. Charlotte was proving to be a difficult teenager and riled her mother up to no end. The fact that Charlotte was still an absolute angel to Amelia and I sowed further discord in their relationship, which I think was starting to also bleed into Samantha's feelings towards us.

"Yes, is something the matter?"

"Can you come over?" she asked. I glanced at the clock.

"Yes, just let me write Amelia a note about where I'm going, and I'll be right over."

Samantha's front door was wide open, which was unusual. I charged in and went straight to the kitchen where Samantha was standing, deathly pale and gripping a piece of paper. She held her arm straight out, handing me the note. I uncrumpled it and looked up at her, biting my lip.

"Does she have any money?"

"She stole what I had hidden in my drawer, $250 or so," Samantha answered.

"How long ago did she leave it?"

"Ellie, I've been standing here thinking I don't even know. I thought first, oh let me call the police, but what do I tell them? I don't know who her friends are. I don't know where she went. I don't know when she went. I must be the worst mother ever. Must be." She reached into a drawer and pulled out a pack of cigarettes. Samantha lit one, hunched forward to protect the match from a non-existent breeze out of habit. I pictured her on her smoke breaks at the hospital, standing outside alone day in and day out. She never did make friends her own age, preferring the company of us old ladies in Scyra.

Samantha sat on the edge of a kitchen chair and leaned, back straight until her shoulders pressed up against the wooden slats, then draped one leg over the other.

I had half a mind to ask for a cigarette. My heart was pounding out of my chest. I don't understand how it could've gotten so bad that instead of turning to us, Charlotte just ran away without a trace.

"Well, we do need to call the police. I can call them and throw my weight around. Write down any names of friends, any places maybe you've taken her. She's been to Chicago with you, right? Have you called your parents or her dad?"

Samantha perked up. "That's a good idea, maybe she went up north to them!"

I nodded vigorously. "Yes, you've went together many times, so she knows how to get there by train."

Amelia came over an hour or so after I did. We made a list of people to call and alternated giving them a ring after filing a report with the police, then sat up with Samantha until she fell asleep. Ever overestimating the strength of human beings, Amelia wanted to carry Samantha upstairs to her bedroom which I silently, but violently vetoed and, instead, wrapped her up in blankets and firmly locked the door behind me.

We crawled into bed immediately and I held Amelia to me as she cried softly into my chest. I felt hot and bitter, brackish sobs rise in my throat and swallowed them down. While Charlotte running away felt like a betrayal to us, to our bottomless wells of love for her, every ounce, every passion, every fit, it was far more treacherous for me to believe it was a betrayal. I knew Amelia was mourning while I was unacceptably furious. Charlotte was fifteen and likely scared and absolutely lonely.

I barely slept and wanted to talk as soon as Amelia awoke. She sensed that I was awake and opened her eyes sleepily. I gave her time for a few blinks before I spoke.

"I have to stay here, Am. I can't leave Samantha." We were due to leave for Chile in a week.

"Even if we find her?" she asked, frowning.

"I think, yes, even if we find her."

"That's very silly, Eloise. We've been planning this trip for years. What are you going to do anyway? Chain her to our house?"

I tried to stay calm and not let fury rise up out of my mouth. "No, but I could at least offer her a place to stay if things are that bad with her mother."

"You and I both know things are not that bad. We're there all the time."

We fought all morning, all afternoon, well into the night, and well into the next day. I was so frustrated that it felt like Amelia had taken a rubber band and wrapped it around my forehead forty-seven times. I was becoming physically ill from being upset, meanwhile she only grew stronger. Helping and comforting Samantha punctuated our fighting.

We had no news until Thursday, three days before we were supposed to leave. A precinct in Chicago called Samantha to let her know they picked up Charlotte attempting to rob a drugstore, along with an older boy. Samantha's parents drove to the city to meet them at the police station while we waited anxiously at home.

I felt that this was so much worse than we could have imagined, running away with a boy and then stealing at only fifteen. Amelia didn't care and argued that we would only be gone for a month. I was firm in my decision, and we spent the last few days not really speaking. Amelia spent most of her time with Charlotte and I left them alone, hoping she was talking some sense into the young lady.

On our last night, I took Amelia's hands in an attempt to make up or at least a little peace. We had not been apart for this long in years, perhaps a decade.

"How mad at me are you, 1–10?"

"El, I'm not even angry anymore." My face softened. Amelia being angry at me was a boulder on my soul. Then she went on, "I'm just heartbroken. I feel so devastated that I can feel it crawling across my skin. It's like a horrible sweater I can't take off. I just want you to come on a trip. It's so simple, such a small ask."

"I can't fight any longer," I said and pulled her to me, which she allowed and sighed into my chest.

"I can't either."

We all waved Amelia off in the morning, pretending to be a happy family once again.

So commenced the most miserable month of my life, where I tried to help mend or assuage the relationship between Samantha and Charlotte and they brushed me off like the pitiful old woman I was. I thought fighting with Amelia was bad, but at least that was to get somewhere together. This was just agony as I came over to tense, quiet dinners and sometimes didn't even have my phone calls answered.

I couldn't tell if the poison surrounding us had been there a long time or was finally allowed to enter now that Amelia had gone. I started to resent Samantha and just seeing Charlotte's pinched, continually furious face made my blood pressure rise. I could hear them screaming at each other and slamming doors from my house and had to close my windows to drown out their suffering, despite my love of a crisp, spring breeze whipping across my aging skin. I felt old without Amelia around and couldn't help but feel greedy for pleasure and fury at being denied it. How many springs did I even have left?

I cried into my pillow almost every night, missing Amelia and understanding her creed better in her absence. I always saw her as a pessimist, not believing you could change or influence human behavior. She often told me I had issues with trying to control everything. I saw myself as an optimist, sure that I could change people for the better. It was hard to maintain that optimism in the face of fifteen years of effort crumbling around my feet.

Later, I found that Amelia wrote to me daily, sometimes twice a day, though I received them all on a delay. I sat down to write her several times a day from the moment she left but found myself devoid of anything to say. I couldn't bear to write about the Becketts and asking about her trip would make me sick with jealousy and regret. I did finally start writing her once I received a few of her letters, but sparsely, asking some questions. She never mentioned my shortness, knowing probably full well how I was feeling and how things were going.

Elqui Valley, Chile – 1965 – Amelia

April 9, 1965

Dearest El,

I write to you from the air. I'll try not to harp on you not coming, as the deed is done, but I was very excited to accompany you on your first airplane ride. Part of me knows you would have been terrified – despite traveling by you know what all these years – and it would've tickled me. But you would've loved it eventually. I can't tell you how exhilarating it is to look down and see tiny mountain ranges.

It's been a very long time since I've traveled to South America, possibly thirty years. It'll be interesting to see how much it's changed. Anyway, landing soon.

Much love,
Amellama Bang

April 14, 1965

Dear, dear, Eloise,

I've made it safely to where I'm staying. My host is a young family with three children all under the age of six. My dream, your nightmare. Maybe it's good you didn't come. Only teasing, missing you like absolute hell. I keep turning to point something out to you and making mental notes to explain something else later. It's silly, but I dreamed, literally, so much about this trip. In those dreams, we were always having adventures while I translated or showed you a fascinating petal or patch of moss.

You're always hard on yourself, but I sincerely feel your gardening skills almost rival mine. Your mind would have been helpful on this trip, I just know it. The blight is so much worse and so much more interesting than I had imagined. We could've learned a lot together. I'm making copious notes to relay back to you. You should see your face when you're poring over a plant, it's delightful.

Dinner time!

Much love,
Tree—melia Waterson

April 19, 1965

Dear Eloi—woo—wee she's sweet,

I expect you'll be receiving my first letter soon. I look forward to hearing from you. Mail seems to be pretty reliable here, thank goodness. I've received a few packets of information from the smarmy professor. Not sure how he's still alive. I would've thought he'd have deteriorated from a venereal disease by now (I know you'd be tsk tsking me at that but it's true!).

The food my host mama cooks is just to die for. It would've taken you a few days, or weeks, to get accustomed to the flavors, but I strongly feel you would've grown to love it, and even taken a few recipes back to the States with you. In fact, let me write down some when I get a chance and we can "have a meal together". May 5, cook the recipe I include in this letter and I'll request my host mother to make it also.

I miss you most at night, the sounds of creatures outside remind me of home, of all those nights in your bedroom. Did you position your bed where it is on purpose? The way the light hits it is magnificent.

I've never shared with you how I knew that I loved you. We've both been through, together and apart, so much and handle it in different ways. You always ask me how I can be so carefree in the face of it all (I gestured vaguely to a phantom El as I wrote this, you would've laughed). My mind likes to poke into all the possibilities, but there's just certain places I don't let it go. Like, before it happened, I never could picture your dad dying because he became such an important part of my life, a security and warmth I never had from a parent.

I knew I loved you because after a few times in my garden, my mind literally could not picture a world or a life without you in it. I can never go there, or I don't even know what will happen. I think I would evaporate into the wind, decimated by too much emotion. I hope you know how much I love you. I hope you've always known that.

I swear those words weren't just to butter you up for my next bit of news. I've decided to stay another couple weeks, maybe another month or two. These people's crops have been devastated and they're suffering. I've left people behind before, but I can't this time after looking into these kids eyes every day. I can't picture a world where I fail them.

Also, I'm still getting acclimated. The altitude knocked me down the first week or two and I didn't get much done. I've also developed a cough. I'm used to the cold, but everything here is just so damp it clogs up my lungs.

Anyway, hope to hear back from you soon.

All my love,
Am

April 25, 1965

Dear El–beau,

The weather has been beauteous the past few days, perfect for collecting specimens. I've made friends with the local healers who introduced me to lots of people who harvest herbs they make their medicines with. I'm hoping to experiment a little, mix some concoctions up and test them on the plants.

It's very hard to tell if it's a disease the plants are born with or if they catch it from each other. My dear, sweet host family has cleaned out a small space for me to turn into a lab where I'm running a few tests. Hopefully they show me what's going on with the spread of the blight. Maybe the plants are born with it but then something in the environment brought it out suddenly? See, you're not even here physically but talking to you is helping me work things out.

Dr. Smarmy sent me more packets of information I need to go read.

My cough isn't better yet, but don't fret, I feel strongly that next week it will clear up. I think I just needed a little sun.

Your beloved,
Amelia Water–some–plants

June 1, 1965

Dear Ellie Bean,

So much has happened the last few days. I feel almost sure that the plants are born with the disease, but I can find a way to prevent it from becoming full–blown. Now I just have to figure out what prevents it. This makes my experiment a little easier actually, knowing that all the plants affected have it. I can take leaves and try different concoctions on them, see which ones are prevented from coming down with the illness.

I wore myself out a bit after trapezing all around town for days on end, so I'm taking a few days to stay around the house and mix together some plant medicines. The people here are so lovely and kind. All my new friends have been dropping different herbs and plants off for me to use all week. They're just as excited as I am for me to start mixing.

I've enclosed some different medicines they make to treat ailments. For example, did you know that ginger can help with nausea? If you find any, chew it next time you're on the train and you might not feel as sick.

My Spanish is rusty. I get by with a lot of face and hand gestures. I forgot how difficult and lonely it can be to be in a foreign country. This is when the homesickness starts sitting in, but I always found that feeling to be sweet. It's nice to know I care about a place and a people so much that I miss it.

The only bad part is being alone with my thoughts so often. I can't communicate complex thoughts or emotions to anyone I see every day. I've been thinking a lot about my mother. I think she accepted us towards the end, after seeing that our "sin" wasn't having any adverse effects on our life. It's strange how I turned out in spite of her, in a good way, but Charli seems to be turning out in spite of her mother in a far different direction. I hope they're okay. I don't feel bad for leaving them, but I do worry. I think Charli just genuinely wants to be left alone. Some people are like that. I think a lot of people that we're close to are like that, but it was harder for them to notice about themselves or express because we were such a tight–knit community.

We were lucky we had each other, so lucky. It took a lot of pressure off of us to be "womanly" when the only opinion that mattered was each other's. I feel less and less feminine as I grow older.

I wonder how my host family sees me, an older, childless, pants wearing scientist. I might as well be a man.

Anyway, time to arrange some leaves for drying.

Your eternal,
Amelia "Genus Genius" Waterson

June 6, 1965

Dear Eloise Scyra,

My arms are so sore from mixing and pounding for days. Now, I just have to swear them all over my sickly (and some healthy!) plants and wait. You'll be happy to know I'm going to take this necessary waiting time to relax and heal. I'm so sick of being sick. This is by far the oldest I've ever felt.

It was a relief to finally start receiving letters from you. I was so afraid that mine or yours were somehow not getting through.

On the theme of things, I hope you know, I hope you know I'm proud of you and all that you've accomplished. I tend towards selfishness; I would've never used all of my strength to mobilize like you did. The sheer willpower it took for you to get a bunch of women in the 10's to sacrifice sleep and walk around at night, magnificent. You pulled it all off with such grace, too. It was unacceptable for us not to act. You always made that clear.

Jed never hurt another woman again because of us. In all my years working with scientists, I never had a better teammate than you. You changed my life. You rescued me from the garden of Eden.

Have you ever thought about visiting your mother using the gem? You wouldn't even have to tell her it was you. I know you're worried about aging if you use it, but maybe have a plan or a few places to visit. This tired argument, when will I stop! I just want you to be fulfilled, El. I'm sure you'd argue you are. I would argue, you are, but isn't there always more?

Anyway, think about it! I'm off to bake in the sun and read We Have Always Lived in a Castle (yes for the millionth time, yes for the second time since I've arrived).

> Your favorite spooky lady scientist,
> Boo–melia Waterson

June 11, 1965

Dear Eloi–gant,

My patience has been rewarded! I have a few treatments that seemed to work on the plants. My plan is to gather the town to mix large batches and then apply them to swaths of land.

Unfortunately, I'll have to try to arrange this feat from the comfort of my cot. I've been very tired. I'm beginning to suspect my cough and fatigue are simply due to the altitude and we'll never agree with each other. The village healer stopped by to leave me a few pills and potions that should help ease my discomfort. She rubbed my feet for a long time. We're too reserved in the States. It was so tender and made all the difference to me for this woman to take a few minutes of her day and unabashedly spend it on my comfort.

Of all the things I'm missing out on from my sick bed, I miss playing with the little ones the most, but I need to save my eeks of strength for work. Sometimes host papa drags my cot out front and I get to watch the kids frolic around from there, which is the highlight of my afternoons. Daily, I tell host mom and dad how lovely their children are. It's our little dinner ritual. I say, "your children are so kind and smart" and they pat my shoulder, one on each side, pull out my chair, and smile and heap food onto my plate.

I wonder who in my family I'm most like out of all my ancestors, if any are looking down amazed at how far I've come from a little gardener in Illinois to a full–blown woman of science, puttering away in Chilean fields. When I come back, we should try to do some family history research. I'm showing my age! Once you start thinking about the past, it's all crotchety and downhill from there. Maybe I'll start yelling at kids on the lawn from your father's old spot when I come back. That sounds fun.

Your gal Friday,
Amelia

June 22, 1965

Dear El,

Tomorrow is the great experiment. My host mother ended up arranging everything while I rested on my sore laurels. My poor joints are finally giving way to age, but at least they allowed me enough strength to get us here. The healer comes by every day with creams and powders. She prays over my body which makes me very uncomfortable, but I'm far too polite to say anything... I can't understand much of what she says, her dialect is too regional, but her face looks worried. I've tried to explain to her that I just need to go home, back to a lower altitude, and I'll heal within the month, but the language barrier is too great for me to even explain that to my host mother to explain to the healer.

Your silence on my suggestion about your mother is deafening! Here's my ideal plan for you, just in case you ever risk it, and then I'll match your tone and zip these wobbly lips.

I think you should visit your mother and tell her who you are, learn what you can about the gem and give her an enormous hug. Then, join me and your father during his last moments. Last, and by far most importantly, join me on this trip. I've enclosed a photo so that you can travel here one day. Some tourists stopped into town and came by the houses. I snagged them the second I saw the camera and begged them to take a polaroid of me and the kids. They're almost as cute as baby Charli, aren't they?

I think, if I used the gem to time travel, I would spend some time in my old garden again, sewing while I listened to you and the birds. I admit, sometimes I would attribute their song to you and imagine us flying off together, having that much freedom. Strange, I haven't thought about that in years.

Would you die with me and come back as birds? We could soar and maybe I'd finally get you to sing to me. I'd pick the ripest berries, the ones sitting right on top of the tree, and bring them back to you to share.

Imagine what the sun would feel like against your feathers, El.

A lover's hug when you haven't touched in years, a first kiss in a lush garden, touching fresh baked bread to your lips. We could feel whole.

>With love, love, love,
>Am

June 26, 1965

El,

As always, you have seen right through me. I am in fact very unwell, particularly the last few days. I hope this is legible. It is a labor to raise this pen. I cannot make it out of town and I absolutely could not muster the strength to get on a plane.

You deserve a proper love letter but, I say this with the utmost confidence, we both know this is the best I can do, an unsentimental cow to the last. A woman who brushed off being stabbed by her mother, that's all I'll ever feel I am. I hope you don't still see me that way. My memory has faded but I know there was a particular look in your eyes after it first happened. I fear it didn't disappear, I just became accustomed to it. Maybe that's the only difference between us. My calm acceptance of my filth and your inability to become dirty.

How did our parents pull off exuding, living, breathing certitude? Meanwhile, uncertainty became so comfortable with me that it made a home for itself right under the thinning layer of my skin. Is everyone's internal voice so goddamn loud? You don't know how much I punished myself, but on my best days, at my best hours, I know that you thought I was enough. God, I love you, Eloise. From the very moment you came brazenly up to my door and asked me to do my best and then never stopped demanding it. Who does that? Four continents, seventeen countries, and you're by far the most audacious person I have ever met.

>With absolutely all the love I have left, none for anyone but you,
>Amelia Waterson Scyra

Part IV

Chicago, Illinois – Charli – 1969

My eyes were bleary from last night's makeup. No matter how hard I scrubbed there were somehow always flecks of mascara piercing the rims of them. I don't know why I bothered. I guess because it helped me fit in better at the restaurant. It was strange enough to be a female bartender at George & Georgetti's, but it would probably be even stranger to be a woman not wearing makeup.

One drink with the guys and next thing I know it's 3 am and I'm stumbling home. Usually, it wouldn't be a big deal, I'd just sleep in all day, but today I had to be up at 8 am to run some errands in the Loop. My manager, Ben, told me I had a week to get an ID or he was firing me. We both knew he never would, but I was tired of him harassing me about it.

Exhausted and starving, I decided to treat myself to lunch and some shitty coffee after I was done. My favorite diner was around the corner, somewhere I'd been a few times as a kid when mom would meet my grandparents in the city. They had a pot roast sandwich that would bring a starving man to tears, loaded with meat and dripping with salty gravy.

I slid into a booth towards the back, dragging all my weight sideways to sit up against the window, and waved the waitress over immediately to order. When she walked away, I bent my head over the hot mug and let steam kiss my nose and nostrils and eyelids. I looked up and blinked to clear the drops from my eyes then noticed an older woman alone in the booth in front of me. She was looking out the window, her eyes underlined by sketches of wrinkles, deep somber curves. Sensing my stare, she turned to me and I scrambled out of the booth to slide in with her. Ten years old all over again, I tucked my head into her fleshy armpit and wept, completely exhausted and overwhelmed. She didn't move and waited to speak until my crying quieted down.

"Charlotte, sweetheart, what's wrong?"

I burst into full body sobs all over again and tried to utter "I just missed you so much, Auntie Ellie." but my words were mush in the quiver of my mouth. I finally calmed down and reached for napkins and noticed my sandwich had appeared in front of me. Aunt El let me dig in. I forgot she was like this, or maybe had never noticed how peaceful and composed she was without the din of the city rushing around us.

"Do you want to come home?" she asked softly as I took my last bite.

"Home? To Oak Park?" I said, frowning.

"I mean I'm not pressuring you to, it's just that you were crying. I thought you needed help."

I laughed. "No! I just missed you. I'm so happy to see you. I'm perfectly fine. I have a job and an apartment with a couple friends."

Aunt El opened her mouth to speak and then closed it again.

"What?" I said, in between fries.

She shook her head, nothing.

"Aunt El, just say it."

"I suppose I'm just wondering why you haven't come back at all."

I shrugged. "I don't want to see mom, reall,y and coming back makes me so sad since Auntie Am died." Aunt El always looked like she was about to say something but was reluctant to; it drove me nuts. She left it alone and we caught up.

After Amelia died, I ran away again and again until it stuck, and I figured out how to make my way in the city. My older friends helped me out a lot, referring me to jobs, styling my hair, letting me borrow clothes, and crash at their places until I finally could pay rent. Basically, all I did was work and party, which I was frank about.

El smiled softly and told me I was more like my mom than I realized. I scowled, demanding she explain her accusation. She just shook her head, silver curls bouncing. There was something eternally young about her, despite her wrinkles and grays. I took her hand and idly traced her palms.

Ellie tipped her head at me and examined my face. "I've actually been thinking a lot about you lately, but I didn't know how to get in touch. I need to make a will. If you'll have it, I'd like you to inherit everything."

I bit my lip and thought about the consequences, the weight of this desire.

She squeezed my hand. "Think about it. No rush, dear. There is at least one thing I'd like to give you, though, if you don't mind. I'm not sure this is the place to talk about it, but I'm getting older and need someone else to know. Amelia was the only person I had ever shared this with."

Even heavier, I pulled my hands back and looked Aunt El in the eyes. She reached into the collar of her dress and pulled out the bag she always wore around her neck. I'd only seen it a few times. She took it off and opened the tiny, velvet bag. Its gape beckoned me to lean forward. Inside, I saw a red glint. When I reached for it, El pulled back slightly.

"You can't touch the gem with your bare hands," she said, then passed it to me. It looked like a little bonfire. The sun wasn't even hitting it but somehow it was glowing. For a second, I thought it was maybe made of plastic because of how red it was, but it was so heavy, there was no way.

"I want you to have it. It would mean a lot to me if you kept it and then passed it onto someone you deemed...worthy. I don't know how much it's worth, but it's extremely dangerous. If I were you, I wouldn't tell more than one person about it, maybe two. It's just as dangerous for someone else not to know."

"Auntie, how in the world is this thing dangerous?"

"You can teleport and time travel with it."

I rolled my eyes and handed it back. "Yeah right, show me."

"Okay, understandable."

El put down enough money for my food and the tip and stood, walking back towards the restroom. I scurried after her. The door closed behind us. El checked the stalls to see if we were alone, then came over and hugged me. Kind of a weird gesture, but I was so deprived of affection that I automatically gripped her back, burying my face in her scratchy wool coat. Suddenly, it was dead silent. I reared my head back and blinked so that my eyes adjusted to the darkness. El let go of me and walked a few steps away, flicking on the light.

I looked around frantically and started gasping, "What the hell? What the hell is going on?"

"We're in my bedroom."

"Absolutely not, there's no way, There's no way." I threw open the door and ran downstairs, checking every single room. Nothing had changed. The tone of my disbelief pitched higher until El finally ran over and clapped her hand over my mouth, surprisingly strong for her age.

"Shhh, shh, shhh. I'm sorry. Shh, I don't want someone to call the police if they hear you. Also, your mother might run over. Shh."

Her mention of my mom immediately shut me up.

I whispered hoarsely, "Auntie Ellie, what the hell?"

She gave me a bewildered look. "Charlotte, I told you what it did."

"Teleporting isn't real."

"We sent men to the moon. Why is this so hard to believe?"

"NASA sent men to the moon. You're my Auntie Ellie."

"So?"

She was genuinely puzzled, like somehow me being shocked was more unbelievable than having your aunt instantly travel miles away using a magical gem.

"How am I going to get home? I have to work tonight."

"Well, do you want to try?"

"Do I want to try? Are you serious? I absolutely want to try."

Her face split into a gigantic smile and she began explaining how the gem worked. I was most interested in how she could differentiate between teleporting and time traveling.

"I've only time traveled once and it was on accident. I did it by accidentally picturing my room as it had been decorated in the past," she said, shaking her head. "It did feel different somehow, physically? But I don't know if there's another way."

I sat on the bed and swung my feet.

"You don't use it to visit Auntie Am?"

The line of her mouth went hard, completely inflexible in the face of that thought.

"It's too risky. I have so many people that depend on me. There's nobody to take over Scyra."

We argued for a bit. There was no way that was true, she just clearly didn't want to let go of the reins. All her older friends had kids I'd grown up around. Many of them still lived around here. My stomach grumbled and I headed to the kitchen, trailed by Auntie Ellie as she rambled about how hard she worked to adjust to how times had changed, all that jazz. I cut her off, shrugging with a mouth full of sandwich.

"Sure, but you loved Amelia. She was the love of your life.

Doesn't that outweigh everything?"

"It's not that simple," she said, back to me as she put away food and cleaned up.

"I really, truly feel like it is that simple. Love versus duty," I replied, putting my hands up like a scale balancing.

Ignoring my scales, she said, "There are other things we need to discuss with regards to the gem that I think you'll be interested in. What time do you need to be home?"

I glanced at the clock. "In two hours, could push it to three."

Ellie put a kettle on, and I went into the living room to get comfortable. She flit in and out of the room, putting out snacks, journals, ripped pieces of paper, letters, and newspaper articles. I flipped through the articles, mostly on crimes in Oak Park. The journal seemed to be Auntie Ellie's diary, so I put it down the moment I realized what it was, just as she was coming into the room.

"It's okay. There are some private matters in there, but not many. Did you read some of the articles?"

I nodded and waited for her to go on.

"I'll try to keep this short and sweet. There's a lot to explain and I'm sure you'll have questions."

Auntie Ellie told me about forming the Scyra Society and catching Jed, in the ultimate surprise of my life. Her and Amelia continued to help Mr. Scyra with cases for years. When he began considering retirement, he picked a successor to work with Ellie and Amelia moving forward. The successor tried to get them to take on a broader range of cases, but they always stuck to sexual assault and domestic violence. It was an open secret amongst Scyra members that Ellie and Amelia were essentially consultants for someone on the force. In addition, many of the "cases" they handled were domestic issues that the police force never got called for.

"So, you and Auntie Am formed a gang?"

"We were not a gang, Charlotte."

"Sorry, a girl gang."

"Anyway."

What it all boiled down to was that I was the closest thing she had to a daughter and she wanted to give me the option to take over the group, the job, the house, and the gem, eventually. I'd never seen her so fired up. She paced in front of me, fully in conversation with herself about how much of an ask this was and how responsible she'd had to be for decades. I guess I understood her not going to see Amelia a little better, but still. I didn't know two people more in love.

I was starting to get bored so I asked if we could talk about Amelia some more. They'd never told me about how they met. I always just assumed they grew up together, like they just sprouted into being best friends, love fully formed. That's how they were in my lifetime. Ellie wanted to keep talking about Scyra. I had to beg, which only worked because I had half an hour left before I had to leave, plus practice with the gem around the house before going all the way to my apartment. She allowed me three questions.

"When did you start dating?"

She wrinkled her face thoughtfully. "I don't think there's a date, per se. We became friends around 1917, she started traveling a few years after that so then it was touch and go. It was not practical to be together."

I rolled my eyes. "Not practical? Love isn't practical. How could you stand that? Was she seeing other people? What if she came home married?"

"Well, homosexual love has to be practical. I suppose since we had no one judging us or to show off to, we got to make our own rules. Of course, I was upset and worried, but I also wanted Amelia to live a full life."

"But she loved you so much."

"I know but loving me and being with me was an enormous sacrifice."

"It also seemed like a gift, though. I mean she couldn't have had a husband and do all those things. And loving you probably stopped her from getting married."

Auntie El worried her sleeve and smiled softly. "Maybe." She looked up at me, then the clock. "One more question, dear, then let's practice a bit. I hope you appreciate how much I'm channeling 'cool Auntie Am' by even allowing this."

"Okay, tell me about your first kiss."

The dreaminess in her eyes alone set me back years. It was the way she looked at Amelia while telling a story, or at my mom when she was fired up. I tried to remember when I'd seen that look on me. Maybe it was something she hid from the object of her joy.

She stood abruptly after going into a more generous amount of detail than I thought she would. Ellie was getting soft in her old age.

"Let's go. We've delayed enough."

We went over how to travel again then prepared to take off. Auntie El made me hug her and travel to the living room. I pictured the room, every detail taken from staring moments ago, and grasped the gem. Heat burst through my hand and we were instantaneously there. The most unbelievable part of the whole thing was how easy it was. Amelia and Ellie had just been zooming around Oak Park for years. What a world of possibilities.

I did it several more times and then thought about my bedroom. I lingered, hugging Auntie El tightly, then grabbed the gem from her pouch. It was immediately dark. I looked around, turned to Ellie, and leaped at her in excitement.

"I did it! I did it!"

"Shhh, shh, shh, your roommates."

I heard footsteps and one of them calling my name while running to swing my door open. In the blink of an eye, Auntie El was gone and I stood there hemming and hawing, trying to explain my excitement, then figure out how long my roommate had been home and how long I should say I'd been quietly, silently, napping in my room this entire time.

Δ

I started meeting El twice a week, taking the train out to her house and sometimes staying entire days. We'd decided that even if I chose not to accept all the responsibility, it was good for one other person to be in the know. Ellie helped me to avoid my mom and didn't ask any questions about the state of our relationship (non-existent), but she did talk about her casually. I don't know if that was her hinting at hope of reconciliation or her accepting the situation and moving on. Things like that were always so hard to tell with her. Sometimes I wonder if Ellie ever knew what she wanted herself.

At first, it was mostly Auntie Ellie answering my questions and talking about all the cases she had solved with Amelia, but after a while I became more interested in figuring out where the stone came from. The library in Oak Park was much better than the one near me in Chicago. I spent long hours there, searching for mentions of time travel or teleportation devices. I also researched other secret societies or women's clubs throughout history.

With total grace, Auntie El let me into every crevice of her life. She gave me Amelia's last letters as well as bundles from all of her travels and left me up to my own devices. The pit in my stomach grew so large that sometimes I had to turn the lights off and just lay on the floor, letting the hole's shrieking stop demanding to be fed. There was nothing to give it but more letters, more Amelia, the best person I'll ever know.

I read them all and then started back from the beginning. Worst of all, the letters made me miss my mom. In letters where Amelia started getting homesick, after I was born, she went into great detail about the comforts she missed at home, like watching me fall asleep in mom's lap and the weight of my body as she tossed me into the air and caught me again. I could taste the meals she described.

All this festered, pooling up around my heart, gangrene feelings. Everything hurt so much but I had no one to tell and nowhere to escape to, except my job where the routine was comforting. Nothing ever changed there but no day was ever actually the same. My roommates were nice, but older and had their own friends. Many of my own friends I made as a teen were starting to get into serious relationships, which exaggerated my lost feelings.

There were too many things to choose from. I could take over and move to Oak Park. I could stay in the city and try harder to feel anchored to my life there. I could even write to Amelia's old contacts and assist with research or travel. Instead, I just read and took the train and bartended and chopped fruit and let the sweetness of joyful memories rot the enamel on my soul.

So, overwhelmed, I did the inevitable and destroyed my life in one giant swing. It was a Saturday, the first cold day of the year. I screamed at my roommates for leaving dirty dishes in the sink again. They kicked me out – my flares of temper the last belligerent straw. I went to work and flipped out on my boss for putting me on the schedule for a day I had asked to have off for a concert and quit.

Then I showed up on Auntie El's doorstep, tears melting down my body. She ushered me inside, took note of my bags, and brought them up to Amelia's old room without a word. Hot tea and a warm blanket to smother my mood was next.

When my sniffling stopped, El sat with me and cleared her throat.

"So, you've decided to come and take over?" she asked, beaming.

I wanted to slap her smile off her face.

"No, I just needed somewhere to go," I said coldly.

Her face immediately fell. She looked old, older than I could ever imagine being. Anger rose in my throat. The only "friend" I had in the entire world to turn to was this pathetic old woman, desperate for a nineteen year old to take over some stupid club because she also had no one else. She'd clearly only been comfortable opening up to me because none of her came with it. All her life amounted to was just letters from someone else, old dusty antiques inherited from people who were long dead, and long hours of thankless, unpaid detective work some officer pushed off onto her. I couldn't see her because there was nothing to see. I didn't fucking want it. I wanted to be me.

I threw the blanket off and told her it was messed up that she acted like it wasn't a big deal if I took over or not, and yet, she had been trying to manipulate me into doing whatever she wanted by giving me Amelia's letters, knowing exactly how much I missed her and looked up to her. Her hands flew up in protest, but I didn't let her speak. I stormed out of the room to go upstairs but heard her following close behind.

"Charlotte, I'm so sorry I made you feel this way. I was just trying to explain everything."

I yelled back, not bothering to turn around. "It's Charli, it's Charli, it's Charli!"

"Okay, Charli, I'm sorry. I just thought you'd enjoy reading Amelia's letters—"

"Enjoy? Enjoy reading about her dying all alone in a foreign country? Enjoy learning about how you failed her? Why would I enjoy that?"

She blinked back tears. Her watery eyes made my stomach hurt.

"Well guess what, it was fucking awful. I hate those stupid letters. Amelia was the greatest and you let her go and you let her get hurt and you suck so much that you won't even take one little risk and go back to see her."

"I told you, I didn't want to let everyone else down. A lot of other people depend on me. I don't even know what she died from. It could have been contagious."

"Contagious? All you can think about is yourself. You don't deserve Amelia." I grabbed a fist full of the letters lying on the desk and screamed at the top of my lungs, shredding my vocal chords to ribbons. "Nobody deserves Amelia." I started ripping the letters apart viciously, taking satisfaction in seeing the horror on El's face. She didn't move to stop me, which made me even more furious. I ripped them all as she watched then stood panting and screaming at her to get out.

She left the room on soft feet, closing the door behind her without making a sound. I opened it and slammed it as hard as I could. The pound was deeply satisfying.

The five seconds it took for me to turn around, see the confetti of destruction around me, and feel my stomach plummet into the depths of hell were the longest, most painful seconds of my life. Worse than the crushing weight of shame that would follow me for decades, worse than losing Aunt El. I grabbed my bags and ran out into the night, leaving everything that reminded me that I was just another disappointment to Eloise Scyra.

Oak Park, Illinois – 1976 – Eloise

Trip sat erect on her favorite chair. It made me sad that she never looked comfortable or relaxed, but I suppose she also never seemed unhappy, so it wasn't my place to mourn or say anything about her physical stoicism. Despite her cold demeanor, I felt a great amount of warmth and affection for her. She was so consistent, quick with practical advice, fully self-assured in every way.

We'd grown as close as we could in the last few years, an old woman and a vigilante from the future. She could read my body language like it was a children's book and was waiting for me to tell her what was on my mind.

My letter to Charli, letting her know that her mother was going to have knee surgery soon, had bounced back. Calling her father and getting her phone number was my last resort. We hadn't talked in years, so I wanted to make the most gentle entrance back into her life that I could. I didn't want her to feel pressured. I could take care of her mother, but wanted to give her the option to make her own choices.

Of course, Trip just said "call her." I nodded and laughed, having already pictured her saying almost exactly that to my concerns several times. We talked about Chicago for a long time. She had just moved to the city and wanted to know how much had changed since I was born. This elicited a second laugh out of me. Everything had changed; I was ancient.

As soon as she left, I called up Charli's father who was happy to give me her telephone number. He asked me to keep him updated on Samantha. They had a nice friendship now, having bonded over their explosive and difficult relationship with their daughter. After leaving me for good, Charli migrated to her father's and caused more hell before he finally kicked her out. She still called him on his birthday and sometimes holidays. It's always easier to forgive yourself for hurting a man; it's less personal.

I took a deep breath and rang the number.

"Hello?"

"Hello, Charli?"

"Yes, who's this?"

"It's Aunt Ellie." I paused, waiting to see if there was a click. Utter silence. "Your mother is having knee surgery this week. I'm too old to take care of her, but we can afford to hire a caretaker, so she'll be perfectly fine. Just thought I'd keep you in the loop."

"How'd you get my number?"

"Your father. Hope you don't mind."

"Why didn't you just have him tell me?"

I laughed, caught off guard. Why hadn't I? "Honestly, I didn't think of that."

"Okay, thank you for telling me. I appreciate it."

"It's no problem, goodbye Charli."

"Bye El."

Δ

Four days later, Samantha was still recovering in the hospital before she came home. I went every morning and then just before visiting hours ended. When I walked into the room, I started to gasp and caught myself, then ushered Charli out gently. Samantha was still asleep.

"Charli, dear, is this your first time seeing her?"

She was perplexed. "Yes?"

"Okay, you might startle her when she wakes up. She's on heavy pain medication. I don't think a surprise would be good."

Her face fell. "You're right." And then she leaned into me, stopping just when I was reaching my weight limit. I wrapped my arms around her and took a deep breath in, smelling tobacco and fake strawberry.

"It's good to see you. I missed you." I held my breath, waiting for her eventual sob.

She tried to choke it back, making the noise even more heart achingly guttural. We stood like that for a long time, nurses and doctors passing us without batting an eye at us, just another pair of mourners.

After a while, I pulled back and Charli let me use my sleeves to wipe tears from her eyes.

"I'm going to see if your mother's awake and let her know you're here."

Samantha was trying to sit up in bed while reaching for a glass of water. I swooped in and caught the water just before she almost tipped it over.

"Samantha, Charli's here," I said, taking her hand. "Are you feeling well enough to see her?"

Her eyes widened in shock. I was taken aback. The medication made her so vulnerable. She stammered sure, send her in. I went out and beckoned to Charli, who bolted into the room, talking a mile a minute, her way of pretending like it hadn't been ten years since she last saw her mother. I left immediately, very uncomfortable and unsure how to help. My plan was to come back in an hour and encourage Samantha to take a nap.

When I came back, Charli was holding her mother's hand and murmuring softly. She stood when I entered. I went on Samantha's other side and pulled up her sheets, adjusted her pillows, and softly told her she must be exhausted. She nodded and Charli and I each took a turn leaning down to kiss her on the forehead. On our way out, we stopped in the parking lot to talk.

"You're welcome to stay with me, if you're planning on staying."

Charli looked away, left of my head, and said, "I'm going to stay at mom's. Can I take your extra key?"

This was too much excitement in one day for me. Charli had driven to the hospital, so I hopped in the passenger's seat. It was a nice sedan, not new, but clean. At home, I grabbed the key from the kitchen and met Charli on the porch. She thanked me and then turned to go.

"Let me know if you need anything. I visit the hospital in the mornings and evenings. Also, I should probably still hire a nurse for when she comes home."

Charli waved her hand dismissively and kept walking away. "I can handle it. The nurse gave me a run down. Also, mom's like fifty pounds right now. Lifting her will be fine."

"Okay, well if you change your mind tell me, please. Also, Charli?"

She stopped on the sidewalk. "Yep?"

"I had written down all of Amelia's letters in a journal, in case anything ever happened to the originals."

She pulled her hood up and walked quickly to her mother's.

Δ

We all fell into a peaceful routine, visiting Samantha, preparing for her to come home. Charli seemed reticent to spend time alone with me, but I was okay with taking baby steps. She let me help prepare the house by recreating Samantha's bedroom in the living room, calling in a favor to put in a ramp on the porch, and laminating copies of the nurse's instructions.

After two weeks, we brought Samantha home together. She was still on heavy pain killers and a little loopy, but not as weak physically. Our routine essentially stayed the same. I came over in the morning and in the evening to rub Samantha's legs and keep her company. Charli usually took that time to run errands or clean. I wondered what she had been doing before that she could just up and leave, but didn't ask.

Her and Samantha seemed to be getting along well, which I wish I could have enjoyed, but I was sure this peace was only in thanks to the drugs. They mellowed out Samantha's often acerbic personality. Her pain increasing over the years made her impatient and sent her sarcastic quips into contemptuous territory. A few words from her could feel like a slap, criticizing things I never would have noticed about me and other people. I felt deeply embarrassed by something she said more than once during Scyra meetings. She always apologized, but I wondered if this side of her was what Amelia and I had missed all those years. I still loved Samantha dearly, but she was challenging to be around for long periods of time. I'm much too old to stand criticism for criticism's sake.

My anxiety reached such a high peak that when the doctor told us they were going to lower Samantha's paid meds, as well as having her start to walk again, I asked Charli to come over while her mother was asleep, feigning an emergency.

She burst through my front door without knocking and caught sight of me in the living room. I briefly felt guilty for making her frantic, her eyes wide and alarmed pushed on my heart.

"Auntie Ellie, what's wrong?"

I motioned for her to take a seat.

"So, the doctor's recommendations. Your mother's going to be in a lot of pain going forward."

Charli shrugged. "Yeah, sure."

"Well, the past few years, your mother's really started to show a new, or perhaps previously hidden, side of herself." I cleared my throat. Criticizing others was not my cup of tea, but I had to protect Charli, who was pursing her lips impatiently.

"She's sometimes not very nice. I think a lot of it was because of the pain she was in, and now I'm concerned about how she'll treat you when it becomes even worse before it – hopefully – gets better."

"What do you mean not very nice?"

"She's very critical. Sometimes she says things that are maybe meant to be joking but cut to the bone."

"Oh yeah, she can be like that. Nothing new."

Charli kept her eyes on me, slightly hooded, like she was working hard to control her face.

"Is that why you left? And ran away? Was she mean to you?"

Charli pressed her palms together in her lap and hunched forward, puffing up her cheeks and then blowing out curtly. "Not exactly. I mean, she's always been pretty critical, just like grandma was. It didn't hurt my feelings, but it did make me feel smothered. I just wanted to be me, but that was hard with her picking at me. It was also hard around all of you. You have such strong personalities. You're all very established in the community. I didn't want any of that."

I laughed, relieved. "Amelia told me that a million times. I didn't really understand it. To me, our group felt like freedom I would've never had anywhere else."

"Yeah, well, I had three mothers. It's a little much. Then Amelia left, and I'm nothing like you and mom."

That hurt a little. A lot more than Charli walked away from me all those times. I always did take comfort in not knowing, in vague directions.

"You think so?"

"I know so, Auntie El. All I do is cry and shout about my feelings, meanwhile you just blink at me. It's almost as bad as mom's criticism."

That set me off, especially after being the recipient of much of that criticism for years. I'd never done that to anybody, especially not Charli. I stood up, angrily.

"Charlotte, my so-called blinking is also called 'listening thoughtfully', 'paying attention', 'being unjudgmental'. Maybe if you cared to get to know me, you'd know all of those things and not run around making assumptions."

Charli's face cracked into a smile and then her jaw dropped

while retaining a jester's curve. "Are you mad at me?"

I stomped my foot. "Hell yes, I'm mad at you Charlotte Beckett and stop laughing at me. This is serious." I swept my arm wildly about me. "Look at the wake you left behind."

She wouldn't stop smiling. I stormed into the kitchen and heard her follow me.

"Okay, I'm sorry. I shouldn't be smiling. You've never been mad at me!"

I was exasperated. Of course, I'd been mad at her. She ripped up all of Amelia's letters.

"Yes, yes I absolutely have been."

"Ellie, look, how am I supposed to know that when you don't say anything? It comes off like you're just judging me."

Now I was waving both arms around at my sides. "What in the world? That is me not judging you. That is me being accepting."

"Okay, great, look now I understand! I understand so much better!"

Cabinets slammed under my clenched hands, but Charli was quiet for too long and I finally slowed down and looked at her now serious face.

"I hurt you? I'm so sorry."

"You should be. Seven goddamn years, Charli. I've been counting."

At that, she burst into pitiful sobs. I sighed and pulled her to me. We stood quietly for a long time, then moved to the living room and talked calmly for a while. She apologized in more ways than profusely, also opening up about the last few years of her life.

After leaving my place, she went to her father's, then bounced to an old school friend's apartment in Chicago. Doing nothing for months drove her into action and she reached out to some of Amelia's old friends, looking for any kind of work as long as it got her out of there. Instead of botany, she went on historical trips, helping to lug equipment mostly, but sometimes going with more lax archeologists and getting to dig or dust. Charli said the quiet, monotonous work helped her work through her emotions, teaching her to control and roll through them like a seal on surf.

We talked through dealing with her mother and perhaps talking to her about being more kind once she nearly healed. Charli just shrugged through most of that conversation, seemingly sure that her mother wouldn't change and being determined to keep her distance once she was better. I asked for holidays, like a divorced father, and she begrudgingly agreed, perking up more when I mentioned asking her father to come. It turned out that he was more like Charli than any of us, including Amelia, and she found a lot of solace in his company. I suspected she also resented her mother for keeping them apart for so long, though, I sincerely believe that was on her father. Samantha never really was that hurt over his infidelity.

I looked at the time and jumped up. We needed to get back over to check on Samantha, who was still almost entirely unable to do anything on her own. Right before we walked into the Beckett's house, Charli turned to me.

"Do you know where your last name comes from?"

I shook my head. "I don't, Greek maybe? I believe my great, great grandparents came over from Greece."

"I think it comes from Themiscyra, where the Amazonian Warriors lived."

"Those women? With spears and such?"

Charli smiled and said "yeah, those women" then broke through the foyer light, obscuring her back in shadows.

Oak Park, Illinois – 1980 – Charlotte

Shit, I was running so late to dinner. Not like anybody would yell at me, but I was trying to prove to Auntie El how adult and responsible I was, so she wasn't rolling over in her grave when I inherited the stone. And I wanted her to take me seriously when I talked to her later.

Dad picked me up from the train station and immediately began making corny jokes about my tardiness. I swatted them away, physically and verbally. He looked healthy. I worried about him being a bachelor, alone in a big house, but he did have a lot of friends who dropped by, old war buddies, and a housekeeper. Somebody would find him if he fell or had a heart attack.

Mom and Ellie gave me hasty side hugs in greeting when I entered the kitchen. They were in a frenzy, throwing open cabinet doors and adjusting knobs. You would think every Thanksgiving dinner was the first they'd ever prepared based on the level of panic that pulsated through the room. This year was particularly bad because my mom and dad replaced all of Auntie El's appliances as an early Christmas present. It was absolutely the most curse words I ever heard drop from El's mouth, mutters of fucking turkey, goddamn stovetop, flippin' pie, shit I just burnt my hand this, damn cranberries that. I just cackled and went to join my dad with two frothy mugs of coffee in the sitting room.

Another technological advancement my parents snuck into El's was a tv in the living room. Her only stipulation was that it had to be on a tv stand with doors so she could hide it at will. There was a fine layer of dust over the buttons and I suspected my father was the only person who touched them a couple times a year.

Mom and I were cordial, friendly even, but I usually stayed at Ellie's. Amelia's bedroom was still the coziest place in the world to me. I'd brought along homework and was working on it when we got called out to dinner. It still weirded me out to see my parents together. Not that they were ever mean to each other, before or after becoming friends again, but it was like two worlds colliding. They cleaned up while Ellie and I went into the living room. Their voices rang throughout the house and I used the cover of their noise to bring up Christmas break with Auntie El.

I asked her if she'd have time for me to maybe help with a few cases and get the hang of traveling over Christmas break. Maybe I could stay for a few weeks. She was thrilled, smiling deeply at me with her eyes and putting her baby soft hand on my knee. I looked at the billows of aging skin on her hand and felt a pang, quickly erased by my parents stepping into the room.

Δ

The next few weeks went by fast, with studying and finals taking up most of my time. Auntie Ellie flung upon the door when I arrived and ushered me in, like I was a guest staying for the first time. She let me unpack, then we spread out in the living room and she briefed me on cases she was working.

Her plan was to give me a few assignments to help with cases she was working, while letting me also work on a case of my own and be the lead on it. A small faction of Scyra helped with cases, bringing ones of interest to Ellie, collecting clues or evidence, and helping to support people after intervention. The breadth of problems they worked on was wide, from young men harassing neighbors to chronic domestic violence. There were rules of engagement, decades of contact information, news articles, even an emergency fund.

Ellie was still the only person who knew about and used the gem. She wasn't going around waving knives and axes at 2 am anymore. The gem was mostly used to spy and gather information, which was to be my first task.

I couldn't sleep that night. Learning all the rules hit home how real this was. It wasn't just a women's club; it was El's life's work that I was without a doubt going to fuck up.

The next week could've been made into a Three Stooges movie reel. I tripped, splat, coughed, screamed, and physically fought my bumbling way through all of my assignments. There was such a massive uptick in home invasions that Ellie's police contact stopped by and asked her to look into it. I sat in the living room, mortified, listening to him sound off on all the homes these reports came from, a nearly identical list to mine.

I was pouting on the couch when Ellie came in, face expressionless as usual. This didn't inspire as much rage in me as it used to, so I sucked in my face, but not quick enough to hide from her hawking eyes. Ellie walked over and sat next to me on the couch, slouching and tipping her head onto my shoulder.

"Are you mad at me?" I squeaked.

"Of course not, dear."

"Are you disappointed in me?"

"No, dear." She took a deep inhale, exhaling through her nose forcefully. "How is your case coming?"

Now this question I felt ready for, since I had plenty of time to think through my answer. I swung off the couch to grab my notes and laid everything out for Ellie, scanning her face for minute signs of approval, even though she had told me she'd remain completely neutral and let me run this.

Martha Jones, nee Reever, had a granddaughter, Joanne, who needed to leave her husband, Jerry, or at least separate from him. He was a lot older than Jo, a war veteran. The family loved him, except for Martha who could sniff out the devil in everyone, likely due to being an absolute spitfire herself. If we let her, she would've marched into Joanne's house and cracked Jerry over the head with a pan.

The abuse was subtle, nothing physical or visible. As the marriage went on, everybody saw less and less of Jo and when they did see her, she was with Jerry. He loomed over her, interrupting any time she tried to speak or tell a story. Martha was grieving the loss of her granddaughter hard. Jo used to visit her every other day. She was like her twin, only a lot younger and a lot wilder. The rest of the family, parents, aunts, cousins, were all thrilled when Jo calmed down. Scyra knew better.

Ellie spent months laying down the groundwork by assessing the situation, making a judgement call, and convincing Jo there even was a problem. Only El could handle something so invasive. I imagined her face serious and drawn tight to the point of her nose, taking every tick of Jo's head, shift of her weight, change in vocal pitch, millisecond of hesitation into account to gather information that Ellie could reform into a dagger, then hand that knife to Jo with her husband's name scratched deeply into the hilt.

Jo was agreeing to take some space so she could set boundaries with Jerry, see if he improves, and pull out of the marriage fully if he didn't change his behavior. My personal hope is that the second she left, joy flooded back into her limbs and she would bounce into a new, better future.

I had Jerry's work schedule and tailed him to make sure he was following it and not checking in on Jo at impromptu times. Martha had a spare bedroom to take her in, which we stocked with clothes, so Jo didn't have to pack much. We had a date set at the end of next week to extradite her. I planned to help her bring her things over to Martha's while Jerry was at work and bring a letter that we worked with her to write, outlining why she was leaving and appointing Jo's dad as the only way to contact her.

I thought it would be good to have a contact other than Martha because I was worried about her temper making things worse if I got her even more involved. Jo told me she was a daddy's girl, he'd do anything for her, even though he really liked Jerry.

The hardest part was meeting with Jo's dad. He paled and closed off his face when I launched into my explanation and plan, but agreed solemnly to mediate any conversations between Jo and Jerry moving forward, using his house as a meeting place, and making sure that Jo was respected and not interrupted during these conversations.

When I finally looked up from my flurry of an explanation, Ellie was beaming. My heart was heating up wildly in my chest, as if it couldn't decide if it was going to melt or explode. She gave me a little clap, rooted left against withered right, paltry compared to my thunderous rhythm but somehow much more powerful.

I tripped less the next week, found out more. Ellie was throwing tasks at me left and right. I put together an agenda for Scyra and zipped around town helping people out. There was a small snag in the back of my head, worried Auntie Ellie had been doing all this running around herself for all these years of her retirement.

I even spent a little time with mom, helping her turn my old bedroom into a more adult guest room. She was doing really well these days and in a lot less pain. I could stand her jabs to the point where I ignored them. Mom was proud of me, I think, that I was going back to school and helping out with Scyra. Christmas was wonderfully uneventful. If I had to live any week again, it would be this one. I want to bury myself in my dad's shoulder, lift my nose up to smell homemade bread, and bury it back in with a smile at the sound of Ellie somehow making my mom laugh so hard she's probably bent over in the kitchen. The only thing that would make it better is having Amelia there, probably getting kicked out of the kitchen by mom and snuggling next to me on the couch, ruffling my dad's hair like he's ten years old and asking me if I've ever heard the story about the cock-of-the-rock mating dance that led to a concussion that ended in a proposal to the wrong woman.

 On the day of extradition, I was calm all over, steady hands, steady heart. Ellie saw me off, giving me a tight hug, and putting the gem around my neck, which I didn't expect at all. I clutched it tightly through the bag on my walk over, tucking it into the collar my coat before I knocked on the door.

 Jo answered and burst into tears, rivers pouring down over the rapids of her face. I ushered her inside quickly and up the stairs, not stopping to ask questions. She was only half packed. I started throwing things into her suitcase, hoping to keep her distracted and in the moment. She wasn't saying anything, just batting back tears and watching me. I slammed her two suitcases shut and hustled her down the stairs in front of me, then handed her a suitcase and walked to the front door.

 The door opened and I stepped back in amazement as Jo's dad and Jerry walked in. Jerry was silent and a ruddy red, drunk on anger like an Irish great uncle at closing time. Jo's dad looked grave and had trouble meeting my eyes while talking. He explained he was here to help work things out and that it wasn't right for Jo to up and leave without at least a conversation. This was the only outcome I hadn't thought through. I was ready to dodge Jerry's anger in case he surprised us at the house or in the street. I had fifteen different ways to coax Jo out if she started rethinking things. I was stunned at the betrayal. Jo listed her dad as the person she trusted the most.

 My shock led to absolute babble falling from my mouth as I tried to protest and block Jo with my body, until I heard a command from behind.

 "Move out of my way, Jerry."

 Jo's dad faltered. "What's that, honey?"

 "I said, move out of the way," she said, voice raised.

 Jerry absolutely lost it at that and started slinging curses. Jo's dad whipped around, more shocked to hear this vitriol than anything. His face started heating up, a wash of embarrassment and understanding and then old man anger, purple and spitting. He pushed Jerry back away from the door. I quickly reached behind me and grabbed Jo's hand, pulling her out to safety. She dragged a little bit when we hit the pavement.

"Should we call the cops?" she asked, worrying her lip.

"Yes, but we need a phone and there's a phone at Martha's. Let's go, let's go. We can run."

We ran six blocks straight, heaving the suitcases behind us. I was deeply grateful Jo didn't have kids. Martha was waiting impatiently on the porch and ushered us in. I ran to the phone to notify the cops that there might be a fight at Jo's house and then had Martha call Jo's parents and leave a message with her mom for her dad to call Martha back as soon as possible.

Jo went to wash her face while I brought the bags to her room. I turned to leave and go downstairs, but Jo was flinging herself at me, grinning wildly with her arms open. She squeezed me so tight that I couldn't breathe.

"Thank you, thank you Charli! What would I have done without you? I was so scared until Jerry showed up and then I just knew I had to get out of there. My heart collapsed when I saw him. I was just so disappointed."

I gave her a squeeze and told her I was happy to help, then hustled her downstairs to talk through next steps with her and Martha. God, I was exhausted. I left as soon as I could and burst into Ellie's house, sobbing. She ran from the kitchen, terrified and asking a million questions. I managed to get out that everything was fine, and she patted my head, then let me cry it out on the couch.

When I calmed down, Ellie brought me coffee and I wailed out the whole story to her, crying again when I got to the part about Jo's dad.

"How could I trust him like that? I put Jo in so much danger. Would you have involved her dad? It felt smart."

Ellie's mouth pulled back, grim. "No...", she said slowly.

I wailed again and pressed my head into a pillow, screaming gutturally.

"Charli, it's okay. I usually use someone from Scyra as an intermediary, but it's okay. Maybe this will work out better. It sounds like Jo's dad will be a solid ally after witnessing Jerry's little episode."

"Why didn't you say anything?" I moaned.

"Well, like I said, maybe this will work out better than having someone more objective. I don't know. We have to mix things up to know what works best."

"But I put her and her dad in danger without even thinking about it."

"I can't hear you when you talk directly into a pillow."

I raised up my head and gave a deep sigh, then shoved it right back in and screamed that I was hopeless.

Every single one of my last few missions during winter break were a disaster. Ellie just grimaced and nervously hummed her way through my mistakes. I went home a day early and had mom drop me off at the train. Ellie insisted on coming along and walked me up to the station. I tried to rush the goodbye, knowing she had some speech coming that would be the final knife wrenched into my heart. She stood in front of me, eyes full, heavy with the weight of me in their gaze.

"Okay Auntie El, let me have it."

She shook her head. "Charli, I think you did really well. I'm so proud of you."

Even worse. How did Ellie always make things epically worse?

She went on, "Look, look at me." She grabbed my chin. "You kept going, Charli. You worked so hard."

I pulled away and waved, while running towards the track. "Train's here."

Δ

I couldn't exactly run away from home anymore, but I basically did the next few months. I didn't talk to anyone except for dad, ignored phone calls, and skipped holidays by saying I had a paper due. I was swimming in shame, letting it gut me every night, an eagle gorging on Prometheus, immature regredience.

One day, I walked into my room, flipped on the light switch and rubbed my bleary eyes to adjust to the light. My scream lit up the house when I spotted Auntie El on my bed. I immediately walked back and shouted out to my roommates that everything was fine, I thought I saw a mouse, but it was just a dust bunny. They came out laughing and tried to rib me for being messy, but I slammed the door in their faces and turned on some music.

"Ellie, excuse my language but, what the hell?"

"I came here to say the same. How dare you?"

I stopped mid step, having automatically walked towards Ellie to hug her. She stood and tread towards me, hands on her hips as I stumbled out a weak "what?".

"You worked so hard for weeks, did a fantastic job, and you just run away again? You're not a child anymore."

"Christmas break was a disas—"

El cut me off, hissing, "It was not a disaster. You are so impatient. I've spent decades building my technique."

"Yeah, exactly, and it only took me a few days to tear it down and have the cops come knocking on your door."

She waved her hand impatiently. "You haven't even checked on Jo. Did you know she's doing great? Hasn't looked back at all and guess who's been there for her every moment? Her father. You did that and then go hide away because you can't handle a few mistakes. You need to grow up."

Now I was riled up. "This is out of respect to you!" I said, putting weight on "to you", leaning into it with my shoulders. "I'm not good enough to handle all of this. You're so much better off finding someone else."

"Charli, how can you say that? You care, you're smart, you did such a good job. Who else could there be? I don't understand your problem."

I huffed, blowing my hair out of my face. "Ellie, I tell you my problem over and over. I don't want to ruin your baby."

"Ruin? You know what might ruin it? Me dying without a successor to the gem. That's it. And even then, there's a network of easily a hundred people to sustain it."

I tried to protest again, but she ran over my words. "All I want is for you to make it yours. That's all I ask. I'm not telling you to become me, to step into my body and just keep running Scyra. I want you to change it. I want you to make mistakes. I want you to take your damn time."

She glanced at the clock by my bed, said "I have to go, meeting," and blipped out of my bedroom without a hug or anything. I turned up my music and sat on my bed, arms crossed tightly until I fell asleep. I slept like a rock, waking up in a puddle of drool at the blare of my alarm.

Δ

Every morning I woke up thinking about Scyra, letting little ideas and thoughts pepper my day, then slept heavily at night. I started journaling about my plans as a hobby to relieve stress while I finished up my last semester of school. Ellie stopped trying to call me, which worked me up so much that I reached out to mom to make sure they were both still alive. My mom's surprise at the sound of my voice made me sick of myself. Imagine, being so self-absorbed that calling your mom is a shocking occurrence.

My parents came into the city to celebrate my graduation. It hurt when my dad said reservation for three. I was sure Ellie would come; she had to. I was basically her daughter.

There was one more month left on my lease. My roommates moved out, leaving me with an entire three bedroom to myself and a little time to relax for the first time in four years. I was bored after three days of walking around naked, blasting music, chugging milk from the gallon, and pounding on things to make beats. Throughout all this, I never stopped journaling. One morning I woke up, found out my Scyra notebook was entirely full, and packed my bags.

Auntie Ellie gave me an unforgettable smile when I showed up on her porch, challenging and welcoming all at once. I shrugged, yeah, I'm here, and got to work.

Oak Park, Illinois – 1988 – Eloise

It was Charli's ritual to hang the necklace back around my neck when she returned. I wasn't allowed to move or touch it while she did this. She gently pulled up my hair, fussing until everything laid properly. She was a flurry of activity at all times, as I faded back over the years. The women who were around my age now sat out on the porch during Scyra meetings. It was too hard for all of us to hear or keep up. Secretly, I still felt spry, and once a week, I had Charli present updates to me, asking for my opinion here and there.

Samantha seemed frailer than I these days. Her other knee was starting to give her trouble. She had become even more of a hermit than I, both overwhelmed by how much Oak Park had changed. I used to enjoy it, but now I just sought comfort. Charli still laughed every time she had to open the hutch that housed the tv. She had her own set in her bedroom, but I kept what she called the "static monster" in the living room.

It was a Tuesday when she came home and let me know she'd be in the city for a few days, draping the chain carefully around my skin. She was working hard to build her network there, even going so far as to rent an apartment. Charli packed a bag and left an hour later. I watched her drive off from the window, then headed up to my bedroom. I pulled a bulging garbage bag out of my closet, opening it gently and taking a deep inhale of what was maybe still my mother's perfume, then pulled a dress out and put it on. I fixed up my hair in the mirror with clumsy fingers. I never did start wearing pants, finding them uncomfortable, but I had forgotten how much I'd changed my hair. The quality of, or lack thereof, the photo on my vanity also amazed me. Luckily, I hadn't changed the house much, but the Christmas decorations mother always put up outside was something father never did. Hopefully I would blip in under the cover of darkness. I tried to picture the shadows properly falling onto our front, pre-screened-in porch, stood straight, and gripped the gem.

Oak Park, Illinois – 1900 – Eloise

I took a deep breath before opening my eyes, straining to hear any shouts or gasps. There was dead silence, no whir of heaters or cars. It was music to my ears, so enjoyable that I forgot to open my eyes.

"Hello?"

I gasped, drawing in cold air that I then choked on. My mother ran forward from the house.

"Ma'am are you okay?"

The ma'am threw me off. I almost protested, forgetting how much older I was than her. She took me inside, helping me walk like I was ancient. I could smell her scent wafting over, peppery and feminine. The house was dark. I had not accounted for my own culture shock and the lack of technology, my being now corrupted with the ease of capitalism.

She fret over me for what seemed like hours, tucking me in, getting me a steaming cup of coffee, even trying to put my feet up, and did not ask me a single question until she finally sat down. The innocence of old age was an even better weapon than youth; maybe I should have been taking on more cases as I got older, rather than less.

Mother's questions were more statement and assumptions than actual questions. Are you lost? I don't recognize you, she said while squinting into my face. Are you visiting family?

"I am, actually." I set down the mug and pulled the gem's bag out from under my many layers. Too scared to hold it, lest I travel, I opened the bag and let her peer in. She looked up, puzzled. I tried to hide my disappointment, but did not hide it well.

"That looks strangely familiar, that odd red color," she said, heavy brow still furrowed. Any more on this topic was just wasting time.

"I am visiting, actually, the Smith's, do you know them?" There were a number of families with the last name Smith, which I hoped would play to my favor.

"Oh yes, yes down a few, down–"

"Yes, right down the street a few blocks." People used to be so much more polite, even my brash mother held back from being too inquisitive. "An old friend of mine, way, way back in the day, used to live here. I just wanted to see the house."

"Oh my! It's too cold to be wandering about. When my husband gets home, he can escort you back home. I think there's some parts of the walk back home that are icy." I would have surely been peeved by being patronized – this is why I almost exclusively spent my time with other old people, or with Charli, who didn't have a maternal bone in her body – if I had not been so enthralled by mother's presence.

I was able to steer her onto herself, lots to talk about when one has a new baby. I coaxed her into talking about how her and father met, watching the gravitas of her hands punctuate each facial expression, the way her generous cheeks moved like putty to make every point. Her eyes held a world of emotions. I could have sat nestled into the couch for hours, but then the front door creaked open. I got up so fast that mother waggled her eyebrows at me, thinking I couldn't see her. Father walked in with a loud "Brr, honey it's mighty cold out there," while I tried to excuse myself, saying it was getting late.

Mother stood, too, and kissed father full on the lips before exclaiming, "Oh, Emma, you said your name is Emma Smith, right? Ms. Smith, now I remember what your gem reminds me of. My husband's mother had one just like it. That giant red one she had?"

Father stopped unbuttoning his coat and looked up at me.

Mother continued on her train of thought, "Anyway, will you walk Mrs. Smith back to her granddaughter's? Leave your coat on." She turned to me and said, "Dear, do you remember how to get back?"

"I do, thank you so much for inviting me in. You have no idea how much I enjoyed being back." I went in for a hug, which I think surprised mother, especially when I took a deep, uninhibited whiff of her.

Father smiled at me, letting me head towards the door first.

"So, this gem my wife spoke of, do you have it with you?"

Reluctantly, I stood under the dull light of the porch and

opened the mouth of the bag. He looked in and then jerked back.

"Eloise?"

I nodded, almost in tears. I missed my father so much, so, so painfully much. He hugged me tight.

"Father, this is yours?"

"It's been in my family for ages. I had heard the lore, but my mother never let me touch it, nor did she talk about it. We used to joke about how fiercely she guarded it, a dragon over her treasure." He added, much more softly, while pulling back to peer into my wizened face, "Now I understand why."

"I have to go," I said.

He nodded and hugged me again. I stepped back into the darkness of the shrubbery and we smiled at each other for one last, long moment.

Oak Park, Illinois – 1950 – Eloise

I landed in the living room of the house and flew out the door, walking as fast as I could to the hospital. This one took some searching, but it seemed like I had finally gotten it right based on my dad's things laying around the living room, looking lived in. Searching through old pictures, I found one of myself holding Charli the day after father died. Sam had stopped by in the morning to offer her condolences again and see how I was doing, and, at some point, snapped a quick photo of Charli sleeping in my arms, one tiny hand gripping a strand of my hair.

In the photo was a hat I'd been knitting, which I used to anchor myself. This was my seventh try at this and I could feel the gem working hard on my body. Trip warned me this may happen, that you could actually feel your body shrivel if you time traveled a lot or for long periods of time.

I rushed into my father's hospital room. Amelia took my breath away. I thought I steeled my soul against this, but I rushed into her arms as she stood, ignoring my father on his literal death bed for almost a full minute. She was sobbing, a low, painful sound that gripped all of my organs.

"Am I right? Is today the day?"

Through tears, she laughed at me, for one last time. "Eloise, how am I really supposed to know that?"

"Yes, right, what day is it?"

"December 3, 1950."

I sighed into her, releasing decades of grief with the push out of my breath, then took her seat next to my father. His eyes were closed, but I could tell he was awake, just deathly tired.

"Father, before you open your eyes, it's me, Eloise, but I am much older than I really am." Seeing my father on my first trip gave me the courage to finally do this, knowing he was familiar with the stone and had at least guessed at what it could do. I hoped this would be less of a shock.

He opened his eyes and his face creased into a weak smile. Amelia and I sat there until he gently passed away, the three of us holding hands. His chest stopped rising and I stood to kiss his forehead. Amelia did the same and then hugged me. I wondered if she had stopped crying at all during the last hour. She sat in the chair and held me on her lap for a while, until I decided I had to go, feeling a new creak in my knee when I shifted.

She gave my hand one last squeeze, said, "See you at home?" and laughed at my initial confusion, getting in a second laugh at my expense.

I took out the stone and she frowned at me. "No kiss goodbye?"

And now I was blushing, a nearly ninety year old woman being embarrassed by her girlfriend.

"Well, I'm just so old."

"Eloise Scyra kiss me goodbye or I'll scream. You're still incredibly lovely."

My eyes stung from welling tears as I kissed her gently on the lips and stepped back into 1989.

Oak Park, Illinois – 1989 – Eloise

It was a testament to how fully Charli had immersed herself into making Scyra her own that she noticed nothing amiss for months, despite being one of the most sensitive people I had ever met. You couldn't hide a thing from her. If I altered my habits even a little when she was a teenager, she'd look at me questioningly until I explained myself.

Over a particularly delicious batch of waffles I took the time to make one morning, that look appeared, her eyes sharpening over every move I made, carving me up. It did ruin my breakfast, distracting me from a flavor I was trying to ingrain into my memory.

"Yes, Charli?" I sighed, while carefully putting down my fork.

"You've been acting weird."

"You're right, I have. I was going to bring it up soon."

She got up and started brewing more coffee. "You sound serious. I'm going to get cozy."

I went upstairs and brought down all my preparations, a big box of papers and titles. I also had a long checklist, whittled down to only a handful of items now.

Favorite blankets were out, furniture rearranged. I tasted my coffee, the perfect caramel color, creamy and bright. My papers were categorized: legal, personal, Scyra, Amelia, historical.

"No miscellaneous?" joked Charli.

I plopped down into the chair and wrapped my favorite blanket around my legs. Charli tucked it in on the sides and I playfully kicked her away. She had relaxed, thinking this was just me preparing for the worst, and plopped down, too.

"So, while you've been gone, I've been time traveling a bit."

Charli raised her eyes in alarm.

"And, frankly, it's making me age very fast. I think my last trip might kill me."

She absolutely lost it, bending over in a great sob. I didn't think it would be this fast. Charli sat up and cried out through tears, "Ellie, how could you tell me like that? You're so fucking blunt. Ugh, why don't you just come punch me in the stomach."

"I'm not sure that would help," I said, pushing myself up to a stand so I could fall onto the couch next to her. She cried on me forever, rivers of grief. Lots of "how could you leave me alone here", "I'm not ready", and the worst one, "I love you". Those words almost made me want to punch myself in the stomach. I messed this up. All this planning, but there's somehow always a small emotional piece I miss, an empathy blind spot.

She ended up with her head in my lap, making a pitiful sound but not crying anymore.

"Where are you going?"

This really isn't what I wanted to talk about. We had many documents to go over and had to plan a visit to my lawyer. The night was a wash, though, with her in that state. I turned on an old movie and made popcorn.

Charli pulled it together after a good night's sleep and we spent the next day talking shop, thank god. Her last thoughts of the day were pleading, asking to not be there when I left. I was crushed. She had to not just be there, but come with me.

Δ

Consciously and unconsciously, I had been saying my goodbyes for years. Once you get to a certain age, you feel the present more strongly than ever. Each bite of a summer strawberry could be the last tart juice to stain your fingers. Every infant's head you smell could be the final one. My bucket list wasn't long. I was a satisfied woman, happy to look on from my porch. My friends were drifting away, into death, disease, and senile seclusion. Charli just wanted to spend quality time with me, laughing, eating, and watching movies. I was sad, wishing these were things she at all wanted from her mother, who had so much longer left on earth.

Trip's first visit years ago told me everything I needed to know about the security of the future. Just her presence gave the rest of my life an easy meaning. It would all be okay. Charli would absolutely be okay.

Two days before I was set to leave, someone knocked on the door and then immediately walked in. I was frightened and picked up a knife. They ran towards me, skating into the kitchen.

"Jesus, Trip. I thought you were an intruder."

"Ma, I thought I'd missed you."

I blinked. "You know about this?"

"Yes, Charli of course told me."

"Charli tells you?"

"Does it matter? I just want to tell you goodbye." She came into my arms, bird-boned. I was worried I would crush her.

"How can you do this? Aren't you scared of just up and leaving Scyra?"

"Not for this. Charli's got it."

"It's a suicide mission. I mean I'd do this for us, for the org, but for love? How do you know?"

I searched her face, trying to figure out what time period she was from, what year. She seemed completely distraught. I shook my head. "I just know."

"But there are no, like, facts about love. I feel like we know more about space than we do love."

"Maybe in the future, space has outpaced love, but not here. You don't look very good." I kissed the top of her head. "You should go."

Trip hugged me one last time and mouthed, "I love you" before teleporting away.

Δ

I had everything I needed, a small bag and a picture.

"Charli, this is the only way, I promise you."

Luckily, she wasn't crying, just meekly protesting.

"Let's go." I waved her over and wrapped my arms around her.

"This is so unceremonious, El."

"I've been thinking about this for decades. Every day was ceremony. Hold onto me tighter."

Elqui Valley, Chile – 1965 – Amelia

I opened my mouth to yell at the kids. My pillows needed adjusting. Whatever this disease was, it was punishing on my joints. A shadow fell over my lounge chair and I felt a hand on my shoulder.

"Am?"

"El? Eloise?" I swung my legs over and shot up so fast that I had to grab the chair. I shielded my eyes from the sun as two people stepped towards me.

"Amelia, it's me. Charli brought me, but she has to go back. Hug, quick. Charli you need to leave."

A grown-up Charli, in the throes of her youth, picked me up and swung me around, sobbing hysterically and saying Auntie Amelia over and over. My body hurt so bad. I sucked in air raspily. Charli finally put me down, said goodbye, and teleported away with no regard for the two children staring at us.

"Uhm, kids, this is my friend Eloise and... oh screw it."

I threw up my hands and turned to El. She swept me up into her arms, much more gently than Charli, and I started weeping.

"Eloise, you're here."

"I am."

"Were you scared?"

"I'm always scared, Amelia," she whispered, while I nuzzled into the utter softness of her neck.

Part V

Chicago, Illinois – 2018 – Trip

"Fine, but let's go somewhere warm first." I stood and held out my hand to help Diana up.

"My husband is on a work trip. We can go to my apartment," she said, taking my hand and pulling herself up.

"Do you want to teleport us there?"

She stared at me. "I can't tell when you're making a joke. You're not good at it."

"I'm dead serious. It's easy. Picture where you want to go while holding onto me and grab the gem."

I loosened the small pouch enclosing the stone and pulled it off. It glowed blood red, bright enough to see in this nearly pitch-black portion of the park.

"So, picture standing in your bedroom, facing your bed. Look at it in your mind's eye, make sure you have current details to anchor it to this time period." She side-eyed me at the phrase "time period".

"Got it? Don't think too much. Wrap an arm around me."

Diana obeyed, wrapping an awkward side hug around my ribs, like King Kong trying to drag me up to the Empire State building. She took a deep breath and snatched up the gem.

"Great job," I said, brushing flecks of grass and her arm off me.

"Holy shit, we're at my apartment."

"Yep, do you have any tea or something?" I asked, walking out of the bedroom, through the living room, and into the kitchen. While she reveled and checked every limb, I popped a mug into the microwave.

Diana eventually followed and sat at the kitchen table. She

tossed a blanket onto the empty chair opposite her, which I wrapped myself in once I found teabags, dunked them into the water, and sat down.

It was a longish story, but not eternal. I lived in a foster home next door to Charli. She didn't have kids of her own and was getting older, in her early fifties. My foster parents were struggling with their own kids plus me (I was bad) and so they opted to return me to the home after my allotted stay. Charli took me in once she found out what they planned to do, and the rest is history. She was the closest thing to a mom I ever had. There wasn't like, fresh baked chocolate chip cookies waiting for me when I got home from school, but she cared that I was happy, and loved and respected me. I think I turned out pretty damn well because of her. The whole respecting a child thing was new to me after being in the system and I just stopped being bad.

"What happened to her?"

I looked down into my mug. "She died in 2011."

"Oh, I'm sorry." Diana averted her eyes from me.

After a while, her curiosity caught back up.

"So, you inherited all your, like rules, customs, the stone, all from her? Where did she get it?"

"From her neighbor, Eloise Scyra."

"Did you meet Eloise?"

"I go see her every once in a while." I shrugged. "She's a badass. Was, was a badass."

"You go see her? Back in time?"

"Yeah, we have coffee and chat."

"Aren't you worried that's going to mess something up in the future?"

I rubbed my eyes and tried to explain. Visiting El was fine, she had the gem almost her entire life and had a sense of how to just live her life, as if teleporting didn't exist, which in turn led to her being good at pretending I don't exist outside of our little visits. Plus, she died before I was even born so she had no influence on my life. As for me, I just make judgement calls.

"Okay, but what if you kill somebody and they were going to be the person who discovered cancer?"

"That's a slippery slope I don't go down. What if the person they hurt was going to cure cancer, but their trauma stopped them from graduating college or moving out of their parents? I don't worry about it. Also, all the important inventions, other people were also inventing them at the same time. It's not just singular humans. It's the time period, it's the place, the need. Anybody could have been Einstein."

Diana scoffed.

"I mean it. There were a lot of other physicists talking to each other, learning the same way, the same things. What's going to happen, is going to happen. And yeah, a lot of random shit does happen that changes the world, but there's also the inverse. I don't have time to just sit around guessing who the next genius is. Also, last point, then we need to talk shop, a lot of times it takes a village. One villager missing isn't going to stop the iPhone from ever being made by a massive team of people. S' that good for now?"

She nodded and yawned. The adrenaline from shock had probably fully drained out of her body by now.

"Get some sleep. Will your husband still be gone tomorrow?"

She nodded, tried to speak, but was interrupted by another yawn.

"Okay, I'll come by at 7," I said, then blipped home.

Chicago, Illinois – 2018 – Diana

I slept like a rock and went through the motions at work the next day, then hurried out to meet Trip. She rang the doorbell promptly at 7 and strode in, a notebook full of plans in hand. I had glasses of water and a cheese spread ready, which Trip sniffed at, bent ninety degrees over, nostrils hovering millimeters away, like she'd never seen food before.

That out of the way, she sat down and ripped out papers from her notebook, then slid them across to me.

"What's this?"

"A travel itinerary," she said, grinning wildly at her handwork.

Trip and I did extensive research that night on the first target, a habit I hoped we kept up for every single person we handled. I was wasted on power, all the joy with none of the hangover.

We took down the criminals first. Trip took me on two and claimed she handled a third, but it was a time travel thing which apparently erased my memory of him.

For our first mission, she let me borrow a wig and taught me how to cover up all of my DNA. She gave me gloves but I noticed that she didn't wear any herself.

"Aren't you worried about fingerprints? You were in foster care."

She held her hands up to me.

"I don't have any."

I bent a few of her fingers back gently, twisted them around, seeing if it was just the lighting. Her fingertips were perfectly smooth.

"Some weird genetic thing?"

"I melted them off. Acid."

The hair on the back of my neck rose and I dropped her hands. She turned to my dining room table and picked up her notebook.

"First target, Jim Flossmoor. He's a cousin of the next target, pretty young, about twenty. We're going to scare the living daylights out of him, sound fun?"

"We'll see about fun."

Trip took a firm hold of my shoulders and teleported us to Jim's backyard. The plan was for her to scope out his bedroom, send me in to scream and wake him up, then teleport in behind me to really get him scared. She said she'd handle talking, just in case they sent him to the precinct or something.

It went off without a hitch. Trip ripped him a new one while I stood in the back holding a knife, making sure the light caught the blade. Later, she said she could actually hear his teeth chattering. One down, twelve more to go.

Chicago, Illinois – 2019 – Trip

I involved Diana just enough for her to think she was helping, letting her come along to scare people. Jim was the first. After I left Diana, I went back and slit Flossmoor's throat. He didn't live in the cops' district, so I doubted Diana would find out. His cop associates would probably chalk it up to his lifestyle catching up to him.

One by one, I mutilated and murdered my way through a nest of vipers. My favorite one, by far, was Bowen. He was a sick fuck with a long record of transfers to cover up his slimy trail and abusing his wife. I took my time tailing him, even visiting him back when he was a teenager. He obviously joined the force to better inflict pain on people. I left his wife the best Christmas present she'll ever get, bound and gagged under their first tree.

Meanwhile, Diana was putting feelers out for a sympathetic ear. I told her nearly every day that she wasn't going to find a single one in CPD, to which she replied with one long finger, somewhere near the middle of her hand. I decided to extend my plan, from days to weeks, spiraling up towards Roberts as he became filled with dread, realizing someone was after his entire organization. Or at least, that's what I hoped he was feeling. Diana was really unhelpful in that regard, personally keeping away from him.

Chen and Roberts, as well as an older man, Don Calhoun, whose name I found in O'Harrell's texts, were my last prize pigs before Roberts. I spent long nights plotting the sickest ways to get back at them. I think Diana was still hoping to take down the higher ups the "right way" as we got closer to bringing about their demise.

I followed her when I had the time and figured out that she was investigating Calhoun on her own, trying to build a case around him. He was like an old crime boss, someone de Niro would play. Respected in the neighborhood, big family, lots of younger guys knocking on his door late at night. It would be hard for her to take him down on anything, as he probably wasn't actively committing crimes at his big age.

Calhoun's death needed to be a message to Chen and Roberts, as well as a symbol of resistance for my clients. I needed to make a splash, pull-off something that would be covered all over the media cycle.

Diana and I spent lunch together most days, now that she accepted that we were literal partners in crime. When her husband was traveling, we swapped lunch for beers at her apartment. It was surprisingly nice to spend time in a normal home. I wrapped myself in her swaths of blankets, poked through her cabinets, and borrowed one of her many pairs of slippers that were far too big for me. She seemed to enjoy it when I teased her about being an old man. Now when I thought of Diana, I pictured her in grandpa slippers, fuzzy blanket around her shoulders, and horn-rimmed glasses, her face steeped in blue light from her laptop. Often, the blanket would slide off of one of her shoulders and I took to fixing it, roughly pulling it up when I got up to go to the bathroom or grab another drink.

We worked well together, although we were both reticent to share too much. Our brains followed similar habits and spotted the same patterns. It was helpful to bounce ideas off of her, even when I was vague about details, for fear of intervention.

Before this period of my life, I never considered myself lonely. Maybe in bed with loneliness, but too busy and too free to actively be lonely. Now, every night felt longer than the last on my closet floor bed. I started to feel the weight of my body trying to force itself to be comfortable on a flat surface. Evenings with Diana made me want to retire, get a dog and a cabin in the woods somewhere. I could start building my library. But this case hammered home how much work I could accomplish. Taking down a sex trafficking ring was beyond my wildest dreams and surely beyond Di's.

Sometimes I caught her staring at the stone around my neck. There was a lot of work to do before I could take her on as my successor and hand over my legacy, namely getting her to not be a kiss-ass cop.

Almost every night, she asked me questions about Scyra,

circling closer and closer to Charli. It felt wrong to share her with Diana at all because I know how much she hated cops and bureaucracy.

I started seeing Ma all the time in an attempt to stave off any feeling about Charli. God, I loved hanging out with her. We had the type of relationship grandmas have with their first born grandchildren. Like no matter who else comes along, you'll always have an understanding the other kids won't have with her. There was still a wall there, though. I couldn't talk freely about myself or even really about Charli, for fear of somehow changing the timeline. And Ma still wasn't a substitute for the woman I considered to be my mother.

To annoy Diana back, I asked her endless questions about her absent husband. Their relationship wasn't real to me. I couldn't imagine her brushing her teeth next to the man scattered throughout her house, or crying while she said her vows to him on their wedding day. She didn't really seem to have friends, either, mostly going from work to home, home to work. The odd date with her husband was scattered in there, as well as getting drinks with random, boring women.

There was an easy intimacy between us, the kind that develops after you commit a crime together. We were conspirators, catching each other's eye when we spotted something strange or funny, someone's outfit, a pet lizard on a man's shoulder on the L. It was a drug to me, adult friendship. After spending my entire life doing absolutely whatever I wanted all the time, I let Diana wash over me, seeping into my needy pores, despite my better judgement. I considered it to be like reaching across the aisle. All of us gem-bearers in Scyra took on someone unlike us and let them transform the society. It had to happen, otherwise we'd still be sitting in the suburbs knitting and talking about how to get so and so away from her financially abusive husband. Not that that wasn't necessary, but it wasn't working to solve systemic issues and it was small. Much smaller than being able to time travel and teleport at will.

Also, I didn't have time to find someone else. My body was disintegrating in front of my very eyes. It's hard to explain. I looked okay, but kind of old for my age. Plus, I was fucking tired. My hearing wasn't as good as it used to be. The other day I found a spot on my scalp where my hair was thinning. Time was ticking by wildly beneath my chest.

I think it was a Wednesday, two days before I took down Calhoun, when Diana asked me why I wouldn't just tell her how Charli had died and how it was obviously not from old age or something normal because of the way I avoided it.

I groaned and put my head in my hands.

"Diana, I don't want to talk about this."

"You run around Chicago being the angel of death, but you can't tell me what happened? That's soft."

This would be a good way to further earn her trust, especially as I got closer to taking down Chen and Roberts.

"It's really fucked up, Diana," I whispered, then got up and walked outside onto the balcony. She followed me, snatching up a pack of American Spirits. She lit one and offered it to me as she stepped outside.

"I'm sorry," she said meekly.

"It's fine." I grimaced towards her and said, "Look, Charli wasn't one of these scummy people I take down. I don't think about them. She was my mom."

"What, really?"

"I mean, not actually, but the closest thing I ever had to a mom."

"Were you there when she died?"

"Yes."

She pursed her lips. "Why don't you just go back and stop it from happening?"

"Because I was there. I can't cross paths with myself. I don't know what would happen. It's not worth the risk."

"How? You loved her. She was like your best friend." She gestured towards my gem. "The things I would do with that."

I turned away and leaned over the balcony, putting my forearms on the cold steel railing.

"Well, let's talk about it. What would you do with the stone?"

No hesitation, she launched into all the people she would visit, her grandma, a friend who passed away from cancer when they were in college, celebrities she idolized. I was internally groaning. Was I wasting my time on Diana?

"Okay, okay," I interrupted, "but like, to help the world, what would you do?"

She lit another cigarette with the one she was finishing and then took a deep drag, closing one eye and peering at me with the other.

"I don't know, I haven't thought about it."

I rolled my eyes and she protested.

"I have a job where I help people!"

I rolled my eyes three more times and leaned back on the railing with a giant sigh. "Seriously, when have you helped people as a cop."

"Hey, I'm a damn good detective. I collect solid evidence. And, I listen to people. A lot of people, the healing mostly comes from being able to report it to someone and feel like they took some control back."

"I know it is, I do it for people all the time." I tossed my butt over the side and turned to leave. I grabbed my notebook from the kitchen table and teleported before Diana could continue the conversation.

"See you tomorrow." I waved.

Oak Park, Illinois – 1989 – Trip

It was hard to see Ma this old. She was a solid woman when I first met her in middle age, deft and strong. Now I couldn't help but peck at her when I visited, making sure her feet were warm and leaping up any time she tried to do something for herself, which she clearly hated.

I let her do most of the talking, being the only person, she could share her time travel plans with. Ma was so excited, leaning forward with a sharp light in her eyes. They danced every time she spoke Amelia's name. After a while, she asked me if something was on my mind.

"I've just been thinking about Charli a lot."

"My advice is always the same, Trip. Go see her."

"I can't. My little desires are mole hills compared to the mountain I could create visiting her."

"Just do it at the end, that can't hurt anything."

"It could though, Ma. What if I stop her death from happening somehow?"

Her eyes drooped downward, and she looked up into my face, painfully searching for something.

"Trip, why would that be a bad thing?"

My cheeks warmed with shame. I lied about Charli's death when I first started visiting, not wanting to hurt Ma and burden her with knowing tragedy loomed large over the head of a person she saw every day. I told her that Charli died quietly in her sleep from a freak brain aneurysm, no pain or struggle. That kept Ma placid, knowing that JCharli eeked out a lot of life, despite having a countdown ballooning in her skull.

There wasn't even a squint of suspicion in Ma's eyes while I hemmed and hawed, images of Charli being impaled racing through my head, her reaching out to me, blood dribbling down her mouth, then slumping forward.

"I waited too long. To me, time is a fabric. I wove my way through a lot of people's lives. If I went back for one person, then who knows what would happen to me, what choices I would have made."

Ma nodded and sat back in her chair.

"That makes sense. I don't know what to say. One part of me understands. I spent my entire life building an organization I am months away from letting go of. My plan has worked out well so far and now I get to make a few visits and go off into the unknown, leaving Charli to her own brilliant devices."

She picked some fuzz off of a blanket, giving herself time to arrange her thoughts.

"But, on the other hand, why do we have so many rules for ourselves? Maybe I'm getting soft in my old age. I'm happy with my choices. All that matters to me now, as a relic of the past, is that you're happy with yours."

I got up to leave, starting to feel sleep pull at the corners of my eyes, and kissed Ma on the forehead. "I am. I always am."

She lifted her chin and took gentle hold of mine, her hand, ice cold and marble smooth. "Who are you, Trip? Are you who you love? What you do? You feel like a ghost."

I was a ghost, dead man walking, doomed to die doing what I was compelled to do. Ma was asking me if what I did was really what I wanted. A surge of feelings stirred in my heart and I turned away.

"What if I'm it? And I give the stone to Diana and she, like, gives it to a museum?"

"Can I ask you a question?"

My body followed her soft, melodic tone, lulled back despite my exhaustion.

"Are you in love with Diana?"

A tsunami of shock hit my body and I hesitated, then burst into laughter.

"I have to go, Ma. I'm fucking tired."

"To use your analogy, relationships between women are like a fabric. With men, you walk a line. Are they a friend? Is it lust or love? It's always easy to tell, that's our secret, written on the walls we put up to stop them from getting too close. Sometimes it's not even walls, it's just emptiness, gaps between our souls that they don't understand. But with other women, there's no end in sight to the places where we can weave across each other's lives. I don't know. This sounds all really silly to me now. I'm not sure what I'm trying to say." She shrugged, not self-deprecating or embarrassed, just elegantly dismissive of herself, a small toss of her chin up in defiance, followed by a sharp shoulder.

"When you spend most of your life thinking about relationships and romance in terms of man - woman, you miss a lot of beautiful patterns? No, that sounds silly, too. It's hard to tease out how you feel in a world where we outwardly define our relationships by who's making love to who. It's not really like that. I didn't know I loved Amelia romantically because I desired her, I didn't even really know what desire felt like back then. I knew because I felt like I could've merged into her body, knit our brains together, and we still wouldn't be close enough. I wanted to relinquish myself to her because I finally realized..."

I shuffled my feet around. "I haven't spent enough time with her to even know if I trust her with my real name, Ma."

She flicked her eyes up to the ceiling in thought. "Well, Olivia, bear in mind, I've known about this Diana woman for twenty years or so, whenever you first told me about her." She smiled. "I've had a lot of time to think about her. Do you feel that lack of trust because of her or because of you? Sometimes it's playing god to not play god. Who do you think you are to be so cautious and think you have control over your feelings, my dear?"

"I love you, Ma, but this whole meta conversation isn't my cup of tea."

I waved and blipped back to the closet, collapsing into my nest of blankets.

Chicago, Illinois – 2019 – Diana

A group of guys were huddled around one desk when I walked in. Ghurt was fighting for a spot and waved me over, desperate for an ally.

"Lendo, take a look at this."

A path cleared as I approached the screen. It must be bad. Everyone was watching my face to see how I would react. I put my hands on either side of the computer and peered at pixel upon pixel of gore.

"Is this our case?"

"No," someone answered. "The pictures have just been making the rounds."

I took my notebook out of my back pocket and took notes. Calhoun had been gutted, his intestines tied around his neck. There was a giant, painted piece of cloth hanging over his bed with Trip's goddamn symbol painted on it. I finished scribbling and went to my office.

Luckily, there was tons of busy paperwork to help settle my anger down. I shredded my fury, shoved computer keys down, wrote like an angry fifth grader in my notebook, pressing so hard that pages and pages after carried my imprint. In all my years on the force, I had never seen something so blatantly brutal. Not even in the movies. Calhoun's eyes were bulging with suffering. Fingers scattered across his plush carpets. It was like someone threw a party with his body, a confetti of bodily fluids.

Removing Calhoun crushed a huge part of the case I was building. I had to get Trip to undo this somehow. She knew I'd been spending hours looking into him, getting ready to squeeze out precious information on Roberts and Chen.

Trip would be over at 7. I went to the gym on lunch then outlined everything in my notebook that I lost with the death of Calhoun. She could make it up to me by finding some of the younger guys Calhoun worked with. Or I could start working with the other department.

Brilliant. I could get in with my pictures of burns from Trip's victims, lead them towards a greater conspiracy and deliver Roberts and Chen into their laps.

I met Trip at my apartment door with a beer and a wry smile.

"You've been busy," I said.

Trip recoiled slightly. "You're not mad?" She skirted me and got her own beer.

"This was for you, goof," I said, waving the beer I was holding in her face. "Am I mad a crime boss got taken down?" I shrugged. "It was inevitable. He was filth."

She sat down and set her notebook on the table, staring at me even after I took my usual seat.

"What?"

"I thought you'd be furious."

"I mean, I'm not happy. But you didn't take out my guys. You do owe me, though, let's be honest. It's a slight wrench in the case I've been building."

"Slight?" Still staring, one eyebrow dusting the ceiling.

"Slight. Will you tail his associates for me, get a list of who I could interview if I need dirt on Roberts and Chen later? Surely, those guys that come around Calhoun's have seen them with him."

"If you're going to yell at me, can you just do it? This is terrible. Mad is like your default mood."

I blew out a puff of air in exasperation. "Look, I was livid this morning. I figured it out. I can't sustain anger. You gave me too long and it's just gone now. Just promise me you won't do this shit with my guys."

"I promise," she said, sticking out a pinkie finger. I reached out and she flinched slightly away automatically, looked up at me, and offered it back. Her little bird bones wrapped around mine. I could crush her if I wanted. Actually, probably not, I thought, remembering the crime scene carnage. If I ever did try to arrest Trip, no one would believe me. There wasn't a man on this earth who could wrap his head around this delicate woman digging her hands into his guts and tying them in a pretty bow around his neck.

We worked in silence for a while. "Trip? Could you reverse Calhoun's death?"

She shoved her hands into her pockets and pressed back into the chair, rolling her neck around before answering.

"I don't know. I don't un-kill people. I think it would fuck up the timeline way worse than their absence."

"Oh, I really just meant could you actually do it. Go back and stop yourself."

"Maybe?"

I let it go then. We had work to do. Chen was next on our list.

Michael Chen was smart and moved much more silently than Roberts. His name only came up a single time in the texts I'd stolen, and it wasn't very incriminating, just a message where O'Harrell said he'd update Chen on his schedule changes. Trip had to trail him for weeks to confirm that he had anything to do with this, but she told me she was sure, and I trusted her instincts, if not her actions.

Our work moved to the couch as the winter grew more bitter by the day. It was my husband's busy season when he spent Monday through Thursday out of town. Trip and I started meeting at museums instead of cafes on the days we spent lunch together, working in front of Monet's lily pads and legions of stuffed animals that lined her favorite wing of the Field Museum.

It was in the depths of one of those wings that Trip let me in. All day she'd been staring at the big cats, idly answering me when I bounced ideas off of her. Towards the end of the hour, she turned to me.

"You asked me how Charli died."

"Who?"

"My mentor."

She was staring intently, somewhat at me. As close to "at me" as Trip could allow herself to.

"Yeah, a long ass time ago."

"It's horrible, but I can't stop thinking about it lately. And you're probably the only person I could tell who wouldn't be bothered by it."

I put my pen down and stretched out, then gave her my full attention. "Bring it."

Trip's left hand was squeezed into a fist. "Okay. We were working a job together. We were so used to teleporting together. She just took my hand and blipped to our target's shed. I don't know why, so stupid. We could've just went to the backyard."

Yikes.

"We landed and I heard a groan and I looked over. Charli had the end of a shovel straight through her chest. I ran over and teleported her home, but it was too late. It was right through her heart."

"That's fucking brutal."

Trip nodded emphatically.

"I miss her so much. But the worst part is that she didn't have a will and I lost my inheritance, Eloise's house. I didn't have any kind of legal claim. Charli technically fostered me, not adopted."

Hot tears slid down her cheeks. I pulled my sleeve over my hand and wiped them away. She reached up and pressed my hand to her face. I froze, surprised by such an affectionate gesture.

"I lost a house that had been in Eloise's family for generations."

"Who is Eloise?"

Trip let go of my hand and I moved it to her shoulder, giving it a squeeze. She covered it with her hand and squeezed back.

"Charli's mentor."

"Ah, jeez. That's awful. I'm really sorry."

She stood and walked over to one of the glass cases, after gently removing my hand.

"It's okay. Maybe now that I said it all out loud, I can be free."

"Yeah, absolutely. Thanks for telling me." Yeah, no, guilt didn't just leave because you told a stranger about it. "Do you want a hug or something?"

Trip laughed and shook her head no, then motioned to the time. I gathered my stuff and joined her at the glass encasing a pride of lions.

"Trip, what's your favorite color?"

She looked at me like I was insane.

"Why would I have a favorite color?"

Chicago, Illinois – 2009 – Trip

It was crushing me that I felt like I owed Diana now. You would think saving her life would set an imbalance in my favor forever. I took ten times as long to make a decision about Chen than I usually would, trailing him and digging hard into his past to figure out when to take him out and how. My first plan was to kill him in 2019 and cause a scene, making sure that CPD connected his death to Calhoun's, as well as the media.

But, in the back of my mind, Diana lounged. I spent hours with her while she worked on this, in addition to her normal case load. It was psychologically cruel to rip him from her hands. So, I went back a decade, ensuring I'd come back to a Diana that didn't remember. Maybe even a new Roberts. Chen seemed like he was the unofficial brains on the police side, not Roberts.

Ten years ago, he was working on his police force application after a stint in the Coast Guard, working at a pizza shop on the west side. I caught him in an alley with an armful of pizzas and smashed my fist through his kidneys. He crumpled, too tall to keep his balance. I kneeled down to pin him and grabbed his head, embedding my fingers into his scalp so I could yank it back and push his spine to its edge of flexibility. He was shaking like a leaf. Probably thought I was much bigger. I let the knife glint in front of his eyes while he moaned, no, please, no.

And then I just sat there, thinking about me and Scyra, and me and Diana, and then just about me.

"What's your favorite color?"

"What?" he gasped.

"Your favorite color, do you have a fucking favorite color?"

"Uhm, blue," he panted.

"Does everybody have a favorite color? Like even adults?"

He was silent.

"Do you not see the knife? Answer the fucking question."

"Probably? I don't know. I'm sorry." His voice was shaking.

I rolled off him and said, "Stay down or I'll shoot you."

"Michael Chen, I'll kill your entire fucking family if you become a police officer. In fact, I'll kill your family and all of your friends if you ever put a single goddamn toe out of line and hurt somebody. Do you hear me? Stand up and look at me."

He stood, wobbling so hard he had to support himself on the dumpster, and raised his eyes to finally take me in.

"Every single fucking one, Chen," I screamed and teleported home.

Chicago, Illinois – 2019 – Diana

Trip strode into my office and started talking before I could even look up and acknowledge her presence. She plopped down into the chair across from me, making herself comfortable.

"We need to talk about Roberts, but first, when did all these women start working here? It's literally, like, half women?"

Wild how fast she could annoy me.

"What do you mean? It's been like this for years."

Trip stared at me and chewed her bottom lip. "Years?"

"Yes, actual years, since I was promoted to Deputy Chief. I made it a priority to up the amount of women we interviewed."

"Okay...well anyway, Roberts."

"What about him?"

"I want to share him with you. Let's do this together, take him down once and for all."

"Marshall Roberts? Together?"

"Let's go to lunch. We can talk this through. Then we probably should take, like, a week off from seeing each other, until we're ready to go. I wouldn't want you to be seen with me."

I stood and grabbed my coat, carefully packing my notebook and my recorder, then followed Trip out. She zoomed through crowds, hesitated in front of my usual cafe, then plowed on and finally found a place she liked.

I settled in, flipped my recorder on, and took out my notebook.

Trip leaned forward and dropped her voice low. "Do you trust me?"

I was caught off guard by this. "Uhm, yeah sure."

"The hesitation is fair." She shifted around, tugging on the scarf around her neck. "I think it's fair I tell you my name. Me offering an olive branch of trust to you. My real name is Olivia," she said, smiling softly.

I smiled back, which she seemed to accept happily

"Okay, let's get into it."

"All ears."

Oak Park, Illinois – 2011 – Charli

I jogged over to open the door. Olivia was standing there awkwardly, like she was waiting for me to invite her in for some reason.

"Forgot your key? I thought you wouldn't be back until 9 or so."

She walked forward and the foyer light washed over her.

"What the hell? Ol you look awful. I thought you were just going to Harold Washington."

"Charli, I....it's me but, like, from the future."

I was absolutely stunned. I ushered her into the kitchen, trying not to stare at the wrinkles wreaking havoc on her eyes and forehead.

"How far?"

She hesitated before answering. "2031."

"Ah, damn. That's hard to wrap my head around. Come here, give me a hug." She collapsed willingly into my arms, pressing her full weight into me.

"Why are you here? What's up? I mean I guess I'm probably dead. There's no way I live until I'm 80, shit."

"Yeah, sorry to break the news this way. You don't make it to 81."

"Hey but look at you! You're in your thirties, probably absolutely thriving. That's great," I said, throwing up my hands and then jokingly pinching her cheeks.

"You just want to visit, hang out?"

"Yeah, any coffee? I can stay for about fifteen minutes."

We made the most of it. I figured it was because Ol was getting older, getting more nostalgic. We talked mostly about her childhood after I took her in. I told her about the first time I met her for the zillionth time. In my time, it had been awhile since I told that story so, of course, I was blubbering by the end. I was old when I met her, sure as shit I'd never have a kid. And then here comes Olivia, shoving her way into my heart.

Ellie always said things just work out. As long as you keep going, keep wanting, keep changing. They work out.

"Did I have a favorite color?" Olivia suddenly asked.

"Oh man, when I first took you in, you were going through a huge purple phase. Sometimes we'd go to stores and I'd lose you. Then I'd have to find the closest salesperson and ask them where the purples clothes were, which always baffled them, but there you were. Trying them on, wrapping yourself in them, like you couldn't get enough joy out of just looking at it. You had to be in it."

She smiled at me, an enormous face ripping smile, my favorite kind.

"You gotta go?"

I stood up and she let me give her an enormous hug again.

Her voice muffled, she said, "Charli, make sure you make a will."

"You were always the worst at goodbyes, but that takes the cake. Jesus Liv."

She laughed and hugged me tighter.

"Yeah, sorry, but just fucking do it," she said, stepping back and teleporting away with a wave.

Chicago, Illinois – 2019 – Trip

I met Diana at 2 am outside of her apartment. We didn't say a word until we were in a secluded backyard a few blocks away.

"Ready? I'll take us to the store, we'll get supplies and stuff, then go right next door to Roberts place. I scoped out an empty apartment next to his, perfect spot to land."

She nodded, so I reached around her waist and took us to the store. I left her in a corner I knew didn't have cameras, pulled my mask on, and ran around grabbing a few things. A new lighter, knives, rope. I already had two syringes tucked into the lining of my jacket, full and ready to go.

God, I was so excited my heart was pumping. Not only did I finally get to take down this sick fuck, but I got to share it with somebody again. We could talk about this all night, maybe even for years to come.

Diana was staring off into the distance when I turned the corner and I felt heat run through my body as she reached up and brushed hair out of her eyes. She didn't spot me until I was only a few strides away, so deep in thought, but her eyes lit up when she saw me, and my heart sped up even faster. As I came closer, she leaned down towards me, taking me into her arms. I pressed back and wildly put my lips on hers, just as I reached down and grasped the gem. We landed in the empty apartment and Diana pulled back, stumbling.

I leaned forward to try to catch her, but her arm shot out into the darkness and grasped something that wasn't there when I came yesterday and talked to the property manager. She pulled hard, yanking whatever it was forward. I threw my arms up and tried to shield myself, but it was enormous and crushed me into the floor.

I felt around as much as I could to get a sense of my situation. It felt like a heavy bookshelf with one of the shelves askew and digging directly into my chest. I was gasping for air and Diana was moaning softly, trying hard to pull it off of me.

"I'm so sorry, Trip. I'm sorry. Shit, shit."

Finally, she rolled it off and I flung myself onto my stomach, trying to smother my hacking and gasping. Diana pat me on the back ineptly.

"I'm sorry Trip, oh my god." She went still. "What if we woke him up? We need to hurry?"

She was right. I dragged in some calming breaths, then leaned on her to get to standing. I took a few turns around the room to make sure I could still move okay.

"See? We're okay. Let's go," I said

"Wait! Let me go first. You're moving slow."

I acquiesced, letting her go first out of the apartment, check the hallway, then move to Roberts door. She pressed her face against the wood, listening for any noises.

"Clear?"

"Clear."

I was in a ton of pain and grabbing the lock-picking tools out of my pocket made it even worse.

"Diana, you'll have to do a lot of this. I'm struggling."

"That's fine, Trip. Sorry again."

She pushed the door open softly and entered. I padded next to her, nudging her towards his bedroom with my body language. Roberts was dead asleep. I kneeled down next to him and took out my syringe.

"Freeze! Hands up, Trip!" Diana screamed, while the lights flipped on, blinding me. I dropped the syringe, grabbed the velour bag around my neck, and stood slowly. I was surrounded by cops with their guns drawn.

I looked into Diana's eyes, pleading for mercy. Her laugh rung through the shell of my body, full of cruel and impersonal joy. Her eyes swiped up to the bag in my hand and she lunged forward, snatching it from me, just as I coughed up phlegm, my lungs still punished from the book shelf. Something warm dribbled down my mouth. I looked down and saw blood dripping onto the hardwood floor from my mouth. I looked up and saw Diana toss my bag on the ground, then stomp iit with the heel of her combat boot.

She looked at me, hoping for a reaction, and gasped when she saw the blood. I doubled over, unable to stand anymore and she cuffed me, shouting for someone to call an ambulance.

"Diana, what the fuck?"

"What do you mean what the fuck? What did you think was going to happen? You waltzed into my office twice to rub this vigilante shit in my face and then the third time you walk in like I'm going to suddenly help you?"

"I saved your life and you couldn't even return this measly favor."

She looked at me with wild-eyed confusion.

"Saved my life?"

Chicago, Illinois – 2019 – Marcelle

Deputy Chief Lendo asked me to run to the apartment and pick up something the perp left before they allowed Roberts back in. Something in a small black bag, should be on the floor.

I was glad I wasn't there from how everyone had described the sting. They all said it was really awkward, training their guns on this tiny, random lady that Lendo was claiming was basically enemy of the state number one and actually laughing out loud while the perp was coughing up blood. None of us really liked her that much in my group of friends. She was kind of old school, liable to say something uncomfortable, trying too hard to connect with the younger women. Plus, who knew how long she would last after this incident. Sure, she didn't kill the woman herself, but it definitely didn't look good.

I searched around Roberts stark bedroom, finally finding a little black bag on his bedside table. Curious, I looked inside. I couldn't see much but felt from just holding the bag that it was all broken up, whatever it was, so I grabbed a book and dumped it out onto it, being careful not to spill any.

I used my ID to move the pieces around. They were dull, a deep, wine red, except for one chunk that was a little larger and brilliant. I took my gloves off for dexterity and picked it up, then remembered I was late on a report I had due and had to get back soon.

I thought to myself, shit, I'm running around for this insane Detective and now I won't even be home until way later. I closed my eyes, picturing my bed, full of pillows and blankets, the first items I bought me and Cassie with my first check, some comfort. I stretched and opened my eyes, then screamed and dropped the shard of glass I was holding. I scrambled onto my hands and knees, shaking, and finally found it glimmering under my bed.

ABOUT THE AUTHOR

k.r. sawyer was born and raised in Chicago, Illinois. She graduated from Ohio State University with a degree in Public Affairs. She doesn't have a favorite color.

Made in the USA
Monee, IL
29 June 2020